Holloway Mountain

Table of Contents

Holloway Mountain

by

Brett Shayler

Written by
Brett Shayler
Book Cover by Karen Shayler
This book has utilized artificial intelligence (AI) programs, including ProWritingAid, Grammarly, QuillBot, Canva, and Adobe Photoshop, to aid in the editing and book cover design process.

Dedication of this book

To the indomitable spirit of the American West, its breathtaking landscapes, and the courageous women and men who carved a life from its unforgiving beauty. This story is a tribute to their resilience, their passion, and their unwavering belief in the power of love amidst hardship and change. I dedicate this story to those who dared to dream, fought for their dreams, and found love in the most unexpected places.

To the women of the frontier, who faced unimaginable challenges with grace and strength, who defied societal expectations, and who flourished even in the harshest environments. This novel is a testament to their courage, their ingenuity, and their unwavering spirit. Their strength and determination inspire every page, every scene, every word. They were not just wives and mothers; they were artists, healers, entrepreneurs, and leaders, shaping the very fabric of a nation. Their stories, often untold, deserve to be heard and celebrated.

This is for the courageous Western men who built communities, protected their families, and sought adventure in the wilderness. This novel is also a dedication to them, to their unwavering spirit of self-reliance, their quiet strength, and their deep-seated love for the land. They faced danger and hardship with an unwavering fortitude that was inspiring. Their stories, interwoven with those of the women they loved, comprise the tapestry of the American West.

To the descendants of those who lived in Shole Creek and similar communities, to those who continue to protect and preserve the heritage of the American West, and to those who appreciate the importance and richness of history, as well as its influence on the lives of those who continue to dream and build upon the foundations laid by those who came before them.

This small token represents gratitude for your efforts, respect for your perseverance, and the power of the human spirit. We wrote this story for those who believe in Western magic, cherish enduring human bonds, and recognize love's transformative strength. This book caters to adventure seekers, admirers of resilience, and those who appreciate the wild and untamed beauty of the world.

Chapter 1: A Meeting in the Mines

The scent of damp earth and crushed rock hung heavy in the air, a familiar perfume to Jen Korte. She sat perched on a sun-warmed boulder overlooking Shole Creek, her sketchbook open on her lap, a half-finished charcoal sketch of the rugged landscape before her. The creek, a ribbon of silver winding through the ochre-colored hills of Holloway Mountain, reflected the harsh sunlight, its murmuring a counterpoint to the rhythmic clang of hammers from the nearby mines. The towering pines, their needles a deep, almost black, green, stood sentinel against the pale blue sky, their branches reaching towards the heavens like gnarled, supplicating hands. Beautiful yet brutal, the landscape showcased nature's power and humanity's resilience.

Charcoal in hand, she swept across the paper, capturing the rocks' rough textures and the gentle sway of the grass. Her brow furrowed and tongue peeking in concentration, she worked with feverish intensity, bringing the scene vividly to life. This was more than just sketching; it transcended the limitations of the medium to become something truly exceptional. A deep connection to the land's strength and vulnerability filled her, forging a kinship so powerful it felt as though she was an intrinsic part of the earth itself.

A sharp clang echoed through the valley from the mine. As Jen looked at the dark entrance to the mine, she noticed a figure slowly emerging from the shadows. He cut an imposing figure, his height and powerful build stressed by broad shoulders, while his dark, long hair flowed down to meet his equally long and dark beard. His gait, while marked by a purposeful urgency, was deliberate and controlled, showcasing a remarkable blend of haste and precision in his movements. A fine layer of clinging dust covered his dark woolen coat, and a dark smudge of grime clearly marked his cheek. Although covered in dirt and grime, he possessed a quiet strength that emanated from him like a palpable force, captivating all those around him. The mixture of worry and resolve carved into his facial features created an interesting yet somewhat disturbing image, one that held the observer's attention. Although the tightness of his jaw betrayed his worry, the dark, intense eyes held a spark of unwavering resolve that suggested a firm determination in the face of adversity.

After a brief pause, during which he surveyed the scene with a sweeping glance, he began walking toward the creek. The name Dr. Tobias Adams, spoken in hushed tones throughout Shole Creek, inspired a complex mix of both admiration and unease amongst its residents. Rumors of his expertise as a trapper and bear hunter preceded him, but Jen was most intrigued by the stories she'd heard about his medical abilities, which were said to be extraordinary. The stories circulating about him depicted a mysterious figure, a stranger who had recently arrived in the lively mining town just a few short months prior, and who had left behind an intriguing and enigmatic aura of mystery wherever he went. There was something about his very being, a certain presence, that suggested a hidden narrative, a secret battle fought and won, that had molded his character and instilled within him not only a quiet strength but also the deep lines etched onto his weathered face, hinting at a life lived with intensity and purpose.

As Jen contemplated the artwork, the stark juxtaposition between the subtle beauty of the charcoal sketch, with its delicate lines and shading, and the grim realities of the miners' lives, hit her with renewed force, creating a powerful emotional contrast. Before her, a vibrant chaos of graceful curves and rough edges unfolded. The captivating contrast and tension between beauty and brutality in the subject fueled her artistic vision and held her attention.

The creek provided a welcome spot for Dr. Adams to pause his journey, and there, he refreshed himself by cleansing his face in its waters. Precision and efficiency characterized his movements; there was not a single unnecessary flourish or embellishment. Although simple and almost mundane, the act somehow perfectly captured the essence of his character.

He glanced behind him, stealing a brief glance over his shoulder. The vast distance separating the intervening landscape, which acted as an insurmountable obstacle, emphasized them, making their connection feel utterly impossible. However, within that short-lived, quickly passing moment, a spark ignited between them, a mutual recognition and a shared understanding of their world blossomed. A secret shared between two souls across the valley, their silent encounter unfolded amidst the clash of steel, the murmur of the creek, and the towering pines which silently bore witness.

With a slight blush warming her cheeks, Jen gently lowered her sketchbook to her side, her eyes downcast. The gentle, subtle pink blush on her cheeks was the ideal complement to her long, flowing, and strikingly beautiful red hair. Although the encounter was brief, lasting only a short time, it felt strangely important and left a lasting impression. The disruption to her work rhythm had broken her artistic concentration, throwing off the smooth flow of her creative process and leaving her feeling unsettled and unfocused. Her heart hammered against her ribs, a frantic and rapid rhythm that stood in stark contrast to the slowly diminishing sounds emanating from the distant mine. The quiet strength that she sensed emanating from Dr. Adams, coupled with the unspoken communication that passed between them across the vast valley, created a sensation that was simultaneously captivating and deeply unsettling.

For Jen, art wasn't merely about capturing the beauty of the landscape; it was about capturing its soul, its very essence of life and death. The mine, with its promise of wealth and its ever-present threat of tragedy, was inextricably bound to the lives of everyone in Shole Creek. She, more than most, understood the precarious balance between the beauty and the brutality of this harsh frontier, between the delicate strokes of her charcoal and the rugged reality of the lives that surrounded her.

She returned to her sketching, but the image of Dr. Adams remained etched in her mind. His imposing figure, the set of his jaw, the intensity in his eyes–it all created an image as interesting and enduring as any landscape she might attempt to capture with charcoal. The accident, the sudden interruption, the fleeting glance–they were all interwoven into the tapestry of her life, threads that were unraveling, revealing a pattern that she had not foreseen. A new, unknown element infused the harsh frontier landscape, creating a sense of mystery and expectation.

Further strokes changed her drawing's focal point. The background, the creek, the mine; these were mere supporting players. The doctor, an imposing figure, dominated her canvas, captivating her completely, a fascinating yet enigmatic presence. The rhythm of her work had changed, her strokes now imbued with a newfound sense of anticipation. Shole Creek's beauty no longer defined her ordinary life. He dominated; the scenery, a mere backdrop, awaited its narrative.

The sun dipped lower in the sky, casting long shadows across the valley. Jen packed away her sketchbook, a sense of anticipation and unease swirling within her. This brief meeting, though seemingly minor, would irrevocably alter her life's path. The image of Dr. Tobias Adams, emerging from the mine, his face etched with worry and determination, became inextricably linked to the vibrant colors and textures of the Shole Creek landscape, a fusion of beauty and brutality, a collision of worlds that would shape her destiny. Her known world merged with mystery; a captivating, unforeseen narrative woven into her life. She felt a thrill of excitement, a nervous flutter in her stomach, as she expected the days ahead and the mysteries that were yet to unfold. The rugged mountains surrounding Shole Creek seemed to stand guard, silent sentinels over the unspoken promises and the unspoken questions that hung heavy in the air. Her life's landscape transformed; a thrilling yet terrifying certainty filled her – nothing would ever be the same.

The dust swirled around his boots as he dismounted his weary mule in front of the Korte mansion. The imposing structure, a stark contrast to the rough-hewn buildings of the mining town, stood as a testament to Stan Korte's wealth and power. Tobias Adams, his dark woolen coat dusted with the red ochre of the Shole Creek trails, ran a hand through his thick, dark hair, the gesture revealing the strength of his arms and the lines etched deeply into his weathered face. His mountain-man appearance, not a physician's, mirrored a life exploring nature instead formal medical training.

His arrival was unannounced, a deliberate choice. He'd sent word ahead only that he was coming, no specifics on time of arrival, a reflection of his independent spirit and the life he'd chosen. He preferred simply appearing, a solitary figure emerging from the wilderness to address the urgent needs of the town. This need was Jen. He carried a small, worn medical bag, its leather softened and scarred from years of use, a testament to the countless journeys it had accompanied him on. His bag contained not only his tools but also a reflection of his character—practical, resourceful, and prepared for any challenge.

Before he could knock, the heavy oak door of the Korte mansion swung open, revealing a stern-faced butler in impeccably tailored livery more suited to London than the frontier. The butler's expression, a mixture of disdain and apprehension, mirrored the initial reactions Tobias often encountered. He was an anomaly in Shole Creek, a blend of refined intellect and untamed wilderness, a paradox that unsettled those accustomed to clear-cut categories.

"Dr. Adams," the butler announced, his voice clipped and formal, "Mr. Korte is expecting you. Please, follow me."

The interior of the Korte mansion was a startling contrast to the rugged exterior. Polished mahogany furniture gleamed under the soft glow of crystal chandeliers, the air thick with the scent of expensive perfume and beeswax. Tobias felt a momentary unease, a subtle dissonance between his rough spun clothes and the opulent surroundings. He had spent years in the solitude of the mountains, his hands hardened by toil, his senses attuned to the subtle shifts in the natural world. This opulent world, with its rigid formality and unspoken rules, felt alien and constricting.

Through hallways adorned with oil paintings and tapestries, he followed the butler. The house itself, a testament to wealth and power, seemed to stand in stark contrast to the unbridled nature that surrounded it. The carefully manicured lawns and meticulously pruned flowerbeds provided a controlled world opposite the chaos of the mines and the untamed beauty of Shole Creek.

Someone led him to a spacious study, dominated by a massive desk cluttered with papers and an ornate inkwell. Stan Korte, a man whose imposing figure mirrored the size of his fortune, sat behind it. A look of impatience and suspicion marked his shrewd, ambitious features as his gaze lifted.

"Dr. Adams," Korte said, his voice gravelly, betraying the strain of years spent bargaining in the ruthless world of mining, "I understand you have a reputation for...resourcefulness."

Tobias met his gaze, his own eyes revealing nothing of his thoughts. "My skills are at your disposal, Mr. Korte. I believe you needed my services."

"My daughter," Korte said, his voice softening slightly, "she's taken ill. A fever, the doctor here says. But something isn't right. I need someone... more thorough."

Tobias remained silent, observing the older man. The tension in the room was thick, a palpable energy born of wealth, power, and the fear that this controlled world, built on ore and iron, could crumble with one unexpected blow. The carefully constructed facade of wealth and success was showing cracks, hinting at the underlying vulnerabilities.

"I've heard... things," Korte continued, his voice low and intense, "about your... past. "The reasons that lead me to believe you are the sole person capable of providing assistance."

Tobias nodded, his expression giving away nothing of his past, a past he guarded closely, a past that involved harsh experiences and hard-won wisdom. He'd arrived in Shole Creek seeking a different life, but the town, like the wild lands he knew so well, had its own way of drawing you into its conflicts and secrets. He sensed increasing unease, this case's complexity exceeding initial appearances.

Korte then dismissed the butler, leaving only Tobias and himself in the room. The unspoken question hung in the air, a heavy silence filled with the untold stories of Shole Creek, its mines, its secrets, and its unexpected links to the rugged doctor who stood before him. The heavy oak door closed loudly, dividing the elegance of the mansion from the outside world, mirroring the delicate balance of Jen's world, a world Tobias was now undeniably part of.

He spent the next few hours examining Jen. The fever was indeed high, but something else troubled him, a subtle irregularity in her pulse, a faint tremor in her hand that suggested a deeper issue. He questioned her, his manner calm and reassuring. The conversation flowed from the ordinary to the extraordinary, touching on the nuances of Jen's life, her artistic aspirations, her anxieties and hopes. The tension between Jen's sheltered life within the mansion and her inherent rebellious nature was evident.

As he examined her, Tobias noticed a small, almost imperceptible scratch on her arm, hidden beneath her sleeve. It wasn't a simple scratch; it was a precise, almost surgical cut, far too clean for an accidental injury. This was no ordinary fever. It was more sinister, hinting at a dark undercurrent of danger hidden beneath the surface of this seemingly tranquil town. The serene facade of Shole Creek was crumbling, revealing a darkness that mirrored the depths of the mines themselves. The gentle murmur of Shole Creek, usually a soothing counterpoint to the life of the town, now seemed to whisper secrets of a hidden danger lurking beneath.

He left the mansion after midnight, the cool night air a welcome contrast to the stifling atmosphere of the Korte household. The full moon cast long shadows across the streets of Shole Creek, revealing a town transformed under the silver glow. The quiet strength that had marked his arrival seemed to emanate from him even more strongly now, intensified by the suspicion that his mission had just taken a sharp and dangerous turn. His seemingly chance arrival would soon profoundly affect many. The landscape, both beautiful and brutal, had revealed its hidden secrets to him, and he was ready to face the challenge, ready to unlock the mysteries and dangers that lay ahead, not only to help Jen but to uncover the truth lurking beneath Shole Creek's pristine surface.

The mountains surrounding Shole Creek seemed to watch him silently, as if they themselves held the secrets to the mystery that unfolded. He turned towards the creek, the murmuring waters a constant presence in the quiet night, its gentle rhythm a reminder of the unpredictable currents of life itself. This was more than a medical mystery; it involved more than just solving a medical puzzle. The adventure was just beginning. And Tobias, the rugged doctor, bear hunter and trapper, was ready.

Korte's gaze, sharp and unwavering, followed Tobias as he moved, assessing the doctor with a practiced eye. His calloused hands, strong jaw, intense dark eyes revealed a life vastly different than his mansion's luxury. The subtle scent of woodsmoke and leather clung to Tobias, a stark contrast to the expensive perfume that permeated the Korte household. That scent unsettled Korte, recalling a difficult, unpredictable former life—one his empire had shielded him from.

"Your reputation precedes you, Dr. Adams," Korte finally said, his voice a low rumble that resonated in the study's stillness. He leaned back in his leather chair, the expensive leather creaking softly under his weight, a sound that seemed to mock the rough spun fabric of Tobias's coat. "I've heard tales of your... unorthodox methods."

Tobias remained silent, his expression unreadable. He knew the whispers that followed him, the stories of his unconventional treatments and his willingness to venture beyond the confines of traditional medicine. He spent years in the wilderness, mastering natural healing, earning both admiration and distrust.

"My daughter," Korte continued, his voice hardening slightly, "is not merely having a fever. The town doctor, a man of... limited experience, assures me it is nothing serious. But I've seen her... changed. She's withdrawn, agitated. There's... something else."

Korte tapped a long, manicured finger on the polished mahogany desk, the sound echoing the unspoken anxieties that gnawed at him. His empire, built on the sweat and toil of countless miners, rested on the precarious balance of his daughter's well-being. Jen was his only child, the heir to his fortune, the symbol of his success. Her illness threatened not only her life, but the future of the Korte dynasty. This involved significantly more than wellness.

He gestured towards a heavy oak cabinet inlaid with mother-of-pearl. He confided, "The town doctor doesn't know everything." He opened the cabinet, revealing rows of neatly organized bottles and jars, their contents labeled in a spidery script. "Rare herbs, experimental concoctions... things I've gained over the years, things I wouldn't trust to just anyone."

Korte's collection suggested unconventional aspects of his personality; he did not limit himself to standard treatments. His wealth and power allowed him access to resources beyond the reach of most, fueling his belief that he could control every aspect of his life, including his daughter's health. This was a man who believed he could command even nature itself.

Tobias examined the contents of the cabinet, his fingers tracing the labels. He recognized some herbs, but others were unfamiliar, their origins shrouded in mystery. The collection reflected not only Korte's wealth but also his deep-seated anxieties, his desperation to protect his daughter and his empire at all costs. The display served as a potent symbol of the vast divide between the opulent world of the Korte mansion and the uncertain realities of the mining town outside its walls.

"I need someone who understands the... subtleties of the human body," Korte said, his eyes probing Tobias's face, searching for a sign of reassurance or doubt. "Someone who isn't afraid to venture beyond the accepted norms."

Tobias met his gaze, his eyes reflecting the flickering light of the fireplace. He understood the unspoken request, the desperate plea masked by a façade of control. Korte pursued something beyond a cure. He was accustomed to success, his existence precisely managed. The illness of his daughter threatened to shatter that carefully constructed order.

"I will do my best, Mr. Korte," Tobias responded, his voice calm and measured, betraying none of the unease he felt. This case went beyond the typical medical one. He sensed a darkness lurking beneath the surface of this perfect world, a darkness that mirrored the volatile nature of the mining industry itself.

A careful examination of Jen consumed the hours that followed. Tobias's skills, honed by years of experience in the harsh realities of the wilderness, allowed him to detect subtle signs that had escaped the town doctor. He noted the faint tremor in her hand, the slight discoloration of her skin, the subtle irregularity in her breathing. These symptoms didn't indicate a simple fever.

He questioned Jen gently, coaxing out details of her daily routine, her interactions with others, her anxieties and fears. He discovered her secret sketches, hidden within the pages of her well-worn journals, revealing a world of beauty and imagination that stood in stark contrast to the opulent prison of her father's mansion. Her art, vibrant and full of life, seemed to be a desperate attempt to escape the stifling constraints of her existence, a silent cry for freedom.

The conversation revealed a strained relationship with her father, a constant struggle for independence and recognition. Jen, despite her privileged life, craved a life beyond the confines of her father's wealth and power. The contrast between her artistic spirit and the rigid formality of her surroundings created a palpable tension, a silent rebellion simmering beneath the surface. The mining town's harshness, juxtaposed with her opulent home, visibly affected her.

He discovered a hidden bruise on her arm, cleverly concealed beneath a layer of silk. It was a bruise that didn't fit the pattern of a simple fall or accident. It spoke of something more sinister, something intentional. His suspicions hardened. This was not a simple illness; it was a calculated attack, an attempt to silence Jen or control her.

Darkness heightened tension within the mansion. The opulent surroundings, once a symbol of security and power, now felt oppressive, claustrophobic. The silence, broken only by the rhythmic tick-tock of the grandfather clock, emphasized the looming threat, the potential for chaos. Tobias felt the weight of Korte's anxieties, his desperate desire to maintain control, to preserve his carefully constructed world.

He departed Korte Manor at midnight, burdened by suspicions, realizing this exceeded a medical matter. A cool night breeze offered temporary relief from the Korte household's stifling atmosphere, but it did little to ease his growing unease. Far greater than he'd initially imagined was the challenge before him. Power struggles and dark secrets within Shole Creek inextricably link to the mystery of Jen's illness. Whispering secrets of hidden dangers and unspoken truths, the rugged landscape reflected the harsh realities of life in the mining town. The adventure was just beginning, and Tobias was ready to face it. The mountains, silent sentinels in the moonlit night, seemed to approve.

A heavy air, thick with dust and the metallic tang of blood, hung in the space. The mine shaft, usually a cacophony of clanking machinery and the shouts of men, was eerily silent, broken only by the occasional groan of injured timbers and the ragged breaths of the survivors. Jen Korte, her usually vibrant face pale and streaked with grime, kneeled beside a crumpled form, her hands gently cradling the head of a young miner. Her fingers, usually deftly wielding a charcoal pencil, now moved with a practiced gentleness, stemming the flow of blood from a gash on his forehead.

Tobias, his powerful hands already tending to another injured man, watched her from across the chaotic scene. He'd seen his share of accidents in the wilds–a bear mauling, a broken leg after a fall from a cliff–but the claustrophobia of the mine, the weight of the earth pressing down, amplified the tragedy. The miners' terror and desperation, thick in the air like coal dust, impacted him as powerfully as the mine cave-in. He saw the way Jen moved, her composure a stark contrast to the panic swirling around her. There was a quiet strength in her, a resilience that resonated with his own rugged spirit. He'd encountered women like that before, women hardened by the unforgiving landscape, but there was also a vulnerability beneath the surface, a quiet sensitivity that belied her courage.

He saw her glance up, her eyes meeting his across the narrow passageway, a flicker of something unreadable passing between them. More than pity or concern; It was a silent acknowledgment of their shared connection to this unforgiving land and the precariousness of existence that bound them.

In that shared glance, a silent conversation took place– a recognition of shared strength. A brief connection hinted at something more profound.

Later, as the injured were being carried out, their bodies stiff and groaning, Jen found herself alone, leaning against a weathered mine cart, her breath coming in ragged gasps. The adrenaline that had fueled her actions was fading, leaving her with a profound exhaustion.

Tobias approached cautiously, his boots crunching on the gravel path. He extended a worn leather canteen. "Drink," he said, his voice a low rumble, barely audible above the moans and the creaks of the wounded.

She took the canteen, her fingers brushing his. She felt an electric shock upon contact, unexpected after such trauma. The contact was brief, but significant. The feel of his calloused hand against hers was both reassuring and strangely exciting. She drank deeply from the canteen, the cool water a balm against the dust and the lingering scent of blood in her throat.

"Thank you," she whispered, her voice barely a breath.

He nodded, his gaze unwavering, studying her face. The grime and the pallor couldn't mask her inherent beauty. Fatigue and the trauma of the day's events clouded her usually vibrant eyes, usually filled with laughter and a mischievous glint. There was a haunting vulnerability in their depth that tugged at something within him. He saw the tremble in her hand as she handed back the canteen, the subtle shaking betraying the toll the accident had taken.

"You were remarkable," he said, his voice soft, acknowledging her quiet heroism. "Your composure... it was astonishing."

A faint smile played on her lips. "It's a skill honed by necessity," she replied, her voice regaining some of its usual strength, but still marked by a tremor. She looked out at the scarred landscape, the mine shaft gaping like a wounded beast. "We learn to cope. We learn to survive."

A sudden understanding dawned on him. That quiet strength, a characteristic that defined him, was something he understood intimately. He grasped the inherent resilience born from confronting danger directly, a resilience forged in the crucible of accepting the world's harsh realities without yielding to fear. They implicitly understood each other, a quiet recognition of their common ground existing between them, with no explicit statement or conversation. The harsh wilderness of Shole Creek served as a crucible, forging both of them into survivors who had endured its relentless trials.

As the sun began to set, casting long shadows across the ravaged landscape, they stood in silence for a moment, taking in the scene before them. Because of their shared experience and the nearness of death that they both faced, a powerful bond had formed between them, forging a connection stronger than ever before. A palpable tension hung in the air, heavy with unspoken emotions and a silent, yet undeniable, awareness of a connection that was just beginning to bloom between them. A heavy silence filled the space, thick with unspoken words, shared history, and the unspoken weight of their mutual respect and admiration for one another. Despite the traumatic events of the day, rather than driving them apart, the shared experience unexpectedly strengthened the bond between them.

As they walked towards the town, amidst the debris and the injured, their steps fell into a rhythm, their paths converging, their glances meeting occasionally, each meeting charged with a subtle unspoken energy. There was an undeniable chemistry developing between them, and a mutual attraction ignited in the disaster's heart. The way they moved, the subtle shifts of their gazes, suggested a deepening connection, hinting at a burgeoning romance amidst the devastation.

Later that evening, as Jen sat by the window of her father's mansion, sketching the rugged silhouette of the mountains silhouetted against the twilight sky, she found herself lost in thought, the image of Tobias's intense gaze still imprinted on her mind. Her brushstrokes depicted both external scenery and her inner emotional turmoil: sorrow, thankfulness, and a newly discovered attraction. Daily occurrences reshaped her perspective, unveiling a man whose strength matched hers; he grasped the resilience needed within their difficult lives.

His hands, rough and strong, were a contrast to the soft brush strokes on her canvas. Yet, the image of those hands holding hers, the brief touch, a moment of physical and emotional contact, remained a profound and unforgettable experience. The accident had upended her world in ways she couldn't yet understand. Meeting Tobias unexpectedly sparked a thrilling sense of change. Deep within her resonated the shared glances, fleeting touch, and unspoken acknowledgment of their strength. She realized she had experienced a connection with him that transcended the accident itself. The memory of their eyes meeting amid the chaos, their silent exchange of shared sorrow, fear, and finally, a flicker of hope, was something profound and unforgettable.

It represented something far exceeding a commonplace shared experience; it was a profound and transformative event that shaped our lives. As the feeling grew, it transcended the boundaries of friendship, hinting at something far deeper, a potential that evoked visions of a future unfolding in the wild heart of the untamed American West. Their shared quiet strength, forged facing life's harsh realities, could build something unimaginably significant. Amidst a stark, difficult terrain, their improbable romance blossomed. As silent witnesses to the burgeoning relationship, the majestic mountains appeared softly to whisper their approval, a testament to the couple's enduring strength and resilience, offering a silent blessing upon a love story born amidst challenging circumstances.

In the days that followed, a whirlwind of activity and events unfolded. As the injured received medical attention, the gaping wound in the earth that was the mine was slowly being secured, marking the grim beginning of the recovery effort. Despite her overwhelming exhaustion, Jen felt a pull back towards the mine, a fascination that transcended mere practicality and bordered on the morbid, a curiosity about the gaping hole that had swallowed whole lives. She would sit on a nearby rock, sketching the ravaged landscape, her charcoal capturing the stark beauty of the destruction, a stark contrast to the vibrant scenes she usually depicted.

It was during one of these visits that she first truly noticed Greg Moore. He was a man carved from the same harsh landscape as Tobias, but where Tobias possessed a quiet strength, Moore exuded a brooding intensity, a barely contained aggression that radiated from him like the heat from a furnace. His eyes, the color of cold steel, seemed to bore into her, assessing, judging. He appeared massive, imposing, granite-jawed, his presence dominating. He moved with a purposefulness that suggested experience, perhaps even weariness, in handling situations like the mine collapse. His uniform, though rumpled and stained with coal dust, still conveyed a sense of authority, a silent reminder of his dual role as mine foreman and sheriff. His presence always seemed to cast a shadow over the scene.

Their encounters were brief, mostly limited to nods and curt exchanges, yet each interaction left her with a lingering feeling of unease. There was a subtle tension in his gaze, a palpable energy that hinted at an unspoken conflict, an underlying rivalry that she couldn't quite decipher. He seemed to observe her, watching her interactions with Tobias with a keen, almost predatory interest. He would linger near her, absorbed in the details of the cleanup, but always within earshot, his presence a persistent undercurrent to their conversations. His questions about the accident, about the safety protocols, were pointed, designed to probe for weaknesses or failures. He didn't take part in the general commiseration, his interactions remaining strictly professional, devoid of empathy, yet heavily saturated with an intense scrutiny.

It wasn't just Jen who felt this scrutiny. Moore's questions to Tobias were equally pointed; concerning his qualifications, his experience with mining accidents, and the efficacy of his medical attention, all veiled under the guise of official investigation. There was a subtle but unmistakable antagonism in his tone, a veiled challenge in his every word, each question carrying an undertone of distrust. It was as though Moore, in his role as sheriff, was attempting to find fault with Tobias, to establish his own dominance, or perhaps even to undermine Tobias's growing relationship with Jen.

One evening, while Tobias was attending to some injured miners at the makeshift hospital in the town hall, Moore cornered Jen in the shadows of the Korte mansion. An unsettling stillness cloaked the night; only the distant howl of a coyote and the rustling leaves made any sound.

Moore's low, rumbling voice vibrated, addressing Miss Korte.

Jen, startled by his sudden appearance, felt a chill run down her spine. "Sheriff Moore," she replied, her voice barely a whisper.

"The doctor... Adams. He's an outsider, isn't he?" Moore's question hung in the air, heavy with implication.

Jen felt her defenses rise. "He's a skilled physician," she countered, defending Tobias's character implicitly. "And a good man."

Moore chuckled, a harsh, grating sound that was more like a rasp. Men who are good don't consistently make good decisions, Miss Korte. This town has its own ways, its own rules. Outsiders don't always understand those rules."

The implication was clear. Moore was warning her about Tobias. He was subtly threatening her, trying to drive a wedge between her and the doctor. He was reminding her of her place in Shole Creek society, suggesting that her attachment to an outsider could lead to unforeseen complications.

"I understand Shole Creek's ways, Sheriff," Jen responded, her voice firm, meeting his gaze with defiance. "And I'll make my own choices."

Moore's gaze hardened, his expression unreadable. He took a step closer, his presence oppressive, the scent of stale whiskey and coal dust clinging to him. "Think carefully, Miss Korte," he said, his voice an indistinct murmur. "Some choices have consequences... serious consequences." He paused, letting the weight of his words hang in the air. Certain relationships threaten far more than reputation.

He turned and vanished into the shadows, leaving Jen alone, the unspoken threat hanging over her like a dark cloud. She stood there for a long time, the chilling words echoing in her ears. That meeting instilled both unease and a defiant spirit. Moore's thinly veiled threats only strengthened her resolve. She refused to be intimidated. She wouldn't allow him to dictate her choices or influence her feelings for Tobias.

The shadow of Greg Moore hung over Shole Creek, his presence a constant reminder of the complexities and dangers that lurked beneath the surface of the quiet town. His actions, his words, his unwavering gaze, all contributed to a growing sense of foreboding. His interference hinted at deeper secrets, hidden agendas, and a potential conflict that would test their resilience and their love. Shole Creek faced another disaster besides the mine collapse. The seemingly idyllic life in the rugged landscape was now threatened by the unpredictable nature of human interaction, the clash of wills, and the secrets that Moore held so closely guarded. The danger rivaled, perhaps surpassed, the mine's collapse. The actual battle for Jen and Tobias would not be against the unforgiving landscape of Shole Creek, but against the human forces that threatened to tear them apart. Greg Moore, enigmatic and powerful, controlled their destiny. A dramatic confrontation was about to unfold with the quiet beauty of Shole Creek, on a path fraught with peril. Moore's weighty presence constantly reminded everyone of the precarious power balance and unpredictable human relationships, particularly in the lawless frontier town. Conflict brewed, setting the stage for a dramatic confrontation that would test the strength of their love, resilience, and shared determination to overcome upcoming obstacles. The wilderness and the hidden agendas of the people in Shole Creek would test Jen and Tobias's quiet strength to its limits, turning their love story into a fight for survival.

Chapter 2: Whispers of Danger

The whispers started subtly, like the rustling of leaves in a late fall wind–barely audible at first, easily dismissed as idle gossip. But gradually, the whispers grew louder, more insistent, weaving their way through the fabric of Shole Creek society, seeping into conversations in the saloon, the general store, and even the hushed corners of the Korte mansion. The rumors spoke of escalating tensions between the Osage tribe, whose ancestral lands bordered Shole Creek, and the ever-growing community of miners.

The initial mine collapse had already shaken the town's fragile equilibrium. Now, this new threat, this simmering resentment, added another layer of unease, a constant hum of apprehension that vibrated beneath the surface of daily life. Jen, ever observant, noticed the change. The usually jovial faces of the miners were now etched with worry, their laughter replaced by hushed conversations and nervous glances towards the hills that surrounded the town. The tense silence in the saloon muted even the jovial banter, punctuated only by clinking glasses and occasional nervous coughs.

Land was the source of the conflict, as Jen pieced together from fragmented conversations and furtive glances. The relentless expansion of the mines, the insatiable hunger for ore, was encroaching upon the Osage hunting grounds, disrupting their traditional way of life. The miners, driven by greed and the promise of wealth, paid little heed to the concerns of the Native Americans, their disregard for ancient customs and sacred lands fueling the growing resentment. Stories circulated about miners trespassing on tribal land, disturbing sacred sites, and even harassing Osage hunters. These actions, however minor they might seem to some, were deeply offensive to the tribe, acts of blatant disrespect that violated deeply held cultural and spiritual beliefs.

Tobias, aware of the potential for conflict, had attempted to understand the situation. Years spent traversing the wilderness brought him into contact with various Native American tribes, fostering respect for their customs and traditions. He knew the Osage was a proud person, deeply connected to their land, and he understood the profound significance of their ancestral grounds. He had witnessed firsthand their deep connection to the natural world, the spiritual reverence they held for the mountains, rivers, and forests which surrounded them. Their intricate relationship with their environment was far more complex than the simplistic view of some miners.

Sharing his concerns with Jen, he explained the precarious equilibrium between the settlers and the native population, an equilibrium easily disrupted, he cautioned, by the twin evils of ignorance and greed. As the sun dipped below the horizon, casting long shadows across the creek, he leaned toward Jen, his voice low and serious, "It's a powder keg waiting to explode," he said, the rushing water a stark contrast to the palpable tension that was steadily tightening its grip on their quiet town. The miners showed a profound lack of respect, and this, combined with the tribe's righteous anger, has the potential to cause a very serious incident.

Jen's artistic sensibility made her keenly aware of the subtle shifts in her surroundings, enabling her to sense the tension in the room as deeply as Tobias. The increased number of armed guards stationed at the mine entrances didn't go unnoticed by her, neither did the nervous glances exchanged between the miners and the townspeople, nor the furtive movements of shadowy figures—all of which served as unmistakable indicators of a conflict that was about to erupt.

One day, while sketching near the edge of the town, Jen encountered a young Osage woman, her face etched with a mixture of sadness and anger. The woman, who introduced herself as Chayton, shared her concerns about the escalating tensions, her words reflecting a deep-seated hurt and fear for her people's future.

Chayton's account painted a far more disturbing picture than the casual rumors spreading through the town. She spoke of sacred sites desecrated, hunting grounds ravaged, and the growing sense of desperation among her people, a desperation that could easily lead to violence. She described instances of harassment and intimidation, tales of miners taunting and threatening her people, the blatant disregard for their traditional practices infuriating the Osage.

Chayton's words revealed the depth of the cultural chasm between the two communities, the miners' arrogant disregard for the Osage culture and their deep connection to the land, a contrast that seemed impossible to reconcile. Raw emotional intensity and a palpable sadness, resonating deeply with Jen's artistic soul, infused the stories. She found herself moved by Chayton's poignant account, the story of a people losing their home, their heritage, their way of life.

Jen, now fully aware of the gravity of the situation, sought Tobias. She shared Chayton's story, painting a vivid picture of the simmering resentment and the potential for a violent confrontation. Tobias listened intently, his own concerns confirmed and amplified by Chayton's firsthand account. The prospect of open conflict filled him with dread. He understood this conflict's potential devastation; it threatened both communities and risked wider consequences, potentially involving the U.S. Army.

The couple sought Sheriff Moore, hoping to find a way to de-escalate the situation before it escalated into violence. They approached him cautiously, careful in their approach, knowing Moore's temperament and his thinly veiled disdain for both Tobias and Jen. They presented their concerns about the growing tensions, emphasizing the need for mediation and understanding, and the importance of respecting the rights and traditions of the Osage.

Moore listened impassively, his cold steel gaze never leaving their faces. He remained unmoved by their pleas, seemingly more interested in maintaining order and control than resolving the underlying conflict. His response was dismissive, echoing his earlier distrust of Tobias. "It's just tribal unrest," he grumbled. " Nothing for us to worry about." His words held an undercurrent of indifference, a chilling lack of concern at the potential consequences. He suggested they mind their own business, a clear sign he was unwilling or unable to address the problem.

Their meeting with Moore proved fruitless, leaving Jen and Tobias more concerned than ever. The sheriff's apathy was both alarming and deeply frustrating, particularly given his knowledge of the potential for violence.

Their response: independent action, defying authority, plunging them into a brewing conflict.

The rumors of tribal conflict were no longer just whispers; they had become a looming threat, a dark cloud hanging over Shole Creek, threatening to engulf the town in violence and chaos. Jen and Tobias, bound by their love and their shared concern for the community, found themselves thrust into the heart of a crisis, forced to confront the harsh realities of life on the frontier and the complex historical context of the Westward Expansion. A deeply divisive conflict now overshadowed the idyllic beauty of Shole Creek, testing the strength of their relationship and the very fabric of their community. The path to reconciliation stretched before them, fraught with danger, uncertainty, and the constant threat of violence. Their choice carried consequences far beyond Shole Creek. Their budding romance now bound the town's fate to two distinct cultures. The whispers of danger were about to become a deafening roar.

The heavy oak door of the Korte mansion creaked shut behind Jen, the sound swallowed by the rustling leaves of the ancient oaks that guarded the property. Her father, Stan Korte, a man his stubbornness matched whose power in Shole only, had forbidden her from visiting the makeshift hospital set up in the old schoolhouse. The recent mine collapse had left a trail of broken bodies and shattered spirits, and while the town rallied to provide help, William remained adamant that his daughter, the jewel of his social standing, remain untouched by the sordid reality of the mining disaster. But her father's rigid expectations would not confine Jen, a woman whose spirit burned as brightly as the setting sun over the Missouri hills.

She clutched a small, worn leather satchel containing her art supplies. Watercolors, brushes, and a sketchbook–tools that were as much a part of her as her own heartbeat. She had spent the last few days sketching the grim faces of the miners, their bodies contorted in unnatural positions from the trauma of the cave-in, the fear and uncertainty etched deep into their expressions. These weren't just sketches; they were documents of suffering, poignant reminders of the human cost of progress.

The cool night air carried with it the invigorating fragrance of pine trees and the rich, damp scent of the earth below. High in the inky sky, the moon, a silvery disc, cast long, dancing shadows all around her as she carefully made her way along the uneven path that led to the schoolhouse. A low hum, barely audible, filled the air, a tangible anxiety that emanated from the earth itself, pressing down on her with a heavy, almost imperceptible weight.

Normally a vibrant hub of learning, the schoolhouse was now transformed into a place of quiet suffering. The air inside was thick with the smell of antiseptic and sweat, a stark contrast to the usual scent of chalk dust and youthful energy. Dim lanterns cast a flickering light on the rows of makeshift beds, each occupied by a miner struggling with pain and fear. Groans and hushed whispers filled the air, a symphony of suffering that tugged at Jen's heart.

A grotesquely twisted leg was what Adams treated on a young miner. He furrowed his brow in concentration, and his hands moved with practiced precision. He barely registered Jen's entrance, his entire focus locked on his patient. Jen, ever the observant artist, approached cautiously, her presence almost imperceptible in the muted atmosphere.

She moved silently from bed to bed, her eyes observing, her hands recording. She sketched the contours of their faces, the lines of pain etched deep into their skin, the hollowed-out eyes reflecting the depths of their suffering. Each stroke of her brush captured not only the physical wounds but also the emotional scars that ran deeper than any visible injury.

One miner, a grizzled veteran of the mines named Silas, caught her eye. Silas slumped over, his breath rattling in his chest, his face pale and clammy. His hand, usually calloused and strong, was now weak and trembling. Jen approached him tentatively, offering a small smile and a gentle nod. Silas, surprised by the unexpected kindness, managed a weak smile in return.

With delicate precision, she sketched Silas, capturing his weary features with a sensitivity that belied her youth. She paid meticulous attention to detail, her gaze observing the subtleties of his suffering–the lines of pain etched around his eyes, the tension in his jaw, the way his breath came in short, ragged gasps.

Her skill with watercolor allowed her to convey a far more profound sense of the miner's pain than a simple pencil sketch ever could. She used soft blues and greens to capture the shadows and highlights on his face, the varying textures of his rough skin, the subtle shifts in his expression as he shifted in pain. The watercolors captured the stark reality of his suffering, and yet, she imbued her work with a quiet dignity, a respect that transcended mere physical documentation.

As she worked, she spoke to the miners, her gentle words breaking through the wall of pain and fear that surrounded them. She listened to their stories, their voices hoarse from pain and fatigue, their tales woven with a mixture of resilience and resignation. Each miner's story, she understood, was a piece of the larger tragedy, a testament to the human cost of greed and ambition.

She spent the entire night at the makeshift hospital, her artistic skill becoming an unexpected tool of healing. More than just documentation, her sketches served as a connection, a silent dialogue between the suffering miners and the woman who dared to bear witness to their pain. Her artistic compassion transcended the physical act of creation, becoming a source of comfort and solace in a world steeped in despair.

As dawn broke, painting the eastern sky in hues of pink and gold, Jen slipped out of the schoolhouse, her satchel heavy with her sketches. The rising sun cast long shadows, but this time, they felt less ominous, less threatening. Defying her father, societal expectations, and most importantly, the limitations of her own circumstances, she had done it. She soothed their pain.

Aware of the risks and potential repercussions of her actions, she knew what she had done. Her father's wrath would be significant, a force that might shake the very foundations of Shole Creek society. But Jen, fueled by her compassion and unwavering conviction, felt no regret. The pain in those men's eyes, the stories they shared, had profoundly altered her understanding of her own privileges. A life of ease, protected from hardships affecting countless others. This was a privilege she refused to embrace any longer.

The sunrise illuminated her determined face as she returned to the Korte mansion. Miners and rescuers faced a difficult, extended recovery. While walking, she took firm steps, inspired by Silas's frail smile and the belief that art, compassion, and defiance can bring light to a shadowy world. Though whispers of danger continued, Jen forged a new strength within her heart—a strength born of defiance and a profound understanding of the human spirit. Consequences were foreseeable; inaction, however, was unacceptable. The battle for Shole Creek was far from over, and Jen, armed with her art and her unwavering courage, was ready to fight.

The flickering lantern light cast long shadows across Tobias's face, highlighting the grim determination etched into his features. He worked with a quiet intensity, his hands moving with practiced ease amidst the chaos of the makeshift hospital. The air hung heavy with the scent of antiseptic, sweat, and the ever-present metallic tang of blood. Around him, groans and gasps punctuated the hushed whispers of the injured miners. Each man bore the physical marks of the mine collapse–broken bones, crushed limbs, deep gashes–but the deeper wounds, the ones etched into their spirits, were far more pervasive.

Tobias, however, seemed impervious to the pervasive despair. His movements were deliberate, precise, his touch gentle yet firm as he examined a miner's mangled arm. In the storm of suffering around them, his low, calming tones acted as a steady anchor. He didn't rush, didn't flinch, his eyes mirroring a compassion that extended far beyond the scope of his medical skills. He was a rock of stability in a sea of turmoil, his presence a quiet reassurance amidst the fear and uncertainty.

Remembering the miners' families and stories from earlier conversations, he addressed each one by name. Though simple, the act demonstrated profound respect and empathy given this shared trauma. He spoke to them not as patients, but as individuals, recognizing their inherent dignity even in the face of their physical devastation.

He skillfully set a fractured leg, his powerful hands maneuvering the bone with an almost supernatural delicacy. His brow furrowed in concentration, but there was no trace of impatience or frustration in his demeanor. The young miner, barely out of his teens, whimpered, but Tobias's voice remained steady, a soothing counterpoint to the boy's pain. He spoke of his family, weaving a comforting narrative that helped distract the young man from his suffering.

His seamless transitions between patients were clear about his work. He listened to their stories, their fears, their hopes, absorbing the collective weight of their suffering without faltering. Each whisper, each groan, each story deepened his connection to them and to the harsh reality of their lives.

His medical bag, worn and well-loved, lay open beside him, spilling forth its contents–bandages, antiseptic, simple surgical tools. The tools themselves seemed to reflect the man who wielded them: functional, reliable, and imbued with a quiet strength. They were not mere instruments of healing, but extensions of his own compassion and dedication.

As he worked, his eyes would occasionally meet Jen's. She stood silently in a corner, her sketchbook open, capturing the scene with strokes of her brush and pencil. Her artistic eye, sharp and observant, noted every detail: the subtle shift in Tobias's expression as he worked, the way his brow would furrow in concentration, the almost imperceptible tremor in his hand as exhaustion took hold. Their gazes met, and a silent understanding passed between them; a shared recognition of the human cost of the tragedy unfolding before them.

Activity blurred the passing hours. The night air, still carrying the scent of pine and damp earth, grew colder. The lanterns flickered, casting dancing shadows that stretched and contorted, mimicking the twisted forms of the injured miners. Yet Tobias remained steadfast, his resolve unwavering. His fatigue was clear, but his spirit remained unbroken.

He was more than just a doctor; his dedication and compassion extended far beyond the confines of his medical practice. Driven by an almost instinctual understanding of the unforgiving wilderness, cultivated through countless years of experience, he worked relentlessly, his hands moving with practiced ease, almost as if guided by an unseen force. He possessed considerable skill, but what truly distinguished him was his remarkable capacity for empathy and his ability to connect with each man on a deeply personal, human level, a talent that set him apart from others truly exceptionally. He understood their pain not just as a medical professional, but as a fellow human being, a fellow inhabitant of this unforgiving land.

His quiet strength was contagious. The room quieted; calm defied despair. The miners, exhausted and wounded as they were, found comfort in his presence. His touch, though often dealing with pain, brought a sense of peace and reassurance. He didn't offer false promises of a quick recovery; he offered something more profound–his unwavering support, his genuine compassion.

As dawn approached, painting the eastern sky in hues of soft pink and gold, Tobias finally paused, his hands stained with blood and dirt. His gaze moved around the room, settling on every tired face, each man battling with pain and fear. The exhaustion was evident in the lines etched around his eyes, but his gaze held a quiet strength. He'd done everything possible; that was it for now. He had provided what he could–care, comfort, and a flicker of hope. However, the battle continued. He had faced dangers in the wilderness before, but this was different. This fight opposed a force; a brutal indifference born from greed and negligence, as insidious as any wild animal.

Tobias understood that the whispers of danger would continue. He recognized the risks that came with living in a town built on the unstable foundation of the mining industry. The mine collapse wasn't just an accident; it was a sign of a deeper, more pervasive issue. Yet he knew he couldn't walk away. He felt a strong connection to these men and this community. He had witnessed their suffering, felt their pain, and embraced their resilience. Now, he considered himself a part of this community; their shared goals and hopes tied him to them. That bond, he realized, was stronger than any danger.

The battle for Shole Creek and its people had only just begun, and Tobias, with his calloused hands and strong spirit, was ready to fight. A symbol of hope in the emerging conflict, he stood tall, his silhouette framed against the rising sun. He had transcended the role of a doctor.

Sheriff Greg Moore, a man whose girth suggested a fondness for hearty meals and whose face bore the weathered map of a life spent under the unforgiving Missouri sun, surveyed the wreckage of the collapsed mine shaft. He wasn't a man known for subtlety, his approach to law enforcement as blunt and direct as a pickaxe wielded by a seasoned miner. His gaze, however, held something beyond the usual gruffness; a flicker of something akin to unease, a subtle tremor in his usually unwavering authority. Even a seasoned frontiersman found the disaster's scale unsettling. The mangled timbers, the scattered tools, the suffocating dust–it all spoke of a tragedy far more significant than a simple accident.

Moore wasn't just the sheriff; he was also the mine foreman, a position that inextricably linked to his personal interests with the well-being of the mine and its workers. This, a detail he conveniently omitted from the official reports, was the underlying current of his investigation, a hidden tributary feeding into the already murky waters of the disaster. He initially reacted with controlled panic, a carefully constructed façade masking his own deep-seated fears about the financial repercussions, potential lawsuits, and damage to his reputation.

He moved through the debris field, his heavy boots crunching on broken rock and splintered wood. Dust, damp earth, and a sharp metallic tang filled the air; explosion remnants lingered from the earlier collapse. With his practiced eye honed by years in the mines, he surveyed the scene, deciphering the subtle clues amidst the chaos. He noted the unusual fracturing of the timbers, the peculiar pattern of the rubble, details that hinted at something beyond a simple cave-in.

His questioning, a subtle undercurrent of distrust present in each tinged each encounter with the surviving miners. His questions were sharp, insistent, his tone bordering on accusatory. He wasn't interested in their pain; he was interested in answers, in finding someone–or something–to blame. The miners, battered and bruised, offered hesitant accounts, their stories often conflicting, their memories clouded by trauma and shock. Their fear of losing their jobs, their livelihoods, hung heavy in the air, adding another layer of complexity to Moore's investigation.

His investigation led him to the mine's ledger, a meticulously kept record of expenses, production, and safety measures–or rather, the lack thereof. He uncovered discrepancies, missing entries, and hastily crossed-out scribbles—signs of systematic negligence and cost-cutting for years. The cost-cutting measures, intended to maximize profits, had undoubtedly played a significant role in the mine's instability. The implications were far-reaching and deeply troubling.

Moore's inherent bias, woven into the very fabric of his being, colored his perspective. A miner, his existence wholly dependent upon mining's success. He understood the pressure to maintain production, to meet quotas, even if it meant compromising safety protocols. It was a tacit understanding amongst the men who worked the mines, a code of silence born of necessity and fear. The silence now carried a heavy price.

His investigation, while outwardly appearing to be thorough, was subtly steered towards a pre-ordained conclusion–one that minimized his own culpability and protected the interests of those above him. He focused on the miners themselves, on their potential errors, overlooking the systemic failures that had created the conditions for the disaster. His questioning was less about finding the truth, and more about shaping the story to fit his own pre-conceived notions.

He interviewed Tobias Adams, his gaze lingering on the doctor's calm demeanor, a stark contrast to the chaos and despair that surrounded them. He probed the doctor for any evidence of negligence, any sign that the miners themselves had contributed to their own misfortune. But Tobias, despite his own weariness, remained steadfast in his unwavering dedication to the injured men. He spoke with quiet authority, a testament to his deep understanding of the human cost of the disaster. His responses, though measured and calm, subtly challenged Moore's assumptions, casting doubt on the sheriff's biased line of questioning.

The tension between them was palpable. A silent battle of wills played out amidst the wreckage of the mine. Moore, accustomed to wielding authority, found himself thwarted by Tobias's unwavering integrity, his unflinching commitment to truth and justice. The Sheriff's complicity in the disaster's systematic negligence was highlighted by the doctor's calm demeanor.

Moore's investigation, far from bringing clarity, only deepened the mystery surrounding the collapse. His attempts to control the narrative only highlighted his own conflict of interest and raised more questions than answers. The questions that were left unanswered, fueled by Moore's selective investigation, cast a long shadow on the lives of the miners, their families, and the entire town. The deeper he dug, the more he realized that the disaster wasn't a simple accident; it was a symptom of a much larger, more insidious problem–a problem that ran deeper than the mine shaft, reaching into the very heart of Shole Creek's social and economic structures. Danger, initially subtle, now loudly threatened the town, foreshadowing coming storms. His actions, or rather his inaction, would set in motion events that would test the strength of Shole Creek and its inhabitants, forever altering the landscape of their lives. The investigation, instead of uncovering truth, only served to further complicate the already intricate web of relationships and conflicts, leaving a trail of unanswered questions and simmering tensions in its wake, setting the stage for a larger, more perilous conflict. A larger drama, with devastating consequences, began with the mine collapse.

The moon, a silver sickle in the inky sky, cast long, dancing shadows across the whispering waters of Shole Creek. The air, still carrying the scent of damp earth and pine, held a unique fragrance tonight–the sweet, heady perfume of honeysuckle, clinging to the air like a secret promise. Jen Korte, her fiery red hair a vibrant contrast to the dark landscape, sat perched on a moss-covered rock, her hands clasped around a worn sketchbook. The canvas lay open before her, a testament to her restless spirit and her keen eye for the beauty that surrounded her, even in the face of adversity.

Tobias Adams found her there, his footsteps muffled by the soft earth. He moved with a quiet grace, a stark contrast to the rough-hewn landscape, his presence as natural and comforting as the gentle murmur of the creek. He settled beside her, the warmth of his body radiating against the evening chill. The silence between them wasn't awkward. The events of the past few days hung heavy in the air, an unspoken weight that bound them together. The mine collapse, the sheriff's heavy-handed investigation, the simmering tensions in the town–all of it was a part of their shared reality.

Jen looked up, her emerald eyes reflecting the moonlight, their depths hinting at the anxieties and uncertainties that weighed heavily on her heart. "They say it was an accident," she murmured, her voice barely a whisper, barely audible above the soft rush of the creek.

Tobias nodded, his gaze fixed on the swirling water. "An accident," he echoed, the word tasting like ash in his mouth. He knew better. Someone hadn't simply let the mine collapse; He had seen the evidence, the telltale signs of cost-cutting measures that had sacrificed safety for profit. But he couldn't prove it. Not yet.

"Sheriff Moore... he's not looking for the truth," Jen said, her voice laced with bitterness. "He's looking for a scapegoat."

Tobias knew she was right. Moore's investigation had been a sham, a carefully orchestrated performance designed to protect the powerful and blame the powerless. He had seen Moore's eyes. He sensed the Sheriff's desperation to cover up something more sinister than a mere mining accident.

Understanding dawned in Tobias's eyes as he whispered, "He's afraid. Afraid of what he might find if he looks too closely."

A shared silence fell between them, heavy with unspoken accusations and unanswered questions. The moon cast an ethereal glow on their faces, highlighting the strength and determination that shone in their eyes. Their connection, forged in the crucible of adversity, had deepened in the past few days. It was a bond built on mutual respect, a shared understanding of the injustices that plagued their community. Their love, once a tentative bud, had blossomed into something capable of weathering the storms that threatened to engulf them.

Jen closed her sketchbook, her gaze drifting towards the shadowy hills that surrounded them. "Father believes in the strength of Shole Creek," she said, her voice barely above a whisper. "He believes in the industry that built this town. But I'm wondering..." She trailed off, her words unfinished, her thoughts lost in the shadows.

Tobias understood her hesitations, her fears. His own ambition, his unwavering belief in the prosperity of Shole Creek blinded Stan Korte, a man of immense wealth and power. He refused to acknowledge the dark undercurrents that threatened to undermine everything he held dear. But Jen, with her artist's eye, her deep empathy, saw the cracks in the façade, the hidden flaws that threatened to shatter the illusion of prosperity.

"He's blinded by his own success," Tobias said, his voice a low rumble. "He doesn't see the consequences of his actions."

"And neither does Moore," Jen added, her voice rising slightly. "They both believe someone can bury the truth and sweep away the consequences." But they're wrong. The truth has a way of surfacing, no matter how hard they try to hide it."

They fell into another silence, the shared knowledge creating an unbreakable bond between them. The darkness around them felt less menacing, the threat less real. In each other's presence, they found a strength they hadn't known they possessed.

Jen leaned closer, her shoulder brushing against his. The touch sent a shiver down his spine, a spark igniting a warmth that spread through him. The shared danger, the shared secret, brought them closer together. They were two souls bound by a common purpose, their individual strengths complementing each other, creating a force that could overcome the powerful forces working against them.

"I noticed something tonight," Jen whispered quietly, her voice almost drowned out by the water's murmur. "At the mine... before the sheriff arrived... I saw a figure... near the collapsed shaft. A shadowy figure, cloaked in darkness... I couldn't make out their face, but I sensed... malice. Something felt...wrong."

Tobias felt a chill run down his spine. The mine collapse, while devastating, felt more like a calculated act of sabotage rather than a simple accident. Jen's observation confirmed his suspicions. This wasn't just about negligence; it was about intent. Someone wanted the mine to collapse, someone powerful enough to manipulate the events, to leave no trace of their involvement.

Tobias' voice was firm: "We must determine their identity. We need to uncover the truth before it's too late."

They spent the next hour huddled together, sharing their fears, their observations, their suspicions. The darkness of the night seemed to mirror the darkness that was consuming Shole Creek, threatening to swallow them whole. Yet, amidst the darkness, their connection burned brighter, a beacon of hope in a world consumed by fear and uncertainty. The whispers of danger that had echoed through the town were now a tangible threat, but their shared secret, their shared concern, their mutual commitment to one another and to the town forged a powerful weapon. Their love became vocal. They were two against the world, their love story unfolding amidst a backdrop of danger, their bond strengthening with each passing moment, each shared secret. They would face the darkness together, their love a beacon guiding them through the treacherous paths ahead. Their alliance, forged in the shadow of the collapsed mine, would become a powerful force, their shared secret a catalyst for the events that were about to unfold. The whispers of danger would grow louder, but so would their determination to uncover the truth and protect everything they held dear.

The quiet rustle of leaves, the soft gurgle of the creek, and the rhythmic chirping of crickets formed the soundtrack to their secret pact. They wouldn't allow fear paralyzing them; they would use it as fuel, their shared determination pushing them toward a future where truth and justice would prevail. The night whispered promises of danger, but it also whispered promises of hope, of resilience, and of a love that would endure, even amidst the most perilous circumstances. The shadows of Shole Creek held many secrets, but tonight, under the watchful eye of the moon, Jen and Tobias shared one of their own, a secret that would change the course of their lives, and the fate of the town itself. Their shared secret was their strength, their shared vulnerability was their bond, and their shared purpose was their guiding light, illuminating the path towards a future yet to be written. The future was uncertain, shrouded in the shadows of the night, but one thing was clear: they would face it together.

Chapter 3: Beneath the Surface

The earth groaned, a low, guttural sound that preceded the cataclysm. One moment, the air hung heavy with the familiar scent of damp earth and coal dust, the rhythmic clang of pickaxes a steady counterpoint to the men's grunts and shouts. Next, a deafening roar shattered the silence, shaking the earth. Dust and debris erupted from the gaping maw of the Korte mine, a geyser of rock and earth spewing into the already darkening sky. A scream, sharp and piercing, cut through the cacophony, followed by a chorus of terrified cries that were swallowed by the echoing roar of the collapsing shaft.

Jen, perched on the hill overlooking the mine, felt the earth tremble beneath her feet. The terrifying spectacle of chaos and destruction shattered the idyllic scene she'd been sketching moments before. A thick cloud of dust, the air thick with the smell of pulverized rock and fear blotted the vibrant hues of the sunset out. Her heart hammered against her ribs, a frantic drumbeat in the sudden silence that followed the initial explosion. The agonizing silence of destruction replaced the rhythmic clang of pickaxes, the silence punctuated only by the desperate calls for help swallowed by the dust cloud.

Tobias, alerted by the tremor that shook the ground beneath his feet, raced towards the mine, his heart pounding in his chest. He reached the edge of the chaos, the air thick with dust and the acrid stench of crushed rock. Men scrambled, their faces streaked with grime and terror, their cries lost in the dust cloud. The scene was one of utter pandemonium–a maelstrom of dust, debris, and desperate men fighting for survival. The rhythmic pounding in his ears wasn't just his own heart; it was the earth itself shuddering from the aftershocks of the collapse.

He pushed his way through the throng of panicked men, his powerful hands clearing a path. The scene before him was horrific. Twisted beams of timber jutted from the earth like broken bones, the mine entrance a gaping wound in the earth, spewing forth a relentless torrent of dust and debris. The air was thick with the screams of the trapped miners, a desperate chorus of agony swallowed by the earth itself. Men wept openly, their faces etched with grief and despair, as they watched the futile attempts to rescue their comrades from the earth's merciless grip.

Sheriff Moore, his face grim and set, barked orders, his voice strained and almost lost in the chaos. His usual bluster was gone, replaced by a stark recognition of the scale of the disaster. Nature's unrestrained power rendered his authority useless. He was a man out of his depth, his carefully constructed facade of control crumbling under the weight of the tragedy. A heavy blanket of silence replaced the normally boisterous activity of the mining town, punctuated only by the desperate cries for help and the rhythmic thud of shovels hitting the earth.

Tobias, his medical instincts kicking in, assisted in the rescue efforts, his hands working with practiced efficiency. He sorted the injured, assessing their wounds with a practiced eye, directing the flow of men and supplies with a calm authority that cut through the panic. He recognized the need to maintain order, to channel the raw energy of fear and chaos into productive action. But amidst the chaos, a chilling realization dawned upon him: the collapse wasn't random. The collapse's precision, the terrifyingly efficient crumbling—suggested something more sinister.

The realization dawned on him that the mine's current state wasn't accidental; instead, it had suffered a calculated and malicious act of sabotage.

He saw how someone had weakened the supports, and he detected telltale signs of tampering that only a skilled eye could spot. He noticed the subtle details, the unnatural fractures in the rock, the carefully placed explosives that had done more than simply bring down the shaft — they had created a devastating, targeted collapse. This wasn't an accident; it was a deliberate act of destruction, a calculated strike aimed at crippling the heart of Shole Creek.

As he worked, he noticed Jen amidst the throng of rescuers, her face pale and drawn, her eyes wide with shock and horror. Her usual fiery spirit was subdued, replaced by a quiet determination as she assisted the injured, offering comfort and aid with a quiet grace that belied the terror that must have been consuming her. The collapse wasn't just a tragedy; it was a personal blow, striking at the very heart of her family's legacy.

Hours turned into a seemingly endless night. A heavy, dust-filled air hung over the devastated town, casting long shadows of despair. The rhythmic thud of shovels against earth became a mournful dirge, a relentless soundtrack to the desperate battle against the earth's unforgiving grip. The flickering lanterns illuminated faces streaked with grime and tears, casting a spectral glow over the scene of devastation. Rescuers won minor victories against impossible odds with each miner rescued. The mountain, once a symbol of wealth and prosperity, now stood as a silent monument to greed and destruction.

The mine's collapse wasn't just a physical catastrophe; it was a societal earthquake. A pall of grief now cloaked the once vibrant town. Now fractured and grappling with loss, the once unified, close-knit community struggled. The economic implications were devastating. The Korte mine was the lifeblood of Shole Creek, and its destruction threatened the livelihoods of countless families.

The sheriff's investigation, predictably, was a clumsy affair, aimed more at deflecting blame than uncovering the truth. He seemed more concerned with maintaining the appearance of order than with finding justice. His attempts to pin the blame on simple negligence were unconvincing, particularly to Tobias, who saw the clear signs of sabotage. He knew that the truth lay buried beneath the rubble, hidden beneath a carefully constructed facade of accidental disaster. The mine collapse was no accident. It was deliberate and sinister. Tobias aimed to expose the truth, challenging those who profited from the town's suffering.

As the sun finally crested the horizon, casting a pale light on the scene of devastation, the rescue efforts wound down. The dead numbered shockingly high. Weeping and the silent sobs of those who had lost loved ones filled the air. Jen stood amid the wreckage, her eyes fixed on the gaping maw of the mine, her heart heavy with grief and a growing sense of dread. This tragedy extended beyond a mining accident;

A chilling certainty gripped her: this was just the start of the mine shaft collapse. Amidst chaos, her love for Tobias shone, a powerful strength against overwhelming adversity. Their shared secret, their mutual determination to uncover the truth, bound them together, forging an unbreakable bond that would see them through the trials ahead. As the town's whispers of danger escalated into a deafening roar, their love stood as a silent commitment—a commitment to uphold justice, reveal the truth, and defend each other unconditionally.

The dust, thick as a shroud, still hung heavy in the air, clinging to everything and everyone like a second skin. The acrid smell of crushed rock and pulverized earth filled Tobias's nostrils, a constant, nauseating reminder of the devastation. Yet, amidst the chaos, a strange calm had settled over him. It wasn't the calm of complacency, but the focused calm of a surgeon preparing for a delicate operation. His medical instincts, honed over years of tending to injuries in the unforgiving wilderness, took over. His practiced and efficient movements formed a silent ballet amidst the frantic activity.

With keen eyes, he assessed the injured, noting a fractured collarbone, a deep gash across a forehead, and a leg twisted at an unnatural angle. He barked concise instructions, delegating tasks to the men who surrounded him, his voice a reassuring counterpoint to the wails of the injured and the cries of the bereaved. He didn't have time for sentimentality; lives hung in the balance, and each second counted. His actions, efficient and calm despite the terror, inspired confidence.

He directed the creation of makeshift stretchers from timber salvaged from the wreckage, guiding the men as they carefully extricated the injured from the treacherous debris. His powerful hands, calloused from years of wrestling with bears and wrangling unruly horses, were gentle yet firm as he tended to broken bones and cleaned festering wounds. He used his own shirt, torn into strips, to staunch the bleeding, his movements precise and economical. He was a whirlwind of controlled energy, a beacon of hope in the maelstrom of despair.

The men, initially panicked and disorganized, found themselves drawn to his calm authority. His presence, a towering figure amidst the dust and rubble, infused them with a sense of purpose, guiding them through their fear and transforming their panic into purposeful action. His skill and courage were palpable, radiating outward, bolstering the spirits of those around him. They worked with a newfound purpose, spurred on by his unwavering dedication and fierce determination. He exceeded expectations as a doctor.

His quiet competence contrasted with the chaotic scene unfolding around him. Sheriff Moore, usually a man of bluster and authority, was a shadow of his former self, his usual swagger replaced by a palpable uncertainty. His attempts to organize the rescue efforts were haphazard and ineffective, his orders lost in the cacophony of cries and the rumble of the collapsing earth. In contrast, Tobias's actions were precise and effective, born of experience and an unwavering commitment to saving lives.

As the hours crawled by, the sun dipped below the horizon, casting long, menacing shadows across the ravaged landscape. The flickering lanterns illuminated the grim faces of the rescuers, their exhaustion etched deep into their features, their clothes stained with dust and blood. But even as fatigue weighed heavily upon them, Tobias's energy seemed inexhaustible. His determination fueled by something beyond simple exhaustion; a deep, unwavering commitment to save as many lives as possible. The darkness only seemed to intensify his resolve.

Amidst this harrowing scene, Jen was a vision of quiet strength. Her usual vibrant spirit was subdued but replaced by a calm, steely determination. She tirelessly moved amongst the injured, offering comfort and aid with an unbelievable grace. She fetched water, cleaned wounds, and comforted the grieving, her quiet presence a calming influence in the chaos's heart. She was a silent partner to Tobias; her help invaluable, her presence a source of strength for both him and the other rescuers.

The bond between Tobias and Jen deepened amidst the devastation. Their shared experience, the horrifying spectacle they were facing together, forged an unbreakable link between them. They witnessed mutual strength, resilience, compassion, and determination despite immense hardship. It wasn't just a shared understanding; it was a profound connection that transcended the chaos and grief that surrounded them. Their gazes frequently met, each time a silent acknowledgment of their shared trauma, their unspoken commitment to each other.

The last hours of the rescue operation were fraught with tension, each body pulled from the earth a grim reminder of the tragedy's terrible cost. As the sun finally rose, casting a pale light over the scene of devastation, Tobias stood amidst the rubble, his body aching, his spirit weary, but his resolve undiminished. The town looked different–ravaged, broken, yet strangely united in their shared grief. He knew that the physical wounds would heal, but the emotional scars would remain. Amidst the darkness, he perceived a shift—the townspeople now viewed him with respect, recognizing his courage and skill. They had seen his heroism, his selflessness, and they knew they could rely on him.

His actions had not only saved lives, but had also transformed him from a respected outsider into a genuine part of the community. He had earned the gratitude of the town, a gratitude that extended beyond words and manifested itself in respectful nods, hushed whispers of admiration, and the trust in his inherent goodness and capacity. The event highlighted his strength, not just his physical strength, but also his emotional resilience, his fortitude in the face of overwhelming tragedy, and his compassionate heart. His heroism solidified his bond with Jen, an unspoken understanding that bound them together in a way that transcended words, cementing their burgeoning romance with the indelible mark of shared trauma and mutual respect.

He anticipated a difficult, protracted investigation, yet remained committed to pursuing justice and uncovering the truth regardless of the consequences. The mine collapse resulted from more than simple misfortune. He knew the fight would be difficult, but he wasn't alone. He had Jen, his newfound friends in the town, and the unwavering strength of his convictions. Justice, like mine survival, demanded courage, skill, steadfastness; Tobias had it all. The whispers of danger that had previously haunted Shole Creek had escalated into a deafening roar; but in the heart of this chaos, he found a renewed resolve, the love he shared with Jen stronger than ever, a shared purpose burning brightly, guiding him towards the dark truth that lay buried beneath the surface. Though the mine is broken, their tragedy-tested courage and strengthened love forged a stronger bond. The community's battle against its demons and adversaries wrote their love story, not in ink, but in blood, sweat, and tears.

The following days were a blur of activity, a chaotic ballet of grief and recovery. The town of Shole Creek, once vibrant and bustling, was now a somber landscape, its heart broken by the mine collapse. Dust still clung to everything, a grim reminder of the tragedy that had befallen them. Yet, amidst the despair, a quiet strength emerged, a resilience born of necessity and fueled by a shared grief. Jen, ever the artist, found solace and purpose in her work. Her sketchbook, usually filled with vibrant depictions of the creek and the surrounding hills, now became a somber record of the disaster.

With meticulous detail, she sketched the ravaged landscape, capturing the raw emotion of the scene. The twisted metal, splintered wood, and grim faces of the mine rescue were all captured in her drawing, etched with exhaustion and sorrow. She depicted the faces of the injured, their expressions ranging from the vacant stare of those in shock to the pained grimaces of those nursing their wounds. She even captured the silent dignity of the grieving families, their faces streaked with tears, their bodies slumped with exhaustion, their spirits broken by loss.

Her art wasn't just a simple record; it was a powerful testament to the human spirit's capacity for resilience. Each stroke of her charcoal pencil, each carefully shading, was a meditation on loss and survival. She captured the horror of the event, but she also captured the unwavering spirit of the community, their collective determination to rebuild, to heal, to remember. Her art inspired hope, showing people that beauty and strength can be found even in the darkest times. The very act of creating, of transforming chaos into art, became a powerful act of healing for her and for the community.

Her artistic talent proved invaluable, exceeding even its role as a memorial. Her detailed sketches became vital tools in the investigation into the cause of the collapse. Sheriff Moore, humbled by his own failings during the rescue, sought Jen's work, recognizing the accuracy and detail within the images. He noted minute details in the rubble, subtle fissures in the ground, and the precise positions of debris that might suggest negligence or intentional sabotage. Artistic renderings provided a much clearer picture of the disaster than official reports. Jen's many previous visits with her father allowed her meticulous renderings to reveal critical anomalies in the mine shaft's structural integrity, anomalies that had been overlooked. Her artistic talent, once viewed as a frivolous pastime, now became an essential element in the search for truth and justice.

Tobias, already deeply impressed by Jen's compassion and quiet strength during the rescue, found himself even more captivated by her resilience and her contribution to the investigation. He saw the meticulous detail in her sketches, the raw emotion conveyed in her art, the profound understanding of the tragedy that infused her every stroke. Their shared experience in the collapse's aftermath deepened their bond, forging an even stronger connection between them. He watched as she tirelessly worked, her slender hands moving with a practiced grace, her concentration unwavering. He found himself mesmerized not just by her skill, but by her quiet determination, her unwavering commitment to documenting the truth, her deep compassion for those who suffered.

He perceived her artistry and exceptional strength. Her art became a bridge between the tragedy and its aftermath, a powerful reminder of the resilience of the human spirit, a testament to the human capacity for hope, even amidst unimaginable loss. He admired her unwavering spirit, her ability to find purpose and meaning amidst the rubble, her extraordinary talent, all of which intensified his feelings for her.

The investigation was a slow and arduous process. Sheriff Moore, still reeling from the disaster, worked tirelessly alongside Tobias, whose medical expertise proved invaluable in assessing the injuries sustained in the collapse. Jen's detailed sketches provided crucial insights into the structure of the mine, revealing subtle flaws and inconsistencies that suggested negligence or even foul play. The testimonies of the survivors were fragmented and often unreliable, their memories distorted by shock and trauma. Yet, Jen's art provided a constant, objective record of the scene, a crucial piece of the puzzle that helped to piece together the sequence of events that led to the collapse.

As the investigation unfolded, a pattern emerged. The collapse wasn't simply an accident; it was a calculated act of sabotage. Evidence pointed to a disgruntled former miner, fueled by resentment and a desire for revenge, who had deliberately weakened the support structures of the mine shaft. The investigation also uncovered evidence of widespread corruption within the mine's management, with cost-cutting measures and disregard for safety regulations, creating a perfect storm for disaster. The truth, when it finally emerged, was a bitter pill to swallow. But Jen's art, stark and unflinching, played a crucial role in bringing the perpetrators to justice.

The trial was a tense affair. The accused, a hardened veteran of the mines, vehemently denied any wrongdoing. But Jen's sketches, displayed as evidence, spoke volumes. They showed the precise locations of the compromised support beams, the subtle signs of tampering, the details that only a trained eye could detect.

Deeply affected by both the victims' stories and Jen's vivid depictions, the jury delivered a guilty verdict. The community, united in their grief and their anger, watched as justice was served. The trial became a turning point for Shole Creek, a moment of reckoning that forced the town to confront its past and to build a more just and fair future. Jen's art, initially born of sorrow and despair, became a powerful symbol of resilience, justice, and the transformative power of art.

The aftermath of the trial brought about a period of healing and reflection for Shole Creek. The community, though still bearing the scars of tragedy, rebuilt, not just the physical structures but also their collective spirit. Jen's art played a vital role in this process, her depictions of the devastation gradually giving way to images of renewal and hope. She depicted the rebuilding of the mine, the additional safety measures implemented, the gradual return of life and vibrancy to the town. Her artwork, once a stark reminder of the disaster, became a powerful symbol of resilience and the enduring strength of the human spirit.

Tobias watched Jen's transformation throughout this period, her artistic journey mirroring the town's own path towards healing. He admired her strength, not only in overcoming personal loss, but also her ability to transform her trauma into something positive and beautiful. He saw the deep compassion that fueled her creativity, the commitment to justice that guided her with every stroke, and the profound understanding of the human spirit that shone through her work. Daily, his love for her intensified; tragedy tested, resilience refined it.

The town's recovery was a long and difficult process, but Jen's artwork served as a continuous reminder of their shared experience, their collective struggle, and their ultimate triumph over adversity. Her art helped heal the wounds of the community, providing a visual narrative of their journey from grief to healing, from despair to hope, from tragedy to renewal. As Tobias and Jen shared more experiences and grew to admire one another more deeply, their relationship strengthened significantly, creating a profound and lasting bond between them. As they journeyed together through hardship, an unbreakable bond formed between them, and their resilience grew stronger than ever before. Their love story, born amidst the dust and the rubble of a shattered mine, was a testament to the enduring power of the human spirit, a love story etched not in ink, but in the resilient hearts of two souls, forever bound by the shared experience of tragedy and the shared victory of hope. Their love, born in the ashes of devastation, became a beacon of light in Shole Creek, a symbol of healing, resilience and the unwavering strength of the human heart. It was a love story whispered on the wind, echoing through the canyons and across the creek, a testament to the enduring power of love, forged in the crucible of a tragedy that tested their courage, and ultimately cemented their bond.

The mine collapse didn't just claim lives; it swallowed fortunes whole. For Stan Korte, the loss was catastrophic, a chasm that threatened to engulf his empire. The initial shock gave way to a simmering rage, a bitterness that settled deep in his bones, coating every thought with a layer of acrid resentment. He'd poured his life, his ambition, his very soul into those mines, and now, they lay in ruins, a testament to his failure, a gaping wound in his carefully constructed world. The financial repercussions were devastating, threatening to unravel years of painstaking work, to shatter the very foundation of his wealth and power. Insurance wouldn't cover the extent of the damage. Whispers of sabotage only amplified his fury, directing his anger towards those he perceived as responsible for his ruin.

His gaze, once sharp and calculating, now held a haunted quality, shadowed by loss and a gnawing sense of injustice. A simmering distrust, a suspicion that tainted every interaction, replaced the jovial camaraderie he'd once shared with other mine owners. He saw betrayal at every glance, a conspiracy in every whispered conversation. His once-imposing figure seemed to shrink under the weight of his misfortune, his shoulders slumping, his gait slower, his movements burdened by a weariness that went beyond physical exhaustion. The vibrant energy that had once characterized him, the steely determination that had propelled him to success, were now replaced by a profound despair, a chilling quietude that spoke volumes of his inner turmoil.

His home, once a symbol of his success, now felt like a gilded cage, its opulence mocking his misfortune. The grand rooms, once filled with laughter and the clinking of glasses, echoed with an unnerving silence, broken only by the occasional sigh or the restless pacing of his footsteps. The portraits of his ancestors, once sources of pride, now seemed to judge him, their unwavering gaze a constant reminder of his failure to uphold the family legacy. Even his beloved daughter, Jen, felt distant, her empathy for the victims of the disaster a constant, painful reminder of his own losses. He struggled to reconcile his grief with her compassion, the chasm between their perspectives widening with each passing day.

His resentment toward Tobias Adams, already simmering beneath the surface, erupted into a full-blown conflagration. He saw Tobias not as a healer, but as a symbol of his misfortune, a constant reminder of his daughter's defiance and his own impotence. The doctor's presence, once tolerated, now grated on his nerves, a constant irritant that exacerbated his already frayed temperament. He saw Tobias's quiet strength, his unwavering support for Jen, as a personal affront, a constant challenge to his authority, a blatant disregard for the devastation he'd endured. He conjured up scenarios in which Tobias was complicit, weaving elaborate narratives of conspiracy and betrayal, his imagination fueled by bitterness and a desperate need to assign blame.

His anger festered, turning into a venomous resentment that poisoned his interactions with everyone. He berated his staff, lashing out at those who dared to cross his path. He canceled business meetings, isolating himself in his mansion, allowing his anger to consume him. The once sharp businessman, renowned for his strategic thinking and unwavering resolve, was now reduced to a shell of his former self, his actions driven by emotion rather than reason. His reputation, once untarnished, suffered, whispers of his erratic behavior spreading like wildfire through the tight-knit community. The financial turmoil further amplified his paranoia, feeding his suspicions that his business rivals were taking advantage of his vulnerability.

His interactions with Sheriff Moore became strained, his questioning of the investigation laced with veiled accusations. He demanded a swift resolution, an explanation for the disaster that would exonerate him from any responsibility, yet simultaneously implicated those he deemed to be his enemies. The Sheriff, a man of integrity, found himself caught in the crossfire, struggling to balance his duty to investigate the collapse impartially with the pressure from a powerful and increasingly unstable man. Moore understood the depths of Korte's despair, but he also recognized the danger of letting his grief cloud his judgment.

As the investigation progressed, revealing evidence of sabotage and negligence, Korte's rage intensified. The unraveling of his carefully constructed world, the public exposure of his company's shortcomings, and the possibility of facing legal repercussions sent him spiraling deeper into despair. He became a recluse, his opulent mansion a prison of his own making, the once vibrant rooms now filled with the oppressive weight of his despair. He spent hours staring out of the windows, gazing at the ruined mine, a stark reminder of his shattered dreams and losing his fortune.

His obsession with Tobias grew, his animosity fueled by a desperate need to find a scapegoat for his misfortune. To undermine Tobias's reputation, he spread rumors and fabricated stories to damage his standing in the community. He commissioned private investigators to dig up dirt on Tobias, hoping to find some evidence of wrongdoing that he could use to discredit him. He saw Tobias as a threat, not only to his financial stability, but also to his pride and his place in society.

The strain on his relationship with Jen was palpable. His outbursts of anger, his irrational accusations, and his constant barrage of criticism pushed her away. Jen, witnessing her father's descent into despair, felt torn between her love for him and her growing affection for Tobias. She tried to reason with him, but he resisted her efforts, dismissing her empathy as naïve idealism. The chasm between them widened. A silent battle fought in the shadowed corners of the grand mansion.

The overwhelming weight of loss and resentment threatened and frayed the once-unbreakable bond between father and daughter. Jen, trapped between her loyalty to her father and her budding love for Tobias, felt the weight of the world on her shoulders. She struggled to reconcile the man she loved with the man her father had become, the compassionate doctor with the resentful mine owner. The future, once bright with promise, now seemed shrouded in uncertainty, clouded by the shadows of financial ruin and familial discord. The tragedy that had struck Shole Creek had shattered more than just the mine; it had fractured the very fabric of Korte's life and his relationship with his daughter. The coming days would determine if this family could salvage the pieces of their lives, or whether the weight of loss would ultimately destroy them.

The days following the mine collapse blurred into a relentless cycle of grief and frantic activity. Jen, despite her own sorrow at the loss of life and the devastation to her community, found herself unexpectedly drawn to the quiet strength of Tobias. He moved through the chaos with a calm efficiency that both impressed and comforted her. While her father retreated into his grief, becoming a recluse within his opulent mansion, Tobias remained a constant presence, a beacon of calm in the storm. He tended to the injured, offering not just medical care but also a soothing presence, a listening ear to those overwhelmed by fear and loss.

His gentle hands, so adept at mending broken bones, also seemed to possess a magical quality capable of soothing fractured spirits. He spent countless hours at the makeshift hospital, his brow furrowed in concentration as he stitched wounds, both physical and emotional. He listened patiently to the stories of loss, offering words of comfort and understanding, his empathy bridging the gap between despair and hope. He was more than a doctor;

One evening, as the last rays of the setting sun cast long shadows across the ravaged landscape, Jen found Tobias sitting alone by Shole Creek, the gentle murmur of the water a counterpoint to the silence of the ruined mine. He had spoken little that day, his usual easygoing demeanor replaced by a thoughtful quietude. The weight of his responsibilities, the constant demand for his medical expertise, had visibly taken their toll. Seeing his exhaustion, Jen approached him cautiously.

"You've barely slept in days," she whispered. She sat down beside him, the cool dampness of the earth seeping into her skirt.

He looked at her, a faint smile touching his lips. "It's nothing a good night's sleep can't fix," he said, his voice husky with fatigue.

"But it's not just the lack of sleep," Jen countered gently. "It's the weight of everything, isn't it? The loss, the anger, the uncertainty..."

He nodded, his gaze fixed on the flowing water. "It's a heavy burden to bear, Jen. I've seen death before, but this... this is different. This feels personal."

Jen understood. The mine was the heart of Shole Creek, its lifeblood pumping through the veins of the community. The collapse represented far more than mere financial disaster.

"I know," she murmured, reaching out to place a comforting hand on his arm. The unexpected touch sent a shiver down his spine, a spark igniting within the weary embers of his exhaustion.

They shared a meaningful silence between them. They sat together for a long time, watching the sunset paint the sky in hues of orange and purple, the vibrant colors a stark contrast to the bleakness of the mine's ruins. In that shared silence, their bond deepened, their connection forged in the crucible of shared adversity.

Over the following weeks, their relationship blossomed. It was a quiet growth, nurtured by shared experiences and mutual support. Mutual comfort stemmed from their talks, covering both the town's practical recovery and deeper thoughts on life, death, and human strength.

They spent hours sketching together amidst the ruins, Jen capturing the poignant beauty of the devastation on her canvas, Tobias sketching the resilience of the people rebuilding their lives. His art, raw and honest, reflected the hardships they endured and yet conveyed a profound sense of hope. Their shared creative endeavors became therapy, a way to process their emotions and find a measure of peace amidst the turmoil.

Tobias's empathy extended beyond his role as a doctor. As Jen struggled with complex emotions, he became her confidante and listening ear. He helped her understand her father's descent into bitterness and anger, explaining that grief often manifested itself in unpredictable and destructive ways. He helped her to see the pain lurking beneath her father's surface, the weight of responsibility and the crushing blow of financial ruin.

The growing intimacy between them was a slow burn, fueled by mutual respect and an undeniable physical attraction. Unspoken emotions charged their stolen moments—a hand brushing against a hand, a lingering glance, a shared smile—a silent acknowledgment of the growing bond uniting them.

Quiet conversations under the vast, star-studded sky filled their nights, their words weaving a tapestry of hopes and dreams for the future.

Their shared experiences forged a resilience that strengthened their connection. They worked side-by-side to help the community rebuild, their efforts becoming a testament to their growing commitment to each other and to their shared home. They volunteered at the relief efforts, organizing supplies, comforting the distraught, and helping those affected find new homes and livelihoods.

Their relationship was not without its challenges. Jen's father remained distant, his anger simmering like a volcanic eruption waiting to happen. He saw Tobias's increasing involvement in Jen's life as a betrayal, a constant reminder of his own failures and the unraveling of his carefully constructed world. Yet, despite the disapproval, Jen and Tobias's bond only deepened. Their shared commitment to rebuilding Shole Creek became a powerful force, strengthening their resolve to face any obstacles that lay ahead.

Despite facing many challenges and hardships, their love story quietly but intensely progressed, serving as a powerful reminder of the enduring strength of human connection amidst adversity. The town's recovery and the blossoming of their romance intertwined, forming a resilient and vibrant love story that mirrored the wildflowers that stubbornly bloomed amidst the ruined mine's rubble, a testament to their shared strength and the town's tenacious spirit. Their love story, far from being simply a romantic tale, served as a powerful symbol of hope, showcasing the enduring spirit of those brave individuals who, despite the hardships and losses encountered in the rugged, beautiful landscape of the American West, dared to forge a new life, filled with the promise of a brighter future. As days bled into weeks and weeks into months, they constructed the groundwork for their future amidst the devastation of the ruins, a future forged in the crucible of shared loss.

Chapter 4: Shadows of the Past

The rhythmic clang of the blacksmith's hammer, a familiar soundtrack to his childhood, echoed faintly in Tobias's memory. He wasn't at the forge, though; he was perched precariously on a rocky outcrop overlooking a raging river, the wind whipping his dark hair across his face. He was ten years old, his small hands gripping a worn leather strap, the other end secured to a struggling, half-drowned pup. The icy water churned around the creature, its whimpers lost in the roar of the current.

This wasn't Shole Creek. This was the wild, untamed heart of the Colorado Rockies, a landscape etched into his soul as deeply as the scars that crisscrossed his back. The sharp, clear memory felt real, like the cool night air settling on his shoulders. He saw the fear in the pup's eyes, a mirror of his own terror as he fought the relentless pull of the river, his young muscles straining against the icy current. He'd risked everything that day, his own life a mere afterthought compared to rescuing the helpless creature. That act of bravery, born from a desperate need to protect something vulnerable, had shaped him, forging the core of his quiet strength.

The flashback shifted. He was older now, fourteen, his lean frame already showing the beginnings of the man he would become. He stood before his father, a mountain of a man, his face etched with lines carved by years of toil and hardship. The blacksmith's forge glowed, casting long shadows that danced menacingly on the walls of their small cabin. His father, his hands calloused and scarred from years of shaping metal, was not shaping metal that day. He was shaping Tobias.

The lesson wasn't in hammering iron, but in enduring hardship, in facing adversity without flinching. His father taught him to harness the raw power of the mountains, the relentless force of the river, channeling it, molding it into something useful, something strong. The lessons weren't always gentle, the words often harsh, born of a gruff love that masked a deep well of concern.

"A man's strength isn't in his size, Tobias," his father's voice, raspy and gravelly, echoed in his memory. "It's in his spirit, in his endurance, in his unwavering will to survive. The mountains don't care for tears, son. They demand respect and resilience."

He recalled his father's fierce gaze, the unwavering belief in his son's capacity for both strength and compassion. It was a peculiar mix; a harsh exterior encompassing a tender heart. A man who taught his son to hunt, to survive, yet who also wept silently over the loss of his wife, a secret sorrow his son had only discovered years later, hidden beneath layers of stoicism. The image of his father, strong but vulnerable, sparked a deep understanding within him.

Another scene flashed before his eyes. He was eighteen, a young man standing on the precipice of adulthood, his hands stained with the blood of a wounded deer, the scent of pine and damp earth clinging to his clothes. It wasn't the hunting that stood out in this memory, but the quiet solemnity with which he tended the deer's wound, his gentle touch a stark contrast to the harshness of the wilderness. He understood the precarious balance of life and death, the sanctity of life, even in its wild and untamed form. This understanding, born from respect for nature and an innate empathy for all living creatures, would become his guiding principle, his moral compass.

These fragmented memories, these glimpses into Tobias's past, revealed a life shaped by loss, hardship, and the unforgiving beauty of the American West. They explained the quiet strength he possessed, the deep well of resilience that allowed him to navigate the turbulent waters of Shole Creek with unwavering calm. His quiet demeanor, often mistaken for aloofness, masked a depth of empathy and understanding gleaned from years spent wrestling with the harsh realities of survival.

He wasn't just a doctor, a trapper, or a bear hunter; he was a man forged in the crucible of the wilderness, his character shaped by experiences that had honed his skills, tested his resolve, and instilled in him a profound respect for both life and death.

The flashbacks ceased, leaving him with a sense of profound peace, a sense of coming home. He was sitting by Shole Creek, Jen's hand resting lightly on his arm. He felt present again; her touch evoked creek whispers, pine fragrance, night's quiet stars. The weight of his past still rested on his shoulders, but now it felt different, less like a burden and more like a foundation upon which he was building his future.

He looked at Jen, her face illuminated by the moonlight, her eyes filled with an understanding that went beyond words. In her presence, he felt a depth of intimacy that surpassed the simple comfort of shared loss. It was a connection that transcended the challenges they faced, a bond that strengthened with every passing day. He understood now, more clearly than ever, why the mine collapse felt personal. It directly attacked the life he carefully built, a life shared with his companion. He'd lost a part of himself in those ruins, and protecting Jen, protecting this fragile new beginning, became the driving force behind his actions.

The unspoken question hung between them, a silent acknowledgment of the shadows of the past that still lingered. He hadn't shared his personal history with her, not in its entirety. He knew that revealing the full extent of his experiences would require immense trust and vulnerability. He was cautious, guarded by years of solitude and self-reliance. Yet, in Jen's eyes, he saw a glimmer of understanding, a sense of patience that encouraged him to slowly unveil his past, revealing his vulnerabilities, and showing her the man he truly was.

The following weeks were a dance between the present and the past. He found himself increasingly drawn to Jen's artistic nature, the way she found beauty in the devastation of the mine. Her vibrant, detailed paintings contrasted sharply with the ruined landscape, showcasing life's resilience. Her art resonated with the deep-seated emotions that he'd struggled to articulate, the quiet resilience of the human spirit, a spirit that he knew intimately from his own life.

He began sharing small fragments of his past, starting with his childhood in the mountains. He described the fierce beauty of the landscape, the thrill of the hunt, the harsh lessons learned from his father. Only wind's howl and hawk's cry broke the silence. Each shared memory revealed a piece of his soul, dismantling the wall of self-reliance he'd carefully constructed over the years. His vulnerability became a bridge between them, creating an even stronger bond.

As he shared his past, he understood more deeply the complexities of his own character. He saw the blend of compassion and hardness, the balance of tenderness and strength. The formerly solitary wilderness man learned community life, his well-being now intertwined with its own. The mine's collapse, the loss, and the grief—all of it had become part of his story, interwoven with Jen's, creating a narrative richer and more profound than either of them could have imagined. It was more than a romance; their love story was. Their love was blooming amidst the wreckage, as resilient and beautiful as the wildflowers pushing their way through the cracked earth of Shole Creek. The shadows of the past were still present, but they were no longer overwhelming; they were part of the fabric of their lives, shaping them, guiding them towards a future that, despite the darkness, promised to be filled with hope and light. Upon facing the future together, hand in hand, they bore the weight of their past as a testament to their strength, resilience, and the enduring power of love.

The rhythmic whisper of Shole Creek, usually a source of solace, felt strangely discordant tonight. Jen sat on the porch of her father's grand house, the imposing structure a stark contrast to the rough-hewn cabins that dotted the mining town. The air hung heavy with unspoken words, the silence amplifying the anxieties that gnawed at her. Tobias's quiet strength had become a comforting presence in her life, a refuge from the turbulent emotions that swirled within her. Yet, there was a chasm between them, a gap bridged only by shared glances and unspoken understanding. The chasm was her family, her past–a past she was now compelled to share.

She had avoided the subject deliberately. Her father, Stan Korte, was a man of immense power and unwavering control, a man who brooked no dissent. The mine, his kingdom, was built on secrets as much as ore. To speak of them was to risk shattering the fragile peace she'd carefully cultivated. Yet, the mine's collapse, the loss of life, had cleaved open the carefully constructed façade of her family, revealing fissures of conflict and betrayal that ran deep.

The story began, not with her father, but with her grandmother, Elara. Elara Korte, a woman whose name was whispered in hushed tones around Shole Creek, a woman of formidable spirit and even more formidable beauty. A portrait of her in the attic showcased fiery red hair falling around a face that hinted at a blend of passion and pain. Jen had spent countless hours studying the painting, trying to decipher the secrets held within those piercing eyes. It was a study that led her to discover a family history far more complicated than she'd ever imagined.

Elara had arrived in Shole Creek, a penniless orphan, fleeing a past shrouded in mystery. She'd found work as a seamstress, her nimble fingers transforming rough spun fabrics into elegant garments. But her true talent lay elsewhere–in her ability to navigate the treacherous social landscape of the burgeoning mining town. She'd possessed a sharp mind, a keen understanding of human nature, and an uncanny ability to extract information from those who held it most closely.

Her wit and independence had captivated Stan Korte, then a young and ambitious miner. He'd seen past her humble beginnings, recognizing the fire within her, a fire that mirrored his own ambition. Their courtship was tempestuous, filled with passionate arguments and reconciliations, their love a volatile blend of attraction and defiance. He was obsessed with acquiring wealth and power, while she dreamed of escaping the constraints of her past, of making a name for herself on her own terms. Their marriage, forged in mutual ambition, was a partnership built on shifting sands, a precarious balance of power and compromise.

Success marked the early years of their marriage, their wealth growing alongside the mine. But underneath the veneer of prosperity, tensions simmered. Elara, ever the independent spirit, chafed under William's controlling nature. Her desire for a life beyond the mine clashed with his relentless pursuit of wealth. She invested her money in various projects he knew nothing about. This financial independence gave her a sense of control in a relationship that constantly threatened to eclipse her personality.

Their only child, Jen's mother, inherited the same fierce independence from Elara. Her name was Isabella, and she was a spirited woman who refused to be confined by the expectations placed upon women of her time. She had a talent for music, a passionate love for the wild landscape surrounding Shole Creek, and a deep disdain for her father's ruthlessness. She'd yearned for a life free from her father's suffocating influence, a desire that put her at odds with William's ambitions.

Isabella's rebellion took the form of a secret love affair with a young geologist, a man named Thomas Ashton. Thomas was everything William was not–kind, gentle, and deeply committed to his work, but uninterested in the mine's potential for wealth, rather he preferred the academic pursuit of understanding the land around him. Their clandestine meetings, conducted under the cover of darkness, became a source of both joy and terror for Isabella. The joy stemmed from a love that transcended social boundaries. William's potential discovery intensified their clandestine relationship.

The discovery of their affair sent shockwaves through the Korte family. William, enraged by his daughter's defiance, banished Thomas from Shole Creek. He forbade Isabella from ever seeing him again, a cruel decree that fueled a silent rebellion within the family. Isabella, her heart breaking, refused to renounce her love for Thomas. The ensuing conflict was devastating; a silent war fought in whispers and stolen glances.

Isabella's defiance ultimately led to her death, a tragic accident that was shrouded in ambiguity. The official report spoke of a fall from a horse. But Jen, piecing together fragments of conversations and hidden letters, suspected something more sinister. The possibility that William's relentless pursuit of power and control had somehow resulted in the death of his daughter was a secret she guarded fiercely.

The secrets Elara kept from William also added another layer of intrigue. Jen discovered a hidden compartment in an old trunk in the attic, containing letters revealing that Elara had a secret son from a past relationship, before meeting William, an unexpected son that she never mentioned to her husband and who disappeared from her life sometime shortly before she married William. Elara expertly concealed the child's existence; the family records remained silent. Jen was now convinced that the mystery surrounding Elara's past, her mother's tragic demise, and her father's ruthless ambition all played a part in shaping the complexities of her family history.

The weight of these revelations pressed down on Jen, a burden of secrets and lies that threatened to consume her. She looked at Tobias, his gaze filled with concern and understanding.

This exceeded a simple account of a family's secret past. It was a story of ambition, betrayal, and the enduring power of love amidst turmoil. It was the story that, she realized, was inseparable from her own life, her own heart. It was a narrative that had shaped her, molded her, and ultimately, forged her own sense of who she was, and who she was becoming. And in sharing this story with Tobias, in allowing him to see the complexities of her past, she felt a sense of release, a sense of hope that, despite the shadows of her family's past, she might finally find a path towards her own future. A future where she could reconcile her own past with her present, and create a life guided by love and truth. Life unfolded, no longer hidden, but revealed. The darkness might linger, but the first faint glimmer of light had broken through. The shadows of the past were still present, but they no longer held her captive.

Sheriff Greg Moore sat on the porch of his small cabin, the rhythmic creak of the wood a counterpoint to the restless turmoil within him. The Shole Creek moon cast long shadows, painting the dusty street in shades of silver and black, mirroring the conflicting emotions that warred inside him. Serving as Sheriff of Shole Creek for five years, he had observed the spectrum of human behavior, noting how greed and desperation could erode a community striving with hope and ambition. Tonight, however, the weight of his responsibilities felt heavier than ever.

The Korte mine collapse had shaken the town to its core. The loss of life was a tragedy that cut deep into the fabric of Shole Creek, leaving a raw wound that threatened to fester. But beneath the surface of public grief lay a simmering undercurrent of suspicion and resentment. Whispers followed him like shadows–whispers of corruption, of negligence, of secrets buried deep within the heart of the Korte mining empire.

Moore knew Stan Korte. He knew the man's relentless ambition, his ruthless pursuit of wealth, his iron-fisted control over the town. He also knew the man's capacity for charm and manipulation, his ability to twist words and events to his advantage. The investigation into the mine collapse was proving more difficult than he'd anticipated. The mine's records were a tangled mess, deliberately obfuscated, making it almost impossible to determine the exact cause of the disaster.

The initial reports pointed towards a simple accident, a sudden cave-in caused by unstable ground. But Moore harbored doubts. He'd seen too many accidents in his time to believe that this was merely a tragic mishap. Numerous inconsistencies and unanswered questions existed. Some survivors' gazes revealed much to him. They weren't fully forthcoming.

He'd spent countless hours poring over blueprints, interviewing witnesses, trying to piece together the fragments of a story that refused to be told. His confusion and frustration grew with each conversation. The miners were hesitant, afraid to speak out against the powerful Korte, wary of retaliation. Their livelihoods depended on the mine, their families' well-being tied to Korte's benevolence.

But Moore couldn't shake the feeling that something wasn't right. He knew that Stan Korte had a reputation for cutting corners, for prioritizing profit over safety. Rumors of substandard materials and inadequate safety measures had circulated for years, whispers dismissed as disgruntled miners' complaints. Now, those whispers echoed louder, amplified by the tragic consequences of the mine collapse.

Beyond the mine's collapse, there was the matter of Dr. Tobias Adams. Quiet strength and integrity characterized the doctor. His presence in Shole Creek was a welcome addition. However, his involvement with Jen Korte, Stan Korte's daughter, added another layer of complexity to the situation. Tobias's integrity was clear to Moore; however, his involvement with Jen created a dangerous situation. The Kortes were not a family to trifle with, and their influence extended far beyond the confines of Shole Creek.

His own past haunted him. He'd seen his share of darkness, both personal and professional. He'd lost a brother to a senseless act of violence, a loss that had left a permanent scar on his soul. That experience altered his perspective, fostering wariness toward hidden depravity, even within seemingly respectable individuals. He'd sworn to serve justice, to protect the innocent, to uphold the law. But the law often felt like a blunt instrument, incapable of reaching the subtle complexities of human nature.

He felt the familiar sting of guilt, a sharp reminder of his own failures. He'd failed to protect his brother, a burden he carried with him always. He'd vowed never to let that happen again. He carried the burden of protecting Shole Creek, a responsibility that sometimes felt suffocating, draining his energy and threatening to consume him entirely.

He knew that uncovering the truth about the mine collapse would not be easy. It would require courage, determination, and a willingness to confront the powerful forces that sought to suppress it. He must confront the town's pervasive darkness, a darkness akin to mine dust.

The personal cost of his profession weighed heavily on him. He was a man alone, his life stripped bare by loss and duty. His nights were filled with restless sleep, his days haunted by the weight of unanswered questions. He yearned for connection, for solace, but found little comfort in the harsh reality of his existence. His days were a battle against the forces of corruption, a fight against indifference and deception.

As he sat there, lost in his thoughts, he saw Jen Korte walking towards him. Tobias Adams, their faces accompanied her etched with a mixture of exhaustion and determination. He knew that their pasts were intertwined with the secrets of Shole Creek, entangled with the web of lies and deceit that surrounded them. He sighed, the weight of his responsibilities heavy upon his shoulders. His past held deep shadows, yet he persevered. Justice would be served, even if it meant facing the darkest corners of his own soul and the most powerful forces in the town. He would uncover the truth, no matter the cost. The fate of Shole Creek, and perhaps his own, depended on it. He had a duty to uphold, and he would not fail. The weight on his shoulders was immense, but the resolve in his heart was stronger. He rose to meet them, preparing to face whatever lay ahead.

The crisp morning air held a bite of fall, the scent of pine and damp earth filling Jen's lungs as she and Tobias rode towards the whispering creek. The recent mine collapse cast a pall over Shole Creek, but the sun struggled to pierce the gloom, offering fleeting moments of warmth. Their horses' hooves drummed a steady rhythm against the packed earth trail, the sound a counterpoint to the quiet tension that hung between them.

Tobias, his usual quiet strength tempered by a weariness that etched lines around his eyes, broke the silence. "Jen," he began, his voice low, "Sheriff Moore mentioned something about a meeting with the Osage. He seemed... concerned."

Jen nodded, her gaze fixed on the path ahead. "He was vague, but implied it was a matter of some urgency. A land dispute, he hinted, something concerning their sacred grounds near the northern boundary of the Korte mining claims."

The Osage Nation, a powerful and proud tribe, had long held a wary peace with the encroaching settlers. Their ancestral lands, rich in history and spiritual significance, were now increasingly threatened by the relentless expansion of Shole Creek and its mining operations. The Korte mine, with its insatiable hunger for resources, stood as a stark symbol of that conflict.

As they approached the designated meeting place–a secluded clearing near the creek, shrouded by ancient oaks–a sense of unease settled over Jen. She saw several figures emerge from the shadows of the trees, their presence both imposing and dignified. The tribal leader, Chief Standing Bear, a man whose bearing spoke of strength and wisdom, stepped forward, his face etched with lines that spoke of years spent battling harsh realities.

He greeted them with a quiet dignity that belied the turmoil within the tribe. "Dr. Adams, Miss Korte," his voice was deep and resonant, carrying the weight of centuries of history. "We humbly request your assistance. The Korte mine is encroaching upon our sacred burial grounds. The tremors from the recent collapse have desecrated ancient sites, disturbing the spirits of our ancestors." He spoke with measured calm, but the pain in his eyes was unmistakable.

Tobias listened intently, his gaze fixed on the Chief. He knew the importance of respecting cultural beliefs and traditions. The clash between the relentless pursuit of wealth and the sanctity of ancient ways was a conflict he understood all too well. He had witnessed firsthand the destructive potential of greed, the disregard for human life and cultural heritage in the name of progress. He recognized necessary action.

"Chief Standing Bear," Tobias responded, his voice firm yet gentle, "we understand your concern. This is a serious matter. We will do everything in our power to help resolve this."

Jen felt deep sympathy for the Osage. As an artist, she possessed a deep sensitivity to the beauty and sacredness of nature, the delicate balance between humanity and the natural world. The desecration of the burial grounds was not merely a land dispute; it violated their cultural heritage, a transgression against their very identity.

"The Kortes will not listen to reason," Chief Standing Bear stated, a hint of despair in his voice. "They only understand the language of power and wealth. They see only the value of the land in terms of minerals, disregarding the significance of the land to our people." He gestured towards the young Osage who stood behind him, their faces etched with worry and fear. These trace their lineage to those buried below. Their heritage, their roots are being torn away."

The weight of the situation pressed down upon Jen and Tobias. It was a situation far beyond a simple land dispute. It represented a deeper cultural conflict, a struggle between two worlds that seemed increasingly incompatible. They were caught in a web of complex alliances, facing the formidable power of Stan Korte, while advocating for the rights and dignity of the Osage.

Tobias, ever the pragmatist, suggested a course of action. "Chief, we need evidence. Documentation of the exact location of the burial grounds, witness testimonies from members of your tribe, anything that can be presented as irrefutable proof. We will then approach Sheriff Moore and seek legal counsel."

The Osage elders conferred among themselves, their murmuring a low hum against the whispering leaves. After a time, Chief Standing Bear nodded. "We will provide you with all the evidence we have gathered. Our sacred maps, the accounts of our elders, all of it." He paused, his eyes filled with a mixture of hope and trepidation. "But we know the Kortes are powerful. Their power extends throughout the town, including its courts. We fear they will not be held accountable."

Jen, ever the artist, understood the significance of visual evidence. "Perhaps I can help," she offered, "I can sketch the locations, create visual representations of the disturbed burial sites. It will be a powerful tool, something that might move hearts that words alone cannot reach."

The elders regarded her with thoughtful consideration. Her artistic talents, usually reserved for capturing the beauty of the landscape, were now poised to become a potent instrument for social justice. These works will be much more than just pictures.

Over the next few days, Jen and Tobias worked tirelessly, gathering evidence, documenting the details of the land dispute. Jen's sketches and paintings, rendered with delicate precision, captured the poignancy of the desecrated burial grounds, the sorrow etched onto the faces of the Osage people. The ancient trees, the wind-swept plains, and the scarred earth became the silent witnesses to their anguish.

Tobias meticulously documented testimonies from tribal elders, preserving their oral history and the weight of their emotional accounts. He compiled maps, historical documents, anything that could substantiate their claim. The weight of their task pressed upon them, the stark reality of a cultural struggle far outweighing the simple confines of a land dispute.

The process of gathering evidence brought them closer to the Osage people. They shared stories, laughter, and tears, forging a bond of mutual respect and understanding. Jen's artistic talents became a bridge, transcending the boundaries of language and culture. Her drawings provided a powerful visual language that touched upon the universal human experience of loss, grief, and the deep yearning for justice. Tobias's medical expertise brought a level of trust, providing practical care for minor injuries and illnesses among the tribe. Their commitment deepened beyond the initial plea for help. They had become allies in a shared fight for the protection of ancestral lands, of spiritual heritage, of a community's very identity.

Facing Stan Korte loomed before them. His power and influence in Shole Creek were undeniable. But Jen and Tobias, armed with irrefutable evidence and united by their shared commitment to justice, felt a growing sense of determination. Challenges loomed, resistance possible, but retreat was not an option. The shadows of the past held power, but the strength of their conviction and the unwavering hope of the Osage people shone brighter. Justice, cultural preservation, love: the fight had just started. Their work remained unfinished. The battle had shifted from evidence gathering to the formidable challenge of confronting Stan Korte, and the forces aligned with him, and securing justice for the Osage Nation. The fate of the tribe, and perhaps the very soul of Shole Creek, rested upon the outcome.

The weight of the evidence lay heavy on Jen's heart. The meticulously rendered sketches, the poignant testimonies, the meticulously compiled maps–they all pointed towards the same undeniable truth: the Korte mine had desecrated the Osage sacred burial grounds. The visual impact of her artwork was undeniable; the stark contrast between the peaceful beauty of the landscape and the brutal disruption of the mining operations spoke volumes. The faces of the Osage elders, etched with generations of history and the present sorrow, mirrored the stark reality of their situation. She had become an unwilling participant in a conflict far larger than herself, a conflict that threatened to tear apart not only the Osage community but also her own fragile happiness.

Her father, Stan Korte, a man driven by ambition and the relentless pursuit of wealth, remained oblivious to the cultural significance of the issue. He saw only the potential for profit, the untapped resources beneath the earth, the endless expansion of his mining empire. To him, the Osage were an inconvenient obstacle, a hurdle to be overcome in his quest for fortune. He had dismissed Tobias's concerns as the ramblings of a sentimental do-gooder, a distraction from the real business of mining. He viewed the land dispute not as a moral transgression but as a business matter to be handled with the same ruthless efficiency he applied to all his operations.

This indifference infuriated Jen. She had always admired her father's drive and ambition, the way he had carved a powerful position for himself in the rough-and-tumble world of Shole Creek. But his disregard for the Osage people and their sacred heritage shocked and disillusioned her. It challenged the very foundation of her belief in her father, in his principles, in the image she had carefully constructed of him. His actions were a stark contradiction to the values she herself held dear.

The confrontation was inevitable. It hung in the air, a palpable tension that vibrated between the quiet respect Jen felt for the Osage and the fierce loyalty she had always felt towards her family. She loved her father, despite his flaws, but she couldn't condone his callous disregard for the cultural heritage of the Osage people. And yet, she knew that challenging him directly would cause an irreparable fracture in their already strained relationship.

The meeting took place in her father's imposing office, a room that mirrored his personality: stark, functional, and devoid of any warmth or personal touch. The air was thick with the smell of coal dust and cigar smoke, a potent symbol of the relentless industry that had shaped Shole Creek. Stan Korte sat behind his massive oak desk, his face grim, his gaze unwavering. He exuded potent power; his dominance was almost palpable. Jen stood before him, her heart pounding in her chest, her hands clasped tightly in front of her.

She had prepared herself for this confrontation, anticipating the resistance she would encounter. She had practiced her words, trying to find a way to convey the moral weight of the issue without triggering his wrath. But as she began to speak, the carefully constructed argument crumbled before her father's unflinching gaze.

"Father," she started, her voice trembling slightly, "I know you believe the Osage are interfering with your operations. But... the evidence is undeniable. The mine has desecrated their sacred burial grounds. This isn't just a land dispute. This is about respect, about cultural heritage. This concerns the community's core identity.

Her father snorted, a dismissive sound that echoed in the quiet room. "Sentimental nonsense," he interrupted, his voice sharp and cutting. "This is business, Jen. And business comes first. Those Indians need to learn their place. They've lived off this land for centuries, but it's time they understood that progress demands sacrifice."

Jen felt a surge of anger, but she forced herself to remain calm. She had hoped for a rational discussion, a chance to appeal to his sense of fairness. But his words revealed an absolute disregard for the feelings and rights of others. He saw only profit, never the human cost of his relentless pursuit of wealth.

"But father," Jen persisted, her voice gaining strength, "Tobias has gathered irrefutable evidence. The Osage have provided maps, witness testimonies. My own sketches show the extent of the damage. We can't simply ignore this. We must do something."

Her father leaned back in his chair, his expression hardening. "Tobias? That... trapper? He's nothing but a troublemaker. He is stirring up trouble." He paused, then added with a cruel smile, "And you, Jen? You're letting your emotions cloud your judgment. You're jeopardizing the future of the Korte family business."

Jen recoiled at the mention of Tobias, a sharp stab of pain. Her father disapproved intensely. She knew, with chilling clarity, the depth of the chasm that had opened between her and her father. It was a chasm that ran deeper than any simple land dispute. It was a clash of values, a struggle between loyalty and conscience.

The weight of her choice settled upon her, crushing her with the full force of its implications. She could remain loyal to her father, accepting his vision of Shole Creek's future, a vision that dismissed the Osage people as an inconvenient obstacle to progress. Or, she could stand with Tobias, with the

Osage people, and fight for justice, even if it meant sacrificing her family's approval, risking her father's wrath, possibly even her inheritance.

The decision gnawed at her, a constant, agonizing pressure in her chest. She had to choose between family and conscience, between loyalty and justice. It was a choice that would define her character, shape her future, and ultimately determine the course of her life and the destiny of Shole Creek. The silence in her father's office stretched, heavy and suffocating, as the weight of her difficult choice hung heavy in the air, pressing down on her like the oppressive weight of the approaching storm.

Chapter 5: The Heart of the Matter

The storm outside mirrored the tempest raging within Jen. The wind howled a mournful dirge, rattling the windows of her father's office, a counterpoint to the silence that hung heavy between them after their explosive confrontation. She had left her father's presence feeling as though a chasm had opened between them, a fissure that threatened to swallow her whole. The weight of her decision pressed down on her, a leaden cloak suffocating her breath. She had chosen conscience over loyalty, justice over family, a path that led her directly to Tobias.

She found him by the creek, his silhouette etched against the fiery sunset, the setting sun painting the sky in hues of orange and purple, mirroring the turmoil in her heart. He was sketching, his brow furrowed in concentration, a familiar scene that always calmed her, but tonight, the familiar comfort offered little solace. The landscape seemed to hold its breath, awaiting the unfolding drama. He looked up as she approached, his eyes, the color of warm earth, filled with a mixture of concern and anticipation.

He rose to meet her, his tall, imposing figure casting a long shadow. His quiet strength, a familiar comfort, radiated from him, a counterpoint to the emotional chaos that swirled within her. She saw a flicker of apprehension, a hint of uncertainty in his usually unflappable demeanor, but beneath it lay a resolute strength that mirrored her own.

"Jen," he said softly, his voice a low rumble that soothed her frayed nerves. He didn't press her for answers, didn't try to fill the silence with meaningless words. He simply let her be, his presence a quiet strength in the turbulent atmosphere. He understood the weight of her choice, the burden she carried. He didn't need words to express his support. His very presence was a testament to his unwavering belief in her, in their shared cause, in the justice they sought.

She opened her mouth to speak, to confess the turmoil in her heart, the conflict between her duty to her family and her commitment to the truth. But the words caught in her throat. The weight of her father's wrath, the potential for family betrayal, was almost unbearable.

Tobias extended a hand, his touch gentle yet firm, and she laid hers in his, seeking solace in his comforting presence. The warmth of his skin sent a comforting shiver down her spine. His simple touch, filled with quiet understanding, conveyed more than any elaborate speech. It was a silent promise of support, a pledge of unwavering commitment.

He led her to a fallen log near the creek's edge, the gentle gurgle of the water providing a melodic counterpoint to the turmoil in her heart. Wind's whisper, leaves' rustle: they sat listening, silent. The stillness was profound, broken only by the natural sounds of the Shole Creek landscape, a tranquil oasis of serenity in the midst of the storm.

Finally, he spoke, his voice a low murmur that barely broke the silence, "I understand what this means, Jen. The weight of your father's disapproval, the repercussions of challenging his authority."

She nodded, unable to articulate the torrent of emotions that welled within her. The conflict raged in her breast: the love for her father battling against her conscience, her commitment to truth and justice.

"I know," she whispered, her voice thick with emotion. I doubt my ability.

Tobias grasped her hand tightly, his touch strengthening her resolve. His eyes, warm and full of understanding, gazed into hers. He leaned closer, and there was a sudden shift in the air, a palpable change in the dynamic between them. The weight of their shared burden seemed to lift, replaced by a burgeoning intensity that threatened to ignite.

He drew a deep breath. "Jen," he began, his voice now stronger, filled with a passion that resonated in the quiet solitude, "I love you. And I'll stand with you, whatever happens. Against your father, against the world. This isn't just about the Osage. This is about us. About our future. Regarding standing up for what is right, even when it involves dealing with the repercussions.

The declaration hung in the air, a bold stroke of defiance against the backdrop of the setting sun, its intensity echoing the raw emotion contained within his words. It wasn't a proposal in the traditional sense. A bold declaration of war against injustice, pledging to stand together through thick and thin, against all odds, and in the face of adversity. He wasn't simply proposing a romantic future, he was offering her a partnership–a pledge of loyalty, support, and unwavering devotion.

His love wasn't a gentle whisper, it was a roar, a defiant challenge thrown at the very fabric of Shole Creek's rigid social structure. He stood firm, facing the potential repercussions with unwavering courage, a symbol of resolute strength. It was a profound and transformative moment, a declaration that would forever change the course of their lives.

Jen stared at him, her heart pounding a wild rhythm against her ribs. The words hung in the air, heavy with meaning, defying the social norms of their time.

The love they shared was a fierce, untamed thing, as wild and untamable as the land around them. It was a love that transcended societal expectations, a love that dared to challenge the established order. It was a love born of shared ideals, of mutual respect, and a deep understanding of the other's soul. It was a love as vast and rugged as the American West itself.

She saw in his eyes not just romantic love, but also a profound respect for her convictions, her determination to fight for justice, for the rights of the Osage. He valued her intellect, her courage, her compassion–qualities that were often overlooked in a society that valued a woman's subservience above all else.

Tears welled in her eyes, tears of relief, of joy, of overwhelming emotion. Hope and renewed determination replaced her earlier fear. She had a partner, a companion, a warrior fighting alongside her. Facing any challenge, conquering any obstacle felt possible; she stood by a murmuring creek beneath a fiery sunset.

His declaration had raised the stakes considerably, placing them squarely in opposition to her father's considerable power and influence. It was a gamble, a dangerous move, but Jen felt a surge of adrenaline, a newfound strength that flowed through her veins. The path ahead remained uncertain, filled with challenges and potential dangers, but she was no longer alone.

She reached out and took his hand, her fingers intertwining with his. His touch sent a comforting warmth through her, grounding her, bolstering her resolve. "I love you too, Tobias," she whispered, her voice filled with emotion, "And I will fight alongside you."

The silence that followed was different now, charged with a new energy, an unspoken understanding that sealed their pact. It wasn't just a romantic union, it was a commitment to stand together in the face of adversity. It was a declaration of independence, a rebellion against the constraints of their society, a testament to their unwavering love and shared commitment to justice.

As the darkness descended, enveloping them in its quiet embrace, they sat by the creek, their hands clasped together, a testament to their unshakeable bond. The storm outside had subsided, but the tempest within them had transformed–it was no longer a whirlwind of conflict but a powerful force, forging a love as resilient as the land they both loved. The weight of their decision still pressed upon them, a burden they would carry together, but in each other's embrace, they found strength, solace, and the unwavering assurance that together, they could conquer any obstacle. The heart of the matter, Jen now realized, was not just the land dispute, but the unwavering strength of their love and commitment, which would guide them on their journey toward justice. Facing an uncertain future, their unwavering determination and love shone brightly.

The next morning, the fragile peace of the previous evening shattered like thin ice under a sledgehammer. Stan Korte, his face a mask of simmering fury, stormed into Jen's small cottage, his heavy boots echoing on the wooden floor, a prelude to the tempest that was to follow. He didn't bother with polite pleasantries, his eyes blazing with incandescent rage. He moved with the swift, predatory grace of a mountain lion, his anger a palpable force that pressed against Jen like a physical weight.

"You little fool!" he roared, his voice raw with emotion, shaking the very foundations of the small dwelling. He slammed his fist on the table, sending a cascade of scattered papers and drawings flying across the room. Jen flinched, but didn't cower. She'd faced down danger before, in the heart of a collapsing mine shaft, amidst the chaos of a stampeding herd, and the threat in her father's eyes felt almost familiar, a twisted echo of the raw, untamed power of nature.

"What you have done... what you have dared to do..." He choked on his own rage, struggling to control his fury. The vein in his temple pulsed like a trapped bird fighting for its freedom. His words were venomous, laced with the bitter sting of betrayal. He saw Tobias as an insidious threat, a poacher trespassing on his territory, a rival claiming his prize.

Jen met his gaze, her own eyes blazing with a defiant fire. She refused to cower beneath his wrath. She stood tall, her chin held high, her spine straight as an arrow. A fierce determination, a stubborn refusal to yield replaced the fear that had plagued her.

"I did what I believed was right, Father," she responded, her voice steady despite the tremor in her hands. She spoke with a conviction that surprised even herself, a newfound strength born of her love for Tobias and her unwavering commitment to justice.

Korte's laughter was devoid of humor, a harsh, grating sound that grated on her nerves like nails on a chalkboard. "Right? Right! You have aligned yourself with those... savages! Those thieving Osage! You have betrayed your own blood, your own family, for a pack of heathens!"

The slur stung, but Jen remained resolute. She knew her father's prejudices were deep-seated, fueled by years of bitter conflict and fueled by the very economic system that he had helped create. His anger wasn't just directed at the Osage; it reflected his fear of losing control, of seeing his empire crumble. To him, the Osage were not human, merely obstructions on his road to wealth.

"They are not heathens, Father," she said, her voice rising in defiance. "They are people. And they have been wronged. Their land has been stolen, their rights trampled upon. And I will not stand idly by while injustice prevails."

Korte's rage escalated, his words a torrent of vitriol. He raged about his financial losses, the threat to his mining operations, and the potential legal battles that loomed. He painted a picture of ruin, of financial devastation, of social disgrace–all consequences of Jen's defiance. He spoke of the shame she had brought upon the Korte name, a lineage he cherished above all else.

The air crackled with tension, thick with unspoken accusations and simmering resentment. The conflict wasn't just about a land dispute; it was a clash of ideologies, a battle between tradition and progress, between blind loyalty and moral conviction. It was a fight for Jen's soul, a struggle for her allegiance.

Suddenly, Korte lunged, his hand outstretched, as if to strike her. Jen flinched instinctively, expecting the blow, but it never came. Tobias burst through the door, his eyes like chips of flint, his broad shoulders squared, his body a wall of protection between Jen and her enraged father.

"Lay a hand on her, and you'll regret it," Tobias growled, his voice low and menacing, a warning that held the cold promise of violence. He stood between them, his very presence a deterrent, a silent challenge.

The confrontation was inevitable. It wasn't merely a clash between father and daughter; it was a battle between two powerful forces. The room throbbed with unspoken threats, the air thick with the scent of violence. The clash wasn't just physical; it was a war of wills, a test of endurance, a fight for the heart of Jen Korte.

Korte, momentarily stunned by Tobias's sudden appearance, recoiled slightly. His rage didn't diminish; it simply shifted its focus. His eyes, narrowed and filled with fury, turned to Tobias, radiating a venomous hatred.

"You!" he spat, the word dripping with contempt. "You, a common trapper, dare to interfere in my family affairs?"

Tobias stood firm, his gaze unwavering, his quiet strength a stark contrast to Korte's explosive anger. He knew that a physical confrontation would only escalate the situation, so he chose his words carefully.

"I am interfering in what is right," Tobias said calmly, his voice low but steady, carrying the weight of his conviction. Mr. Korte, rectifying the Osage people's injustices requires acknowledgement and amends.

Korte laughed again, a harsh, bitter sound. "Justice? You speak of justice? This isn't about justice. This is about my livelihood, my empire! You threaten my very existence!"

He paced the room, his anger a raging storm, his movements wild and unpredictable. He painted a picture of economic ruin, of social ostracization, of the potential loss of everything he had worked for. He made it clear that Jen's actions jeopardized not just his fortune, but the very fabric of their family.

Tobias met his gaze, his own eyes filled with a quiet strength and determination that belied his calm demeanor. Korte's wealth or power did not intimidate him. He had seen too much death, faced too much danger, to be cowed by mere threats. He anticipated a difficult, prolonged fight, yet felt ready.

"Your empire is built on injustice," Tobias stated firmly, his voice unwavering. "And it will crumble under the weight of its own corruption. You may have wealth and power, Mr. Korte, but you lack something far more valuable–integrity."

Korte's rage reached a fever pitch. He lunged again, his face contorted with fury. Tobias reacted instantly, his movements swift and precise, his powerful hands deflecting the blow. The two men grappled, a silent, brutal dance of anger and determination, a clash of wills that threatened to erupt into open violence.

Jen watched in horror, caught between the two men she loved, her heart torn between loyalty and justice. She saw the raw pain in her father's face, the deep-seated wounds of betrayal, but she also saw the unwavering conviction in Tobias's eyes, his fierce commitment to what he believed was right.

The struggle continued, a whirlwind of fists and fury, a testament to the intense emotions that fueled their conflict. Jen's love, and Shole Creek itself, were at stake; a fight for justice in the wild West. The result defined involved parties' futures, a precarious future. The clash was brutal, a fierce testament to the depth of their animosity. The fight continued, a struggle for dominance, mirroring the larger struggle for control of Shole Creek and its resources. The town's dynamics and its people's lives will be irreversibly altered by this confrontation.

The struggle ended as abruptly as it began. Tobias, with a surprising display of restraint, managed to subdue Korte without inflicting serious injury. He pinned the older man against the wall, his grip firm but not brutal, a calculated demonstration of strength rather than a display of brute force. Korte, breathless and defeated, sputtered incoherently, his rage spent, replaced by a stunned silence.

Jen rushed to her father's side, her heart pounding with a mixture of relief and fear. She helped him to a chair, her touch gentle, her concern evident. Shame and exhaustion, a stark vulnerability revealing years of unspoken anxieties and pain, now replaced the anger in her father's eyes.

"Father," Jen began, her voice soft, yet imbued with a strength that belied her fragility. "Please, listen to me." She kneeled beside him and touched his hand, feeling the tremors that ran through his body, the echoes of the tempest that had just raged. "I know you don't understand, but I love Tobias. He's not the enemy you see him as."

Korte remained silent, his gaze fixed on the floor, his face a mask of conflicted emotions. The carefully constructed facade of strength and control had crumbled, revealing a wounded, vulnerable man. He looked up, his eyes, red-rimmed and weary, met Jen's. The years of unspoken words, of unbridged chasms, seemed to hang heavy in the air between them.

"He is a good man, Father," Jen continued, her voice filled with a quiet intensity. "He's kind, compassionate, and he truly cares for me. He respects the Osage people, he doesn't see them as enemies. He understands their plight, and he's willing to fight for what's right, even if it means risking everything."

Jen went on to detail Tobias's work with the Osage, his efforts to help them navigate the complexities of legal disputes surrounding their land. She spoke of his integrity and his courage, of his quiet strength and his unwavering commitment to justice. She painted a picture of a man who was deeply principled, and who, despite his rugged exterior, possessed a tender heart and a noble spirit. She recounted instances where Tobias had demonstrated his kindness and compassion, not just to her, but to others in the community–small acts of charity that illuminated the true nature of his character.

She spoke of his healing touch, his skill as a doctor, his unwavering dedication to relieving suffering. She described how he had risked his life more than once to rescue those trapped in mine collapses and the tireless efforts he made to help the poor and the destitute in Shole Creek. He wasn't dramatically heroic; She depicted his life vibrantly; every detail revealed his character.

Jen knew she needed to break through her father's deeply ingrained prejudices. She needed to appeal to the part of him that still valued family, that still cherished the bonds of love. She spoke of his own values, reminding him of the times when he had himself stood up for the downtrodden, when he had shown compassion and kindness, in his younger years before the relentless pursuit of wealth had hardened his heart.

"You've always taught me the importance of standing up for what's right, Father," Jen said, her voice trembling slightly. "And this is what I'm doing. I advocate what I deem just and true. And Tobias is fighting alongside me, not against you."

She spoke not only of Tobias's commitment to justice, but also of his love for her. She described their shared experiences, their laughter, their quiet moments of intimacy, the deep connection they shared. She spoke of the strength she found in him, the security, the comfort, the understanding. She painted a portrait of a love that was both passionate and tender, resilient and true. She described their shared dreams for the future–a life built on love, respect, and a shared commitment to creating a better world.

She spoke of their mutual desire to establish a home, to raise a family, to build a life together in the heart of Shole Creek. It wasn't just a romantic ideal; it was a practical vision, a tangible goal. They envisioned a future where they could use their combined skills and talents to help others, to build a community that valued justice, compassion, and mutual respect.

Her voice filled with emotion, her words poured forth like a river breaking through a dam. Tears streamed down her cheeks, yet her gaze remained unwavering. She was pouring her heart out, laying bare her soul, pleading for her father's understanding, for his acceptance, for his love.

Finally, Korte spoke, his voice barely a whisper. "I... I don't understand," he confessed, his words revealing the depth of his turmoil. The years of unspoken anxieties and suppressed emotions seemed to overwhelm him. He was struggling to reconcile his own deeply rooted prejudices with the love he held for his daughter. The conflict within him was evident, a painful struggle between his own ambition and the love he felt for Jen.

"I've been so blinded by my own ambitions, by my greed," he continued, his voice thick with remorse. "I've let my anger and prejudice cloud my judgment." He looked at Jen, his gaze filled with a mixture of regret and love. The realization of his own failings seemed to weigh heavily upon him. He admitted that his disapproval of Tobias wasn't just about his social standing or his relationship with the Osage. It was also about the threat Tobias represented to his absolute control over his daughter.

"I... I was afraid of losing you, Jen," he whispered, his voice cracking with emotion. The weight of his unspoken fears, his insecurities, and his regret hung heavy in the air. His failings humbled him; he wrestled with his mistakes' enormity.

Silence filled the room; only the old house's gentle creaks interrupted it. Long-held tension dissipated; fragile peace, nascent hope emerged. Jen reached out and took her father's hand, her touch a silent reassurance, a symbol of forgiveness and understanding.

"I'll never understand why you treated the Osage people the way you have," Jen said gently, "but I believe you can change. I believe you can learn to see them, not as enemies, but as human beings who deserve respect and justice."

Tobias, still standing nearby, stepped forward, his demeanor still reserved but his eyes softer than before. He extended his hand to Korte, a gesture of reconciliation. "Mr. Korte," he began, his voice calm and respectful, "I understand your anger. However, I hope you will believe me when I say that I only want what's best for your daughter. And I promise to always treat your daughter, and your family, with the respect and love that they deserve."

Korte hesitated for a moment, his gaze shifting between Tobias and Jen. Despite lingering prejudice and bias, he appeared more tolerant. He reached out and grasped Tobias's hand, a silent acknowledgment of Jen's choice, a reluctant step toward reconciliation.

Unspoken words hung heavy, but the storm had passed, leaving behind a fragile peace, a fragile hope that a new dawn was breaking over Shole Creek. A clear understanding emerged; challenges remain, yet the path to reconciliation has begun.

A sharp rap on the door shattered the fragile peace in the Korte cottage. Before Jen could even rise, the door swung inward, revealing Sheriff Greg Moore, his broad frame filling the doorway. His usually jovial face was etched with concern, his eyes scanning the room, taking in the aftermath of the recent struggle. He'd heard the commotion from his office, the shouts and the sounds of a physical altercation, and he'd come running. He was a large man, his build suggesting years spent working in the mines and enforcing the law in Shole Creek. His presence commanded attention, a silent assertion of authority that calmed the tense atmosphere, though it also added a layer of complexity to the already delicate situation.

Moore, a man known for his fairness and his pragmatic approach to conflict resolution, immediately assessed the situation. He saw Korte, slumped in a chair, his face pale and drawn, Jen kneeling beside him, her eyes still glistening with unshed tears, and Tobias, standing tall and composed, but with an undercurrent of tension radiating from him. The air itself seemed charged, still humming with the residual energy of the conflict. His keen eyes, honed by years of experience in mediating disputes in this volatile mining town, picked up on the subtle nuances of the scene—the unspoken words, the lingering tensions, the simmering resentments.

"What in God's name happened here?" Moore boomed, his voice echoing in the quiet cottage, cutting through the heavy silence. His voice, though loud, held a note of concern, not anger. He knew this family, knew their history, knew the volatile nature of their relationship, and he understood that the issues were deeply rooted, going far beyond a simple disagreement.

Jen, ever the composed daughter of the mining magnate, wasted no time in explaining the situation, carefully choosing her words to present a balanced picture, neither excusing her father's actions nor minimizing Tobias's involvement. She narrated the events of the evening, detailing her father's violent outburst, Tobias's surprisingly restrained response, and the ensuing discussion that had led to a fragile truce. She highlighted her father's long-held prejudices and fears, carefully contextualizing his anger within the framework of his deep-seated anxieties about her future and his own dwindling influence in the town.

Moore listened patiently, his gaze shifting between Jen and her father, observing their body language, their subtle expressions, and the unspoken currents of emotions that flowed beneath the surface of their words. He knew Korte well. He'd seen the man's ruthless ambition in action, his relentless drive for wealth and power, and he understood the potential for violence inherent in that kind of unbridled ambition. Korte's kinder side occasionally surfaced, a possibility destroyed by his wealth obsession.

When Jen finished her account, Moore turned his attention to Korte. "William," he said, his voice softening, but the firmness in his tone remained, "Jen's told me what happened. You need to understand that while I understand your concerns about your daughter's choice, resorting to violence isn't the answer." He knew that direct confrontation wasn't the way to deal with Korte's deeply rooted prejudices. He needed to find a way to appeal to his sense of responsibility, his awareness of the potential consequences of his actions, and his desire for order in his own life.

He spoke of the repercussions of Korte's actions, the potential for legal ramifications, the damage it could inflict on his reputation, and the impact it would have on the town's already delicate social equilibrium. He didn't lecture or scold, but used a calm, authoritative voice to appeal to Korte's sense of self-preservation, his concern for his reputation and the stability of his business empire, and his inherent need for control. He also pointed out that Korte's reputation was already taking a battering because of the ongoing conflict with the Osage nation.

Moore then shifted his attention to Tobias. "Dr. Adams," he said, "I understand you acted in self-defense. However, I urge you both to exercise restraint. This town can't afford any more violence, especially between two influential men like yourselves. This town needs peace and stability."

He recognized that Tobias, though possessing an almost legendary strength, had displayed surprising self-control in his handling of the situation. Moore understood that this wasn't simply a romantic conflict. It was a struggle for power and influence in the town. Korte, deeply entrenched in the mining business, viewed Tobias's growing influence and his rapport with the Osage as a threat to his own dominance. Moore, being the Sheriff, was well-aware of the simmering tensions between Korte and the Osage, which could easily ignite into a full-blown conflict.

He suggested a meeting, a mediated discussion between Korte, Tobias, and representatives from the Osage nation, aimed at fostering mutual understanding and resolving the conflict peacefully. He knew that finding a solution required more than simply addressing the immediate confrontation. He had to delve into the root of the problem, which involved the deep-seated prejudices held by Korte and the historical injustices experienced by the Osage people. He proposed a framework for reconciliation that addressed the broader societal issues underlying the conflict. He offered to facilitate negotiations, aiming to create a lasting peace within Shole Creek.

Korte, subdued and weary, offered a grudging nod. The events of the evening had clearly taken their toll on him, leaving him drained and emotionally spent. The conflict, though resolved, had opened a wound within him, exposing his deepest fears and insecurities. He began to understand that his anger wasn't just about Tobias; it was about the changing landscape of Shole Creek, his loss of control over Jen, and his failing ability to maintain his dominance.

Tobias, ever pragmatic, accepted Moore's proposition. He understood the importance of maintaining peace in the community, and he saw the wisdom in Moore's proposal. He also understood the crucial role he needed to play in bridging the divide between Korte and the Osage. Reconciliation offered significant benefits—for Jen, her father, and the town. He agreed to participate, hoping that a peaceful resolution could be achieved.

As Moore left the cottage, a sense of uneasy calm settled over the room. The immediate threat of violence had passed, but the underlying tensions remained, like smoldering embers waiting for the right conditions to flare up again. The future was uncertain, the road to reconciliation long and arduous, but thanks to Moore's intervention, a path towards peace had been opened, a glimmer of hope in the tense atmosphere of Shole Creek. The heart of the matter, while exposed, still required careful tending, a delicate balance between forgiveness and justice, love and ambition, reconciliation and the ever-present threat of conflict in the untamed Wild West. Danger persisted, yet temporary calm reigned. The mountains looming nearby and the constant whispers of Shole Creek suggested additional challenges on the horizon. The future of their relationship, and indeed the future of Shole Creek, remained uncertain, balanced on a knife's edge between hope and despair.

The silence that followed Sheriff Moore's departure was thick, heavy with unspoken words and unresolved feelings. Jen, her hands still trembling slightly, rose from her kneeling position beside her father. Stan Korte remained slumped in his chair, his eyes fixed on the worn rug, the lines etched deep into his face a testament to the relentless strain of his life. He succumbed to ambition's relentless pursuit, letting fear consume him.

Jen approached her father cautiously, her heart aching with a mixture of anger and compassion. She understood his fears, his anxieties about her future, his inability to let go of the control he had always craved. But she also understood the pain he had inflicted, the emotional wounds he had opened.

A profound sadness tempered the anger, though still present. She saw the defeated slump of his shoulders, the weariness in his eyes, and a wave of empathy washed over her.

Gently, she reached out and placed a hand on his arm. The touch was tentative, a fragile bridge across the chasm that had opened between them. Korte flinched momentarily, a reflex action born of years of hardened resolve, but he didn't pull away. His gaze, still fixed on the floor, seemed to soften slightly.

"Papa," she whispered, her voice barely audible above the ticking of the grandfather clock in the hall. The word held a lifetime of memories, a tapestry woven with love, conflict, and unwavering loyalty.

Korte didn't respond immediately. A quiet, broken only by the hearth's soft crackling, filled the space. Emotion hung heavy in the cottage's air; unspoken words and years of built-up resentment. That moment offered healing potential, yet also risked causing more pain.

Finally, Korte looked up, his eyes meeting hers. There was no anger in their depths, only a profound weariness, a deep-seated sadness. What he saw in her eyes was not judgment but understanding, a glimpse of the love that had always united them.

"Jen," he murmured, his voice raspy, strained. The word was a plea, a fragile offering of reconciliation.

She sat beside him, pulling a worn shawl over his shoulders. The gesture was simple, almost mundane, yet it carried a weight of affection that transcended words. It was a silent affirmation of their bond, a promise of support and understanding, a gesture of healing.

"I know you're afraid, Papa," she said softly, her voice a balm to his troubled spirit. "Afraid of losing control, of losing what you've built."

Korte nodded slowly, a tear tracing a path through the wrinkles on his cheek. His composure, the carefully constructed façade of strength and control that he had cultivated over the years, began to crumble. The mask of the powerful mining magnate fell away, revealing the vulnerable man beneath.

"I've always tried to protect you, Jen," he whispered, his voice breaking slightly. "I just... I didn't know how to do it anymore."

His words were a confession, a raw and honest admission of his failure, of his inability to adapt to the changing times, to accept the changes within his own family. He had built his empire on control, on dominance, and he was losing both. He was losing his daughter, his influence, and his grasp on the world around him.

Jen took his hand, her fingers interlacing with his. The touch was a silent reassurance, a promise of unwavering support. "I know, Papa," she said gently. "And I forgive you."

The words hung in the air, simple yet profound, a testament to the enduring power of love and family. Forgiveness proved difficult; pain and wounds lingered. But they were a starting point, a foundation upon which a new relationship could be built, a new understanding forged between father and daughter.

Tobias, watching from a distance, felt a wave of relief wash over him. He had expected resistance, anger, perhaps even more violence. Instead, he witnessed a raw and honest display of human vulnerability, a painful yet necessary step towards reconciliation. He understood that his involvement went far beyond romance; it was a catalyst for a deeper transformation within the Korte family, within the very fabric of Shole Creek itself.

The truce, fragile as it was, offered a moment of introspection, a chance for both Korte and Tobias to examine their motives, their fears, and their shared aspirations. For Tobias, it was a chance to reflect on his own feelings for Jen, and the implications of their relationship within the volatile landscape of the American West. He understood that the road to true reconciliation lay not only in resolving the conflict with Korte but also in finding a way to mend the deep-seated divisions within the community, a path which he realized demanded more than just his physical strength, but his careful diplomacy.

The next few days were a period of quiet contemplation. Korte, still shaken but noticeably calmer, began to reassess his relationship with his daughter and the town. He saw Jen's connection with Tobias, not as dangerous, but potentially beneficial to all, himself included. He started to understand how his own narrow-minded views, fueled by his thirst for power, had driven a wedge between them, between him and the burgeoning peace that Shole Creek so desperately needed.

Tobias used this period to strengthen his ties with the Osage tribe. He understood that the conflict between Korte and the tribe was intrinsically connected to the larger conflict within his relationship with Jen. In an act of both diplomacy and sincere friendship, he offered his medical expertise to the tribe, tending to their sick and injured. This action showed compassion; it was also clever strategy. His relationship with the Osage was not only personal but became a powerful political tool. The respect and friendship he had cultivated among the tribe made him a force to be reckoned with, a counterbalance to Korte's influence. His ability to bridge the gap between the two factions would be crucial in his pursuit of peace, and in his attempt to win over Korte's trust and acceptance.

The atmosphere in the Korte household shifted subtly, the air clearing slightly, the pervasive tension beginning to dissipate, replaced by a fragile sense of hope. The wounds remained, the scars a constant reminder of the conflicts that had divided them, but the wounds were slowly starting to heal, the scars fading under the gentle touch of reconciliation and understanding. A fragile truce offered a chance for reflection, healing, and future peace in the Wild West. The mountains stood silent witness to the unfolding drama, their stoic presence a constant reminder of the vastness of the landscape and the resilience of the human spirit. Shole Creek still whispered, yet a gentler current of hope now flowed, hinting at better times.

Chapter 6: The Weight of Secrets

The fragile peace in the Korte household was shattered one crisp fall evening. A chill wind howled outside, mirroring the storm brewing within. Jen, absorbed in a delicate watercolor painting of the Shole Creek valley, barely registered Silas, an old, weathered prospector known for his penchant for gossip and an uncanny ability to unearth secrets. He stood awkwardly in the doorway, his face etched with a mixture of apprehension and grim determination.

Silas, a man who usually greeted Jen with a boisterous chuckle and a wink, was unusually somber. His eyes, usually twinkling with mischief, were clouded with a heavy weight of unspoken knowledge. He cleared his throat, a sound like dry leaves skittering across cobblestones. "Miss Jen," he began, his voice a low rumble, "I... I have something to tell you. About your father."

Jen lowered her brush, her heart pounding a restless rhythm against her ribs. That hesitant, serious expression—she recognized it; she'd seen it before in the eyes of those who witnessed tragedy. "What is it, Silas?" she asked, her voice barely a whisper.

Silas hesitated, his gaze drifting to the flickering fire in the hearth. He took a deep breath, as if bracing himself for the weight of his words. "It's about a claim... an old claim, near the Widow's Gulch. A claim your father... well, he never spoke of it. But I saw it... I saw the deed."

Jen's breath caught in her throat. Her father had always been secretive about his past, his business dealings shrouded in an almost obsessive veil of privacy. She had often wondered what secrets lay hidden beneath the surface of his gruff exterior, the impenetrable wall of ambition that he had constructed around himself. A forgotten past emerged as the wall crumbled.

Silas continued, his words slow and measured, each syllable laden with the weight of years of suppressed knowledge. "It was a rich claim, Miss Jen.

King-making gold. But... it wasn't found legally. There was... an incident. A dispute. A man died."

The revelation hung in the air, a heavy cloud of unspoken accusations and buried truths. Jen felt a cold dread creep into her heart, a chilling realization that her father's success, his empire built on the back of the Shole Creek mines, might have been stained with blood. The image of her father, the man she knew as a powerful and ruthless mining magnate, began to blur, replaced by a shadowy figure, a man steeped in secrets and shadowed by a violent past.

Silas, noticing her shock, continued. He was a partner, you see, the man who passed away. A man your father worked with. They struck it rich, but a disagreement over the spoils... it ended badly. The sheriff then ignored problems. Minor financial contributions and subtle persuasion resolved the issue.

Jen struggled, processing this new information about the man. This was a different Stan Korte, a far more ruthless and dangerous figure than the man who, despite his flaws, had shown signs of remorse and vulnerability in recent days. The weight of his secrets felt heavier than the gold he had amassed.

Silas, seeing her distress, placed a comforting hand on her shoulder. "I wouldn't have told you, Miss Jen, but... Tobias... he deserves to know. He needs to understand the kind of man your father truly is. And what he's capable of."

The mention of Tobias jolted Jen back to reality. Their burgeoning relationship, the tender moments of reconciliation, felt threatened by this newfound knowledge. Could she ever truly trust her father? Could Tobias ever accept her father, once he learned the full extent of his past? The weight of the secret felt insurmountable.

The next day dawned cold and gray, mirroring the turmoil within Jen's heart. She decided to confront her father, but the conversation was far more difficult than she could have anticipated. Stan Korte didn't deny the accusations; instead, he confessed, his voice heavy with guilt and regret. He spoke of a reckless youth, a thirst for wealth that overshadowed all morality, and a cover-up born of fear and desperation. He admitted involvement, plus a lifetime burden: his success stemmed from dishonesty and brutality.

Korte's confession was a painful unraveling. He discussed his past self, his errors, the decades-long burden of his secret. He spoke of the constant fear of exposure, of the relentless pressure to maintain his carefully constructed façade. The seemingly impenetrable, stern patriarch, controlling every facet of his own and others' lives, succumbed to his past. His fracture stemmed not from his secret's exposure, but from confessing his guilt. His power, his wealth, his carefully constructed empire, seemed insignificant in comparison to the burden of his conscience.

Jen listened, her heart aching with a mixture of anger, pity, and understanding. She saw the profound sorrow in her father's eyes, the genuine remorse that transcended his attempts at justification. She perceived his vulnerability, hidden beneath ambition and control; the man who always shielded her, despite questionable methods.

The revelation changed everything. The fragile truce between Jen and her father was once again threatened, not by anger or conflict, but by the sheer weight of their shared history. It was a history that Jen would have to confront, a history that would shape her future, and a history that would irrevocably alter her relationship with Tobias. The weight of the secret hung over them, a dark cloud threatening to engulf their lives, but even amidst the storm, a flicker of hope remained–the hope for forgiveness, reconciliation, and the potential for redemption.

The revelation also cast a long shadow over Jen and Tobias' relationship. Tobias, upon learning the truth from Jen, reacted with a complex mix of emotions. Initially, there was anger, a righteous fury at the injustice and the violence inherent in Korte's past. But he had seen the man's vulnerability, his capacity for change. He recognized that while Korte's actions were reprehensible, his remorse appeared genuine. Tobias struggled to accept this revelation regarding a man he'd grown to admire, a man displaying newfound love and compassion.

The weight of this secret tested the strength of their love, threatening to tear them apart. The conflict between their feelings, the clash between their love and the harsh reality of Korte's past, threatened to destabilize their relationship. Jen found herself torn between her love for Tobias and her loyalty to her father, her feelings a tangled web of conflict and compassion.

Tobias, meanwhile, had to grapple with his feelings for Jen, the moral complexities of the situation, and his responsibility to the community.

The town of Shole Creek also felt the tremors of this revelation. The news spread like wildfire, the secret once buried beneath layers of wealth and influence now out in the open. Whispers and speculation ran rampant, the fragile peace shattered by the uncovering of this dark chapter in Korte's history. The Sheriff, Greg Moore, found himself once again caught in the crossfire, his position of power tested by the need to uphold the law and his complicated history with Korte. The townspeople were divided, some quick to condemn Korte, others more willing to offer a measure of understanding, fueled by a mixture of fear and loyalty.

The unveiling of the truth didn't destroy the relationship between Jen and her father, nor did it entirely destroy her and Tobias' budding romance. Rather, it became a crucible in which their love, their families, and the very fabric of Shole Creek was tested. It forced them to confront the complexities of forgiveness, the weight of the past, and the challenging path towards a better future. It underscored that in the Wild West, and in life itself, the pursuit of justice and redemption is a long, arduous road, one that often demands courage, perseverance, and an unwavering belief in the power of love to heal even the deepest of wounds. The mountains remained steadfast witnesses to this ongoing drama, their silent sentinels standing guard over the unfolding narrative of Shole Creek, a town wrestling with its past while desperately clinging to the promise of a brighter future.

The initial shock of Silas's revelation had given way to a simmering unease that pulsed beneath the surface of her daily life. The vibrant colors of her paintings seemed muted, the beauty of Shole Creek dimmed by the shadow of her father's past. She had confronted her father, a confrontation that had been as agonizing as it was revealing. He hadn't denied the accusations; instead, he had confessed, his voice a low, gravelly rumble that spoke volumes of guilt and regret. He hadn't offered excuses, only a heart-wrenching account of his past, a past she had never known, a past that had shaped the man he had become.

He spoke of a reckless youth, a time fueled by ambition and a thirst for wealth that had blinded him to morality. He described a partnership gone sour, a dispute over a gold claim that had escalated into violence, culminating in the death of his partner. The details were grim, the language stark, devoid of the usual bluster and self-aggrandizement that characterized his public persona. Youth consumed by greed, his crimes hidden by cleverness and power; an empire forged in treachery and brutality.

His confession offered more than a factual account. There was a profound sorrow in his eyes, a genuine remorse that cut through the carefully constructed façade of power and control. He spoke of the years of living with this secret, the constant fear of exposure, the relentless pressure to maintain his carefully constructed image. He confessed not to justify his actions, but to unburden himself, to finally acknowledge the weight of his guilt. He spoke of the sleepless nights, the gnawing guilt that had followed him for decades, a relentless torment that no amount of wealth or success could ever alleviate.

He didn't ask for forgiveness, not explicitly. He didn't expect it. His confession was an act of self-flagellation, a desperate attempt to shed the weight of his past, to finally confront the man he had been and the man he had become. Jen unexpectedly found empathy in her vulnerable, honest admission of guilt and regret. It wasn't easy. Resentment simmered; his actions, unjust. But beneath the anger, a different emotion began to emerge, a flicker of understanding, of compassion.

She perceived a broken man behind the ruthless mining magnate, a man tormented by his history and its repercussions. His face showed pain; his eyes, exhaustion. His weary bearing spoke volumes of a life lived secretly. She realized that his ambition, his relentless drive, had been fueled not only by greed but also by a deep-seated fear, a fear of losing everything, of exposing his dark past. She understood that his ruthlessness, his controlling nature, had been a defense mechanism, a way to protect himself and those he cared about from the consequences of his actions. This presented not an excuse, but another viewpoint, showing the human heart's complexities, even her father's.

Her understanding deepened as she reflected on her own life, on the sacrifices her father had made, even those born of questionable motives. She recalled the unwavering support he had given her, the opportunities he had provided, the way he had always strived to protect her, even if his methods had been flawed, even if his morality had been compromised. She had never doubted his love for her, even amidst the conflict and misunderstandings.

This newfound understanding didn't erase the past, didn't diminish the gravity of his actions. But it added layers to her perception of him, softening the edges of the man she had known only through his public persona.

This new perspective altered her relationship with Tobias. She shared her father's confession with him, not expecting immediate absolution or even understanding. She braced herself for his anger, for his rejection, but Tobias's reaction was more nuanced. He was initially furious, his righteous anger a palpable force. The injustice of her father's actions, the violence and deception, ignited a fire in his soul. He observed the victims: a man stripped of his life, a town betrayed. Justice fueled his anger.

But Tobias's anger was not directed solely at Jen's father. He understood the broader context, the harsh realities of a frontier society where the rule of law often yielded to personal ambition and ruthlessness. He personally witnessed the desperation and compromises necessitated by survival. He saw the remorse in Stan Korte's eyes, the genuine sorrow that transcended any attempts at justification. He grasped the secret's gravity, Korte's long-carried burden.

Tobias, with his inherent empathy and his understanding of human nature, could reconcile his anger with a degree of compassion. He grasped Korte's multifaceted nature: a blend of cruelty and remorse. He understood that Korte's actions were reprehensible, but he also recognized the man's genuine attempt at redemption, the possibility of a transformation. This didn't mean condoning his past, but acknowledging his capacity for change. It wasn't easy for Tobias, but his love for Jen, his belief in her, and his own capacity for compassion allowed him to navigate the treacherous terrain of his emotions.

The revelation of her father's past did not destroy their relationship; it tested it, refined it. It forced them to confront the complexities of their feelings, to navigate the moral ambiguities of their situation. It challenged their belief in each other, in their ability to navigate the turbulent waters of their love story. But it also strengthened their bond, deepening their understanding and respect for one another. Their love became a beacon, a guiding light through the storm. They learned to trust each other implicitly, supporting each other through the turmoil, their love a testament to their resilience.

The news spread through Shole Creek like wildfire, igniting a storm of speculation and judgment. The whispers in saloons and the hushed conversations in homes created a divided community, opinions sharply polarized between condemnation and understanding. The sheriff, Greg Moore, found himself once again navigating a precarious political landscape. He knew Korte, understood the man's complex nature, but his sworn duty to uphold the law clashed with his personal relationships, creating a moral dilemma that would test his integrity. The townspeople were divided; some sought justice, others sympathized with Korte's repentance. The weight of the secret extended beyond the immediate family, rippling outward, affecting the entire community.

Through it all, Jen remained steadfast. Her newfound empathy and understanding didn't diminish her father's wrongdoing, but it shaped her response. She didn't shield him from the consequences of his actions, but she offered him her compassion. She chose to approach the situation with maturity, understanding, and a sense of forgiveness that transcended the anger and resentment..

She had learned that forgiveness, whether granted or sought, is a complex, deeply personal process, a journey that requires courage, self-reflection, and a willingness to confront painful truths. This process had ultimately strengthened her character, making her stronger, more compassionate, and even more resilient. Her love story with Tobias, though tested, was proving to be as enduring as the rugged landscape that surrounded them. The weight of the secrets, the challenges, the complexities–all these would shape their future, but their love, steadfast and unwavering, would weather the storms. The mountains, silent witnesses to their struggles, would remain, a testament to their enduring love and the resilience of the human spirit in the face of adversity.

The initial wave of anger had subsided, leaving behind a residue of quiet contemplation in Tobias's heart. He had paced his small cabin, the rhythmic creak of the floorboards a counterpoint to the turmoil within him. Jen's confession had been a revelation, stripping bare the layers of Stan Korte, revealing a man far more complex than the stern, unyielding mining magnate he presented to the world. He saw the ruthless businessman, the man who had built his empire on a foundation of questionable ethics, but he also saw the father, the man who had loved and protected his daughter fiercely, even if his methods were flawed. Years of guilt weighed heavily upon him, his secrets palpable.

Tobias understood the desperation that drove men in the West. He'd seen it in the eyes of the trappers, the miners, the settlers–a hunger for survival, a willingness to take risks, to bend the rules, that sometimes blurred the lines between right and wrong. He had, himself, skirted the edges of legality in his own life, pushing the boundaries of self-preservation when faced with the harsh realities of the wilderness. He understood the weight of hidden truths. The constant vigilance, the ever-present fear of exposure, the gnawing guilt that ate away at one's soul–he understood it all.

But unlike Stan Korte, Tobias had never taken a life. He fought nature's harshness, a relentless battle for survival. The guilt he carried were of a different sort–the regret of lost opportunities, the pain of failed relationships, the shadows of a past that clung to him like the dust of the trail. His sins were those of omission, not commission. The knowledge that his hands were clean of blood made it easier to extend compassion, to understand the intricacies of a man whose past was stained crimson.

It wasn't about condoning Stan Korte's actions. It wasn't about excusing the violence and deception. It was about understanding the man, seeing beyond the surface, recognizing the complexities of his being. It was about acknowledging the remorse, the deep-seated regret that etched itself onto his face like canyons carved by time and sorrow. It recognized a cruel man's capacity for change, for redemption.

Tobias wasn't naïve. He understood the gravity of Korte's actions, the impact they had had on the lives of others. He saw the injustice, the pain, and the anger simmering in the community. But his understanding of human nature, his own capacity for forgiveness, allowed him to navigate the emotional labyrinth. He knew that true forgiveness wasn't about forgetting; it was about letting go, about releasing the anger that poisoned the soul.

He reflected on his journey from city to wilderness, a journey ending at Shole Creek, with Jen. He had found solace in the mountains, in the quiet strength of the land. He had found purpose in healing, in easing the suffering of others. It was that same strength, that same purpose, that guided him now, helping him navigate the turbulent waters of Jen's confession.

He had seen the fear in her eyes, the vulnerability she had displayed in sharing her father's secret. That vulnerability, that unyielding faith in him, had resonated deeply within his soul. It strengthened his resolve to stand by her, to support her through the storm. Their love, born amidst the rugged beauty of Shole Creek, was being tested, but it was proving to be strong, as enduring as the mountains themselves.

The acceptance wasn't immediate. It wasn't a sudden shift from anger to forgiveness. It was a gradual process, a journey of understanding that unfolded over days, punctuated by moments of quiet reflection and heartfelt conversations with Jen. They spoke late into the night, their voices hushed whispers in the dimly lit cabin. He listened, he empathized, he sought to comprehend the complexities of the situation from her perspective, acknowledging her own struggle to reconcile her love for her father with the gravity of his actions.

He sought to understand the burden of her family legacy, the pressures she faced as the daughter of a powerful mining magnate. He acknowledged her struggles, validating her feelings and experiences. He didn't try to diminish her pain or minimize the severity of her father's transgressions. He simply offered her a sanctuary, a place where she could be vulnerable, where she could grieve, where she could find peace.

He recognized that their love was being tested by the weight of secrets. This love story wasn't typical. He realized romantic gestures would n't only measure that their love but by their capacity for empathy, forgiveness, and understanding.

Their nights were filled with quiet moments, long gazes across the flickering lamplight, hands clasped in silent comfort. He read to her from his well-worn books, sharing stories of resilience and hope, reminding her of the strength she possessed, the ability to heal and move forward. He listened to her fears and anxieties, offering reassurance and calm amidst the chaos. He encouraged her artistic pursuits, recognizing that her art was an outlet for her emotions, a way of processing the complex emotions that swirled within her. He gently encouraged her to continue her work, seeing in her paintings a reflection of her inner strength, her tenacity in the face of adversity.

The acceptance wasn't just an emotional acceptance; it was also a pragmatic one. Tobias understood the implications of Stan Korte's confession. He saw the storm brewing in Shole Creek, the social unrest and division that was likely to follow. He knew that the sheriff, Greg Moore, faced a difficult task in maintaining order and justice. He also understood that Jen would need his support now, more than ever, as she navigated the treacherous social currents and the emotional fallout from her father's confession.

Their love wasn't a naïve, untouched idyllic romance. It was a complicated, nuanced tapestry woven from threads of passion, understanding, and empathy. It was a relationship forged in the fires of adversity, strengthened by shared burdens and mutual support. It was a love story worthy of the rugged beauty of the West, a testament to the resilience of the human spirit in the face of conflict, a love story that mirrored the enduring strength of the mountains surrounding them.

The coming days would bring new challenges, new storms to weather. The weight of the secret would continue to cast its shadow, but Tobias was prepared. He stood by Jen, his love unwavering, his commitment resolute. He had found his place in the wildness, not just in the mountains and forests but in the heart of Jen Korte, a woman as wild, as strong, and as resilient as the land itself. Their love story was far from over; in fact, it was only just beginning, its trajectory carved by the turbulent events of Shole Creek, yet its destination guided by the enduring strength of their love and mutual understanding. Their journey had only just begun. The weight of the secrets had tested them, but had also forged an unbreakable bond between them, a bond that would stand the test of time, a love story for the ages.

The late afternoon sun cast long shadows across the dusty main street of Shole Creek, painting the wooden buildings in hues of orange and purple. Sheriff Greg Moore sat on the porch of the saloon, a half-empty glass of whiskey sweating in his hand. The usual boisterous chatter of the town seemed muted, replaced by a low hum of apprehension. The revelation of Stan Korte's past, whispered amongst the townsfolk, hung heavy in the air, a palpable tension that even the whiskey couldn't entirely numb.

Moore wasn't a man given to introspection. He preferred action, the crisp authority of his badge, the satisfying thud of a well-aimed punch. The evening's silence and unspoken thoughts pushed him to face a ghost from his past, a regret lingering on him like trail dust. It was a story he rarely shared, a burden he carried alone, hidden beneath the veneer of stoic resolve he presented to the world.

He'd been a younger man then, barely out of his twenties, full of youthful bravado and a reckless disregard for consequences. He'd arrived in Shole Creek with dreams of making a name for himself, of carving a life out of the raw, untamed wilderness. He'd found work in the mines, his strong hands and even stronger will quickly earning him respect among the rough-and-tumble miners. He'd seen the brutal realities of the mining life–the back-breaking labor, the dangerous conditions, the ever-present threat of accidents. He'd seen men lose their lives, swallowed by the earth they toiled to conquer.

But it wasn't a mining accident that stained his soul. It was a woman, Sarah. She was as vibrant and fiery as the setting sun, her laughter as bright as the gold they sought in the depths of the earth. They'd fallen in love amidst the dust and grime of the mines, their romance a flickering candle in the darkness. He vowed her a life beyond mining, comfortable, secure, free from disaster's constant threat.

He'd been a fool, young and arrogant, convinced he could conquer anything. He'd pushed her away, driven by a misguided ambition that blinded him to the love he held in his hands. He'd been focused on his career, on climbing the ladder of success within the mining operation, believing that he needed to achieve a certain level of financial stability before he could offer Sarah the life she deserved. He'd told himself it was for her own good. It was a lie, a cruel and self-serving justification.

Then came the accident. A cave-in, sudden and brutal, swallowing several miners, including Sarah. The memory of her face, pale and lifeless, haunted his dreams. The grief was a crushing weight, a constant reminder of his folly, a testament to his lost opportunity. The guilt gnawed at him, a bitter reminder of his youthful arrogance and short-sighted ambition.

He'd chased success, but all he'd found was emptiness. He'd achieved the position he'd craved, becoming Sheriff of Shole Creek, a position of authority and respect. But the emptiness remained, a vast chasm in his heart, filled only by the bitter regret of a love lost. He'd used his badge as a shield, a way to bury his grief, a way to distract himself from the gnawing guilt that consumed him. He'd found solace in his work, in the authority he wielded, but it was a futile attempt to silence the whispers of his conscience.

The events surrounding Stan Korte's confession had brought his past sharply into focus. He'd seen the pain in Jen's eyes, the struggle she faced in accepting her father's actions. He noted simmering anger among Korte's victims. He'd felt a kinship with Jen's pain, a shared experience of bearing a heavy burden, a shared understanding of regret.

Moore understood the complexities of human nature, the capacity for both cruelty and compassion. He had seen firsthand the devastating consequences of poor choices, the impact of unchecked ambition. He had lived with the consequences of his own mistakes. He'd realized that true justice wasn't simply about punishing the guilty; it was about understanding the circumstances, acknowledging the complexities of human behavior, and seeking a path towards healing. Korte erred gravely; however, Moore's past held comparable failings.

The knowledge that he wasn't alone in carrying such a burden lightened somewhat the weight of his secret, a heavy cloak of guilt. Seeing Tobias's patient approach to Jen and her situation, his ability to understand and empathize, inspired Moore to reflect on his own past.

He thought of the many times he'd judged others too harshly, too quickly, failing to see the nuances of their stories, ignoring the mitigating circumstances that contributed to their actions. He realized that true justice wasn't about retribution but about restoring balance, about healing the wounds inflicted by past actions. He had spent years hiding behind his badge, his authority a shield against his own inner turmoil. He'd worn his stoicism like armor, protecting himself from the pain of his past. But the events of the last few days, the unfolding drama in Shole Creek, had forced him to confront his own demons.

He drained the last of his whiskey, the burning liquid a fleeting comfort against the persistent ache in his soul. He knew the path ahead wouldn't be easy. The anger in the community was palpable, the desire for retribution strong. But he also knew that he couldn't simply dispense justice; he had to help guide the community towards healing, towards forgiveness. He had to act as a bridge, bridging the divide between anger and understanding, between retribution and restoration.

The moon rose high in the inky sky, casting a pale light over the sleeping town. Moore remained on the porch, the cool night air a welcome contrast to the heat that simmered beneath his skin. The weight of his secret remained, a constant companion, but it no longer felt so heavy. It was a part of him, a reminder of his past mistakes, a testament to his capacity for growth and change. He was no longer just a sheriff; he was a man grappling with his past, seeking redemption, striving to create a more just and compassionate future for Shole Creek.

He stood up, the creak of the porch boards a sound that mirrored the subtle shift in his inner landscape. The work ahead was monumental, the challenges numerous, but Moore was ready. He was ready to confront not just the criminals of Shole Creek but also his own demons. He faced the future, not hardened, but vulnerable—a man learning from past errors, seeking self-redemption. He would be a shepherd of justice, but also a guide toward healing and reconciliation in this rugged, beautiful land, ensuring that the tragedy of Stan Korte's actions did not repeat itself. His regret wouldn't be his ruin. This would underpin a more compassionate, just future for Shole Creek. Sheriff Greg Moore felt a glimmer of hope and a newfound sense of purpose as he faced the long and uncertain road ahead, one that went beyond just the badge and the gun. He felt healing, true forgiveness—both others' actions and self-acceptance—finally possible.

The rising sun cast a warm, golden light on Jen's face as she sat by the creek, her sketchbook open in her lap. The usual vibrant strokes of her charcoal were absent, replaced by hesitant, lighter lines. The weight of her father's confession, the shattering revelation of his deceit and cruelty, pressed heavily upon her. She'd known him as a stern but ultimately loving man, a pillar of strength in their family, a prominent figure in the town. That image shattered, replaced with a stark understanding of his shadow self—a side she'd always ignored. The idyllic landscape of Shole Creek, once a source of inspiration, now felt tainted, a reflection of the turmoil within her heart.

Tobias found her there, his presence as comforting as the warm morning sun. He sat beside her, offering a silent companionship that spoke volumes. He understood the depth of her pain, the struggle she faced in reconciling the man she knew with the man he truly was. He'd seen firsthand the complexities of human nature, the capacity for both good and evil, residing within the same individual. The West's harshness, his trapping, and bear hunting prepared him. He knew that survival in the wild demanded resilience, an ability to adapt, and a willingness to confront harsh realities. Now, facing uncomfortable truths—this resilience—defined their relationship.

He reached out, gently taking her hand. Her fingers were cold, despite the warmth of the morning. He held her hand, feeling the tremor in her grip, the silent plea for comfort and understanding. "It's alright to grieve, Jen," he said softly, his voice a balm to her troubled spirit. "It's alright to be angry, confused, hurt. Feelings vary in this situation.

She looked up at him, her eyes red-rimmed and swollen, yet reflecting a flicker of something akin to hoped amidst the pain. "I don't understand," she whispered, her voice barely audible. "How could he? How did he accomplish all those tasks and still maintain that gaze, those eyes that were constantly there for me?

Tobias knew the question was not merely directed at him; it was a question she posed to herself, a question she desperately sought an answer to. He understood the confusion and pain that stemmed from betrayed trust and shattered illusions. He also knew this particular hardship. The harsh realities of the frontier had taught him that life was a cruel mistress, and trust wasn't easily given or earned.

"Some people," he began, choosing his words carefully, "wear masks. They hide their true selves behind a facade of respectability, of success. They build walls around their hearts, protecting themselves from the pain and the guilt of their actions. Your father may have been one of those people."

He paused, allowing his words to sink in. No easy answers existed, no simple explanations could alleviate her suffering. He wasn't trying to justify her father's actions, merely offering a explanation, a different perspective. He grasped the distinction between understanding and acceptance.

"But he's still my father," Jen insisted, a tear tracing a path down her cheek. "And a part of me... a part of me still loves him, despite everything."

"And that's alright, too," Tobias reassured her. "Love is not always rational, Jen. It's not always easy, and it certainly doesn't always make sense. You can love him and still be angry with him, still hurt by his actions."

Their conversation meandered, touching upon the complexities of family relationships, the burden of secrets, and the resilience of the human spirit. He spoke about his own experiences, the losses he'd endured, the hardships he'd faced. He shared memories of his childhood, a childhood marked by loss and a yearning for connection, mirroring a similar vulnerability within Jen's own experiences. His stories, far from being boasts of bravery, revealed a man struggling with his own past traumas. He spoke of his brother, lost to a mountain avalanche, a loss that haunted him to this day. This shared vulnerability allowed a new kind of intimacy to emerge between them, a bond forged not just in romantic love but in shared human experience.

As the sun climbed higher in the sky, casting long shadows across the valley, Jen felt a sense of peace descend upon her. The weight of her father's actions a constant reminder of a broken trust. Talking with Tobias gave her a different perspective. She viewed her father's actions as his inner demons manifesting, a consequence of past trauma, not simply betrayal.

Tobias provided comfort; It was a moment of profound insight into the complexities of love and forgiveness. He showed her that forgiveness, if it was to come, couldn't erase the past or condone her father's actions, but it could allow her to find a path towards healing and acceptance, both for herself and for her relationship with her father.

Quiet contemplation filled the remaining hours. Jen resumed her sketching, her charcoal flowing across the paper with renewed energy, a fresh perspective shaping her art. Lines remained uncertain; however, clarity and strength emerged from vulnerability. Tobias watched her, a quiet contentment settling over him. They had faced a storm that threatened to tear them apart, but they had weathered it, their love emerging stronger and more resilient.

Later that evening, as they sat on the porch of Tobias's cabin, watching the stars emerge in the darkening sky, Jen spoke. "I think... I think I understand now," she said softly. "I can't erase what he did, but I can... I can try to understand it. I can try to forgive him, not for him, but for myself."

Tobias took her hand, their fingers intertwining. "And that's the beginning of healing," he whispered, his voice low and comforted. "The road ahead may still be long and difficult, but you won't have to walk it alone."

Their love story, once a delicate blossom threatened by harsh winds, had become something stronger, more enduring. Having confronted the burden of secrets, they gained a fresh insight, a stronger bond, a rekindled dedication to one another, and a joint resolve to tackle future obstacles as a team. The challenges remained - the volatile nature of the mining industry, the simmering tensions with the local Native American tribe, and the complexities of life in Shole Creek. But now, armed with a new perspective, strengthened by a love tested and refined by hardship, Jen and Tobias stood ready to face them, hand in hand, their bond as strong and resilient as the rugged landscape that surrounded them. The weight of secrets hadn't disappeared, but it no longer threatened to consume them. They had learned to carry it together, their love a beacon of hope amidst the darkness, a testament to the enduring power of human connection in a world of hardship and uncertainty. Their journey had only just begun, but they were ready, their love a guiding star in the unforgiving beauty of the American West.

Chapter 7: Forging Alliances

The days that followed were a whirlwind of activity, a stark contrast to the quiet introspection that had consumed Jen in the wake of her father's confession. Stan Korte, his usually iron demeanor softened by a flicker of vulnerability, sought out Tobias. The meeting took place in the dimly lit study of Korte's imposing mansion, the air thick with the scent of aged leather and pipe tobacco. William, usually so imperious, sat hunched in his leather armchair, his hands clasped tightly together, a stark image of a man wrestling with his conscience.

"Dr. Adams," Korte began, his voice a low rumble, "I... I owe you an apology." He paused, clearing his throat, the words choked back by a lifetime of suppressed emotion. "My behavior towards you, my... my judgment, has been... unacceptable. Jen has told me... she's told me things."

Tobias remained silent, observing the older man with keen eyes. Korte's burdened expression showed guilt and regret. He saw a man stripped bare, power intact, yet his long-maintained facade gone.

"I've been a fool," Korte continued, his gaze meeting Tobias's. "Blind to the obvious. I focused on the wrong things–wealth, power, the success of the mine–and I neglected... well, everything else. Especially my daughter."

The confession hung heavy in the air, a stark acknowledgment of Korte's past mistakes. Tobias saw the genuine remorse in Korte's eyes, a flicker of the humanity hidden beneath the layers of his harsh exterior. He sensed an opportunity, not just for personal reconciliation, but for a larger alliance that could benefit the entire town.

"Mr. Korte," Tobias began, his voice calm and measured, "your daughter's happiness means a great deal to me. Shole Creek's health matters most. He paused, choosing his words carefully. "I understand you've been a man of...

strong convictions, perhaps even stubborn." A hint of a smile played on his lips.

Korte chuckled, a dry, rasping sound. "Stubborn is one word for it. Obstinate, perhaps. And utterly blind to my own shortcomings."

"But," Tobias continued, "I also see a man who cares deeply for his daughter and his town. A man who, despite his flaws, is capable of change."

He outlined his vision, a plan that involved Korte using his considerable influence to quell the simmering tensions with the local Native American tribe. The ever-expanding mine encroached the tribe's ancestral lands upon, leading to mistrust and escalating conflicts. Korte, with his wealth and power, could negotiate treaties, secure land rights, and foster peaceful coexistence. In return, Tobias would use his influence to reassure both the tribe and the townsfolk that peaceful resolutions were possible.

Korte listened intently, his initial skepticism slowly melting away as Tobias painted a vision of mutual benefit and lasting peace. The proposal addressed both their individual concerns and those of the entire community. It was a risky gambit, a delicate dance between conflicting interests, but it was a dance both men were willing to engage in.

"An alliance," Korte murmured, stroking his chin. "An unexpected one, indeed."

"One built on mutual respect, understanding, and a shared goal," Tobias corrected. "The well-being of Shole Creek, and the happiness of your daughter."

The agreement solidified that night, sealed not with a formal contract but with a shared bottle of Korte's finest whiskey, a potent symbol of their newfound camaraderie. This marked a pivotal moment, impacting not only Tobias and Korte's bond, but Shole Creek itself. A cautious optimism replaced the town's oppressive tension.

The news of the alliance spread like wildfire, generating a mixed reaction amongst the townsfolk. Some were skeptical, hesitant to trust Korte's sudden change of heart. Others, particularly those who had suffered because of his harsh dealings, were outright suspicious. Most welcomed peace, wanting conflict to cease. Greg Moore, the town sheriff, a man known for his stoicism and impartiality, was among those who remained cautiously optimistic.

"I've never known Korte to back down," Moore commented, leaning against the bar at the saloon, a glass of whiskey swirling in his hand. "But there's something different about him. Something... broken. Perhaps, that brokenness mends into something improved.

The following weeks were dedicated to the meticulous task of repairing damaged relationships. Tobias, utilizing his innate diplomacy and understanding of human nature, worked tirelessly to mend fences, build bridges, and foster mutual trust between the miners and the tribe. He spent long hours in the camp of the Native American tribe, learning their customs, their fears, and their aspirations. He saw the pain caused by the encroachment on their sacred lands, he heard the stories of broken promises and violated treaties. He saw a people desperate for peace, just like the townsfolk of Shole Creek.

Korte, for his part, used his considerable influence to ensure fair compensation for the tribe, a deal that addressed their land rights and secured their future within the community. He facilitated the creation of a new agreement that respected the tribe's cultural heritage and acknowledged their sacred ground. He invested in tribal education and infrastructure, fostering a new sense of hope and possibility.

The transformation in Korte was palpable. The cold, hard edge to his personality softened, replaced by a newfound sense of empathy and responsibility. He still possessed his strength and determination, but now, they were tempered by a genuine concern for the well-being of his community and his family. He viewed Jen's joy and her bond with Tobias, not threateningly, but with pride and satisfaction; proof love alters even inflexible systems.

The alliance wasn't without its challenges. Old resentments simmered beneath the surface, and there were moments when the delicate peace was threatened. But through it all, Tobias and Korte held firm to their commitment, their newfound partnership acting as a bulwark against the ever-present dangers. Their combined influence, along with Tobias's diplomacy and Korte's power, ensured that peace remained a viable possibility.

As the summer sun cast its golden rays on Shole Creek, an atmosphere of tentative peace settled over the town. Mining continued, now in concert with nearby residents. The once-fraught relationship between the miners and the Native American tribe slowly evolved into a cautious truce, and eventually, a newfound respect. The unexpected alliance between a rugged doctor and a powerful mine mogul had not only changed the lives of those directly involved, but it had reshaped the destiny of an entire frontier town. The future still held uncertainties, but now, Shole Creek faced them with a newfound unity, a sense of hope born from an unlikely alliance forged in the heart of the untamed American West.

The shared goal wasn't simply about appeasing the Native American tribe or silencing the growing dissent among the townsfolk. It was about forging a new identity for Shole Creek, one built on mutual respect, understanding, and a shared vision for the future. This meant tackling the underlying issues that had festered for years, issues that ran deeper than mere land disputes or economic disagreements. It demanded a complete overhaul of the social fabric, a restructuring of power dynamics, and a fundamental shift in perspective.

Tobias, ever the pragmatist, understood the complexities of the situation. He understood a simple treaty was insufficient. He understood the necessity of open communication, empathy, and mutual compromise. He spent countless hours with the tribal elders, learning their history, their grievances, and their hopes for the future. He listened patiently as they recounted generations of broken promises, of treaties violated and lands stolen. He saw the pain etched on their faces, the deep-seated distrust that had been cultivated over years of conflict. He came to understand that their resistance wasn't born of malice but of a profound sense of injustice, a desperate struggle to protect their ancestral heritage.

His interactions were not confined to formal meetings or official negotiations. He sought out informal encounters, sharing stories and meals, engaging in casual conversations that fostered a sense of human connection. He learned about their traditions, their spirituality, and their deep connection to the land. He learned to appreciate their resilience, their strength, and their unwavering determination to preserve their identity in the face of overwhelming adversity.

Meanwhile, Stan Korte, under Tobias's astute guidance, undertook a transformation that surprised even himself. He began to shed his arrogant exterior, replacing it with a newfound humility. He acknowledged his past mistakes, admitting the errors of his ways in a public forum, an act of contrition that shocked many but won the respect of others. He established a fund for the tribe, offering financial support for education, healthcare, and infrastructure development. He even began attending tribal ceremonies, participating in rituals that celebrated their rich culture and history. Political expediency didn't fully explain this man's actions.

The process was far from smooth. Old grudges and ingrained prejudices died hard. There were moments of tension, moments when the delicate peace teetered on the brink of collapse. But Tobias and Korte, now bound by a shared goal and a mutual respect, worked tirelessly to prevent any escalation. They acted as mediators, calming tempers, diffusing conflicts, and finding common ground. They became an unlikely team, a powerful force for positive change in Shole Creek.

Their collaboration extended beyond the Native American issue. They addressed the problems within the mining community, focusing on worker safety, fair wages, and improved working conditions. They implemented new safety regulations, reducing the risks associated with mining accidents. They worked with local businesses to create new opportunities for employment and economic growth, bolstering the community's overall prosperity.

Their efforts weren't just limited to practical solutions. They fostered a spirit of collaboration, encouraging the miners and the tribe to work together on joint projects. They organized community events, bringing people together to celebrate their shared heritage and forge stronger bonds. They encouraged intermarriage, breaking down social barriers and fostering a new sense of unity.

The changes were gradual, but the once-tense atmosphere in Shole Creek began to ease. The air, once thick with suspicion and resentment, began to clear. Hope replaced long-standing despair and uncertainty within the community.

Jen, watching her father's transformation with a mixture of awe and pride, found her own role in this new era of peace and cooperation. She used her artistic talents to capture the spirit of the changing times, creating paintings that depicted the newfound unity between the miners and the tribe. Her artwork became a powerful symbol of hope, a testament to the transformative power of collaboration. Her portraits of both her father and Tobias became iconic representations of the unexpected alliance that had shaped the destiny of Shole Creek.

Tangible achievements did not simply measure the success, but by a palpable shift in attitudes and beliefs. The people of Shole Creek, once divided by prejudice and conflict, began to see themselves as part of a larger community, bound together by a shared destiny. They learned to value diversity, to appreciate different perspectives, and to find common ground in the face of adversity.

The journey towards a truly unified Shole Creek was far from complete, but the alliance between Tobias and Korte provided a solid foundation for lasting peace and prosperity. The shared goal had transcended its initial purpose, morphing into a powerful force that reshaped the social, economic, and political landscape of the town.

The impact extended far beyond the immediate community. The story of their collaboration spread throughout the territory, inspiring other settlements to adopt similar strategies for conflict resolution. Shole Creek became a beacon of hope, a testament to the transformative power of unity and the possibility of achieving peace even in the harshest of environments.

Tobias and Korte, once adversaries, had become unlikely partners, their shared success a testament to the enduring power of collaboration and the transformative potential of a shared goal. Their story became a legend whispered across the vast expanse of the American West, a tale of redemption, reconciliation, and the remarkable ability of human beings to overcome their differences and build a better future together. Shole Creek's harsh beauty, once a battleground, symbolizes unity's triumph over past conflict, a Western beacon of peace. The once-divided community stood together, a testament to their shared vision, a vision made possible by the unexpected alliance between a doctor and a mine mogul, two unlikely heroes who reshaped the destiny of Shole Creek.

The air hung heavy with the scent of pine and damp earth, a stark contrast to the acrid smell of gunpowder that had so recently permeated Shole Creek. The tension, however, remained, a palpable presence clinging to the edges of the newfound peace. The formal treaty signing, a meticulously crafted document outlining land rights, resource sharing, and mutual respect, was merely the first step on a long and arduous journey. True reconciliation required more than just ink on paper; it demanded a fundamental shift in hearts and minds.

Tobias, ever the pragmatist, understood this implicitly. He knew that the signing ceremony, while a significant milestone, was merely a symbolic gesture. The real work lay in fostering genuine understanding and empathy between the townsfolk and the members of the Lakota tribe. He initiated a series of cultural exchange programs, inviting tribal elders to share their stories and traditions with the community. These weren't formal lectures but intimate gatherings, held in the comfortable setting of the town hall, or sometimes even in private homes, fostering a sense of familiarity and trust. The elders, initially hesitant, slowly warmed to the doctor's genuine interest and respect. They spoke of their history, their deep connection to the land, their spiritual beliefs, and their anxieties about the future. Their words, mournful, defiant, painted a vivid picture of a people struggling to preserve their heritage in the face of relentless change.

Jen, meanwhile, played a crucial role in bridging the cultural divide. Her artistic talents proved invaluable in capturing the essence of the Lakota people, their resilience, and their rich cultural heritage. She painted vibrant portraits of tribal elders, capturing the wisdom and strength etched on their faces. She depicted scenes of traditional ceremonies, showcasing the beauty and spiritual significance of their rituals. Her artwork, far from being mere depictions, became powerful symbols of understanding and empathy. It transcended language barriers, speaking directly to the heart and fostering a deeper connection between two vastly different cultures. Her work was displayed prominently in the town hall and at the annual Shole Creek fair, becoming a focal point for discussions and promoting a new level of cultural appreciation.

The miners, initially wary of the tribe, gradually began to see them not as adversaries but as fellow inhabitants of the land, each with their unique traditions and contributions. They learned about the tribe's sophisticated knowledge of herbal remedies and medicinal plants, knowledge that proved invaluable in treating common ailments and injuries. They shared stories and skills, demonstrating a growing camaraderie and respect. Joint projects, like the building of a new community irrigation system, provided opportunities for cooperation and collaboration, strengthening the bonds between the two groups. The successful completion of these endeavors not only addressed practical needs but also symbolized the growing unity and cooperation that permeated the community.

Stan Korte's role in this process was nothing short of transformative. He had initially opposed any form of reconciliation, viewing the tribe as a threat to his mining operations. However, Tobias's patient guidance and the gradual shift in the community's attitudes helped him see the error of his ways. He actively participated in the cultural exchange programs, listening intently to the elders' stories and openly acknowledging his past mistakes. His genuine remorse and willingness to make amends won over many skeptics, showing that change, even on a personal level, could be profound and lasting. He established a scholarship fund for Lakota children, ensuring access to education and paving the way for future generations to participate more fully in the community. His actions were not simply political gestures but a reflection of his genuine desire for redemption and his commitment to building a better future for Shole Creek.

Greg Moore, the town sheriff, played a vital role in maintaining order and ensuring a smooth transition. His presence, while authoritative, was tempered with fairness and understanding. He worked closely with both the tribal leaders and the community, fostering communication and mediating any disputes that arose. He understood the importance of maintaining law and order while respecting the sensitivities and needs of both groups. His actions demonstrated the ability to balance competing interests, ensuring that the process of reconciliation moved forward in an orderly and peaceful manner.

There were moments of tension, disagreements over land boundaries, and occasional misunderstandings that required careful negotiation and mediation. Each hurdle cleared only made participants more determined, showcasing the value of perseverance and empathy during conflict. The elders, initially hesitant, came to view Tobias and Korte as allies, not as invaders. They began to trust their intentions and see them as genuine partners in the endeavor to build a better future for their people. Their participation in the community events, initially symbolic, became more significant over time, with an increasingly active role in shaping the town's social and cultural fabric.

The sense of closure that followed the reconciliation was palpable. The air was no longer heavy with tension but light with a newfound sense of community. The sharp divide between townsfolk and Lakota faded; mutual cultural appreciation blossomed. The success of their reconciliation was not simply a matter of signed treaties or formal agreements. It was a manifestation of a profound shift in the social and cultural landscape of Shole Creek, a testament to the transformative power of empathy, understanding, and shared commitment to a common goal. The shared experience of overcoming adversity and working together to build a better future for all strengthened the bonds of the community, creating a legacy that would resonate for generations to come.

Jen's acclaimed artwork portrays Lakota history, culture, evolving communal understanding, and respect. She captured the faces of both the miners and the tribal members, their expressions reflecting not just the shared joy of peace, but also the deep respect they had developed for each other. Her portraits became symbols of this new-found unity, representations of the journey towards peace and understanding. These paintings exceeded mere artwork; They served as a constant reminder of the hard work, perseverance, and unwavering commitment that brought about this remarkable transformation in Shole Creek.

The story of Shole Creek's reconciliation spread, carried on the winds that swept across the prairies and whispered among the mountains. It became a legend, a beacon of hope in a land often marked by conflict and division. It inspired other communities to pursue similar paths, to embrace dialogue and empathy as a means of achieving lasting peace. The reconciliation held broader importance than just local success. Shole Creek powerfully illustrates that despite challenges, reconciliation creates fuller, more meaningful lives through peace and understanding. The spirit of Shole Creek, once defined by conflict, now embodied the ideals of unity, tolerance, and enduring peace. This rugged landscape, marked by two years of strife, now silently testifies to a community's remarkable achievement, forged in adversity, strengthened by reconciliation. The harmony achieved was not a mere absence of conflict but a positive, thriving embodiment of peace built on mutual respect and understanding.

The initial tentative peace, fragile as a newborn fawn, needed nurturing. The signed treaty was a crucial first step, but true reconciliation required more than just legal agreements; it needed hearts and minds to change. Jen, with her quiet strength and keen artistic eye, saw a path where others saw only impassable chasms. She understood the power of art to transcend language, to speak to the soul where words often failed. While Tobias engaged in pragmatic diplomacy, forging practical alliances through shared projects and cultural exchanges, Jen worked on a deeper level, focusing on emotional connections.

She began by creating a series of sketches, capturing the daily lives of both the townspeople and the Lakota. These weren't perfect pictures. These simple sketches, displayed prominently in the town's general store, served as silent ambassadors, fostering a sense of shared humanity. People stopped to look, to ponder the similarities they discovered between these seemingly disparate lives. They saw shared emotions—joy, sorrow, weariness, hope—reflected in every line and shade.

Jen didn't stop at sketches. She began painting larger canvases, depicting scenes of shared activity. A painting showcased a Lakota elder teaching a group of children, including both Lakota and settlers, about the medicinal properties of local herbs. Another depicted a joint effort to build a new bridge across Shole Creek, miners and Lakota working side-by-side, their hands rough but their spirits united. These weren't mere depictions of events; they were powerful narratives, weaving together the threads of two cultures, highlighting their interdependence and their shared humanity.

Her work extended beyond the visual. Jen initiated storytelling sessions, inviting both Lakota elders and townsfolk to share their stories, their memories, their fears, and their hopes. She would record these narratives, then meticulously transcribe them, weaving them into a rich tapestry of voices, creating a document that served as a chronicle of both the conflict and the emerging reconciliation. These written accounts, along with her artwork, became invaluable tools in fostering understanding and empathy.

She understood that reconciliation was a journey with its ups and downs. There were times when old prejudices resurfaced, when misunderstandings arose, threatening to derail the fragile peace. Jen, however, never wavered in her commitment to bridging the divides. She acted as a mediator, patiently listening to both sides, helping them articulate their concerns, and guiding them towards solutions that respected the needs and rights of everyone involved.

Her compassion and empathy were remarkable. She learned to speak some Lakota, allowing her to communicate directly with the tribal members, fostering deeper connections and understanding. She learned about their traditions, their spiritual beliefs, their anxieties about the future, and she incorporated this knowledge into her artwork and storytelling, further strengthening the bonds of understanding.

One particularly tense moment arose when a dispute over grazing rights threatened to reignite old hostilities. Jen, working alongside Tobias and Sheriff Moore, acted as a mediator, skillfully navigating the complex emotions and competing claims. She helped both sides see the other's perspective, highlighting their shared dependence on the land and the potential consequences of further conflict. Through patient negotiation and a willingness to compromise, she helped forge a solution that satisfied both the townspeople and the Lakota, preventing a potential crisis and strengthening the bonds of trust.

Her artistic talent wasn't just about creating beautiful images; it was a tool for diplomacy. She painted a series of portraits of the tribal leaders, showcasing their dignity and strength. These portraits were presented as gifts, not just as artwork, but as symbols of respect and acknowledgement. They sparked conversations, encouraged dialogue, and helped dispel negative stereotypes. She painted portraits of the townspeople as well, capturing their hopes and anxieties, their willingness to engage in a path of reconciliation.

Jen's influence extended beyond the immediate community. News of her work and her diplomatic efforts spread throughout the region, attracting the attention of government officials and other influential figures. Her artwork and the written accounts of the Shole Creek reconciliation were showcased at exhibitions, attracting widespread attention and inspiring other communities to pursue similar paths of peace. Her efforts brought about a wave of goodwill, promoting further collaboration and understanding between different cultures.

But the true measure of Jen's contribution was the intangible shift in attitudes and perspectives. She created an atmosphere of empathy, where previously there had been only suspicion and fear. She inspired trust, where previously there had been only animosity. She demonstrated the transformative power of art, not merely as an aesthetic pursuit but as a potent tool for social change. Her work transcended the immediate context of Shole Creek, representing a model for reconciliation and understanding that could be applied to many other conflicts and divisions.

Jen's journey in Shole Creek wasn't merely a romantic subplot to a larger story; it was the core of the narrative. Her strength of character, her artistic skill, and her profound empathy were as integral to the reconciliation as Tobias's pragmatism and Stan Korte's eventual remorse. She proved that a single person, armed with compassion and the power of art, could forge peace where others saw only conflict, weaving a future built not on dominance, but on mutual respect and enduring understanding. Her legacy would live on not just in the artwork she created but in the spirit of peace and reconciliation that she helped to establish in the heart of the American West. The canvas of her life, as vibrant and ever-evolving as the landscape around her, was testament to a woman who dared to bridge divides, not just with paintbrush and pen, but with the unwavering strength of her spirit.

The air in Shole Creek, once thick with tension, began to thin, carrying the scent of pine and damp earth, instead of the acrid tang of fear. The fragile peace, painstakingly forged through diplomacy and the quiet revolution of Jen's art, started to blossom into something stronger, something resembling true community. The shared experiences of hardship, the near-misses with disaster, had paradoxically brought the townspeople closer. They had faced the brink of chaos together, and in that shared vulnerability, they had found a newfound respect for one another.

The miners, their faces etched with the grim realities of their profession, started to smile more readily. The weariness in their eyes, once a reflection of constant struggle, began to soften, replaced by a cautious optimism. They gathered in the evenings, not just to drink and recount their day's toil, but to share stories, laughter, and even music. The saloon, once a haven for hushed anxieties and bitter complaints, now echoed with the sounds of camaraderie, a testament to the healing power of shared experience.

The women of Shole Creek, who had initially been divided by class and background, found common ground in their shared anxieties and hopes for their families. They formed a support network, helping each other with childcare, tending to the sick, and sharing recipes and gossip over steaming cups of coffee. Their collective strength, previously fragmented, now formed a powerful force, contributing significantly to the town's rejuvenation.

Even Stan Korte, initially resistant to the changing dynamics, began to thaw. Witnessing the positive transformations in the town, seeing the renewed spirit in his daughter's eyes, and recognizing the folly of his past prejudice, he started to participate in community events. He contributed generously to charitable causes, supporting initiatives that benefited both the townspeople and the Lakota. His presence, once a symbol of intimidation, became a reassuring sign of his acceptance of the new, more inclusive Shole Creek. He saw the economic benefits of a harmonious community, the opportunities that arose from collaboration, and he started to invest in projects that fostered unity. He even commissioned Jen to paint a large mural depicting the history of Shole Creek, a collaborative piece that incorporated elements of both settler and Lakota heritage.

Tobias, relieved by the easing tensions, found more time to focus on his medical practice. His clinic, previously a place of hushed anxieties and pain, became a hub of healing and community. He treated both settlers and Lakota members alike, dispensing medicine and care without prejudice. His strong physique and gentle hands, once symbols of strength and defense, now became emblems of comfort and compassion. He participated actively in community gatherings, earning the respect and affection of the townsfolk, his quiet strength forging bonds of trust and friendship.

Sheriff Moore, ever the pragmatic observer, also noticed the shift in the town's atmosphere. He had played a crucial role in maintaining order during the turbulent times, but now his efforts focused on fostering cooperation and harmony. He organized community events like hunting parties and fishing expeditions, creating opportunities for both settlers and Lakota to interact in a relaxed setting. His authority, once a symbol of control, transformed into a reassuring presence, a guarantee of fairness and justice for everyone.

The changes weren't just cosmetic; they were profound and lasting. Children, once wary of strangers, played together, regardless of their background. The lines that had once sharply divided the community began to blur, replaced by a shared sense of belonging. The creek itself seemed to reflect this newfound harmony, its waters flowing more freely, carrying away the sediment of conflict and nourishing the seeds of a brighter future.

Jen's influence continued to ripple outwards. Her artwork, once a tool for diplomacy, became a powerful symbol of the town's transformation. She organized exhibitions featuring both her own work and pieces by other local artists, both settlers and Lakota. These exhibitions served as celebrations of their shared heritage, showcasing the beauty and diversity of their combined cultures.

The storytelling sessions continued, becoming a cherished tradition, a testament to the importance of sharing memories and preserving their collective history. Jen ensured that both Lakota and settler stories were recorded and valued, creating a unique oral history that captured the essence of their shared journey.

The bridge that had been built jointly across Shole Creek became a physical manifestation of this newfound harmony, a symbol of their shared success and collaboration. Every time a wagon crossed, it was a reminder of the power of unity.

Tobias and Jen's relationship flourished amidst this environment of renewed hope. Their love story, once threatened by conflict and prejudice, now became an inspiration to the community, a symbol of their shared journey towards reconciliation and understanding. Their commitment to each other mirrored the town's commitment to rebuilding itself, creating a profound and enduring love story intertwined with the fabric of the community.

Even the landscape seemed to participate in the healing. The mountains, once silent witnesses to conflict, appeared to stand taller, their peaks bathed in the golden light of a brighter future. The wildflowers bloomed with vibrant colors, as if celebrating the town's resilience and renewed hope. The very air seemed lighter, carrying the promise of a peaceful coexistence.

The economic benefits were undeniable. With cooperation and trust established, trading between the settlers and the Lakota flourished. New business ventures emerged, capitalizing on their shared resources and skills. The mines, once a source of tension and conflict, became engines of prosperity, generating wealth and opportunity for everyone. The improved relationships brought about a more efficient and productive mining operation, boosting economic development for the entire community.

The story of Shole Creek's transformation spread far beyond its borders. Other communities, struggling with similar conflicts, sought inspiration from their example. Delegations arrived from neighboring towns, eager to learn from the Shole Creek experience, seeking advice on fostering reconciliation and building stronger communities. Jen's art and the town's story became a powerful testament to the resilience of the human spirit, inspiring similar transformations elsewhere in the American West.

The once volatile frontier town became a beacon of hope, showcasing the power of unity, empathy, and forgiveness. The journey hadn't been easy, but it had resulted in a stronger, more vibrant community, a testament to the endurance of the human spirit and the transformative power of love, art, and understanding. The spirit of Shole Creek was forever changed, forever marked by the vibrant tapestry of cultures woven together by the threads of reconciliation. And in the heart of it all, the romance of Tobias and Jen served as a symbol of enduring love, a beacon of hope shining brightly against the rugged landscape of the American West. Their story became an integral part of the town's evolving narrative, one of healing, growth, and ultimately, triumph. The future, once uncertain, now unfolded with the promise of prosperity and peace, built not on division, but on the solid foundation of a stronger, unified community.

Chapter 8: A Test of Faith

The tranquility of Shole Creek, so painstakingly achieved, proved to be a fragile peace. The sun dipped below the horizon, casting long shadows across the newly revitalized town, painting the scene in hues of orange and purple, a deceptive beauty that masked the brewing storm. It began subtly, a whisper in the wind, a subtle shift in the atmosphere that even the most optimistic couldn't ignore. The jovial chatter in the saloon was muted, replaced by hushed conversations and wary glances exchanged across the room.

The first sign was the disappearance of several Lakota hunting parties. They had been venturing further afield than usual, venturing into territory known to be hazardous. Days turned into weeks, and the initial concern morphed into a gnawing fear. Whispers spread through the town, fueled by anxiety and uncertainty. Had they encountered an unforeseen danger? Had an old enemy resurfaced? The unease spread like wildfire, threatening to undo all the progress that had been made.

Sheriff Moore, his usually stoic face etched with concern, called a meeting. The air in the town hall was thick with apprehension. The miners, who had so recently celebrated their newfound camaraderie, sat silently, their faces grim. The women huddled together, their quiet murmurs a testament to their shared anxiety. Even Stan Korte, his demeanor still bearing the scars of his past prejudices, sat with a noticeable tension, his usual bluster replaced by a quiet intensity.

Tobias, his medical bag resting beside him, scanned the faces of the assembled townsfolk. He sensed a familiar darkness creeping back into their eyes, a darkness that threatened to engulf the fragile hope they had so recently found. He had witnessed the healing power of community, the transformative effect of unity, but this new threat cast a long shadow over their hard-won peace. Jen, her usually vibrant spirit subdued, sat beside him, her hand resting reassuringly on his. Her artistic talent, which had played such a vital role in bringing the community together, seemed powerless against this unseen adversary.

The silence was finally broken by Old Man Hemlock, a grizzled prospector who had witnessed countless hardships during his years in Shole Creek. His voice, raspy from years of shouting above the din of the mines, carried a weight of experience. "It ain't just the Lakota who are missing," he rasped, his words hanging in the air like a dark omen. "Supplies have gone missing from the mine too. Tools, food, explosives... everything's disappearing."

A collective gasp rippled through the room. The disappearance of the Lakota hunting parties had been troubling, but the theft of supplies from the mine pointed to a far more sinister threat–a deliberate act of sabotage, intended to cripple the town's economy and sow discord. Fear and suspicion again fractured the once unified community. Who was behind these acts? And what were their motives?

Suspicion fell on several groups. Some whispered of rival mining companies, seeking to undermine Shole Creek's success. Others spoke of disgruntled miners, seeking revenge for past grievances. But the most unsettling whispers spoke of a resurgence of an old enemy—a band of outlaws, rumored to be operating in the surrounding mountains, waiting for an opportunity to strike.

Tobias, ever the pragmatist, suggested they organize search parties, combing the surrounding areas for any sign of the missing Lakota and investigate the mine thefts. He insisted on a joint effort, involving both settlers and Lakota, reminding them of the strength they had found in unity. This time, however, the cooperation wasn't as effortless as before. The shadow of suspicion hung heavy in the air, poisoning the well of trust.

The search parties ventured into the rugged wilderness, their progress hampered by the treacherous terrain and the pervasive sense of unease. They found no trace of the missing Lakota, but the evidence of the sabotage at the mine was clear–broken locks, scattered tools, and a chilling sense of violation. It was evident that the perpetrators were well-organized and knew the mine's layout intimately.

Jen, unable to stay idle, used her artistic skills to document the scene, sketching the details of the sabotage and the expressions of fear and uncertainty on the faces of the miners. Her sketches became a visual chronicle of the town's fear, a testament to the insidious nature of the threat they faced.

As days bled into nights, the tension in Shole Creek reached a fever pitch. The sense of community, so carefully built, began to fray at the edges. Old prejudices resurfaced, with accusations and counter-accusations flying. Suspicion and fear replaced the harmony that had reigned. The vibrant tapestry of unity began to unravel, threatening to plunge the town back into the chaos of its troubled past. Tobias and Jen, their love story once a beacon of hope, now found themselves battling not only an external threat but also the insidious threat of internal division.

The discovery of a hidden cache of weapons near the mine further fueled the anxieties. The weapons were sophisticated, far beyond the capabilities of any local outlaw gang. This pointed toward a more organized, and more dangerous, threat. The possibility of a powerful external force, intent on destabilizing Shole Creek, loomed large.

The situation demanded swift and decisive action. Tobias, drawing upon his experience as a trapper and hunter, developed a plan, using his knowledge of the terrain and his keen observational skills. He proposed a strategic defense of the town, using the natural features of the landscape to their advantage. He also suggested a concerted effort to identify and neutralize the threat before it could strike again.

Jen, despite the fear that gnawed at her, found strength in her art. She created posters depicting the stolen supplies, urging the community to remain vigilant and to report any suspicious activity. Her art, once a symbol of hope and reconciliation, was now a vital tool in their fight for survival.

The townsfolk, initially hesitant, rallied to Tobias's call to action. They remembered the lessons learned during the previous hardships and recognized the importance of collective action. Old grudges and prejudices were momentarily forgotten as they united against a common enemy.

As the sun rose on Shole Creek, casting its golden light on the town, it also illuminated the determined faces of its inhabitants, their resolve hardened by the emerging threat. The battle for the survival of Shole Creek had begun. The fight would not only be for the town's physical safety, but also for the preservation of the hard-won unity and the fragile peace that had been achieved. The upcoming confrontation would test the strength of their bonds, their faith in each other, and the endurance of their collective spirit. The future of Shole Creek, and the love story of Tobias and Jen, hung precariously in the balance.

The weight of the town's anxieties pressed heavily on Tobias. He wasn't just a doctor anymore; he was their shield, their protector. He walked the dusty streets, the silence broken only by the creak of his boots on the parched earth, a stark contrast to the lively town he'd helped build. The faces he saw mirrored the fear that gripped Shole Creek–fear that threatened to unravel all they had achieved. He sought Jen, needing her strength, her unwavering optimism, as much as he needed his own resolve.

He found her in her small studio, the flickering candlelight casting dancing shadows on her canvases. She was sketching, her brow furrowed in concentration, her usually vibrant spirit dimmed by the pervasive unease. The sketches, however, were not of the idyllic Shole Creek they had envisioned. These were grim depictions of the sabotage, the missing Lakota, the fear etched on the faces of the townsfolk. Her art, once a celebration of life and community, now served as a chilling record of their desperate struggle.

"Jen," he said, his voice soft, yet firm, "we need to be stronger. We need to show them that we won't be broken."

She looked up, her eyes filled with a mixture of fear and determination. "I know, Tobias. But this... this is different. It feels... calculated. Too organized."

He nodded, his gaze settling on her sketches. He understood. The haphazardness of a simple robbery, or even an attack by a lone outlaw, was absent. This was a deliberate attempt to cripple the town. The sophistication of the stolen weapons confirmed his suspicions. This wasn't the work of disgruntled miners or common criminals. This was a calculated attack, planned by someone with resources and a deep knowledge of Shole Creek.

"We need to find out who's behind this," he stated, his voice resolute. "And we need to do it fast."

Sheriff Moore, his face interrupted their conversation grimmer than Tobias had ever seen it. He spoke of a new development–a series of threatening letters had been delivered to several prominent townsfolk, including Stan Korte and Old Man Hemlock. The letters were anonymous, but they contained thinly veiled threats, hinting at further sabotage and violence if their demands weren't met. The demands themselves were vague, hinting at a larger, more sinister plan.

The threat felt like a tightening noose around Shole Creek's neck. Tobias knew the situation demanded more than law enforcement. He needed a strategy, a plan to not only protect the town but to also uncover the identity of their enemies. He knew he could rely on Jen's perceptiveness. Her artist's eye saw details others missed.

"Jen," he said, "I need your help. We need to analyze these letters, look for any clues, any fingerprints, anything that could lead us to the culprits."

Jen nodded, her artistic skills suddenly transformed into investigative tools. She meticulously examined the letters, her keen eyes scanning the paper for any trace of the writer's identity. She found nothing obvious–no fingerprints, no unusual markings. But she did notice subtle inconsistencies in the handwriting, suggesting the possibility of multiple authors or a deliberate attempt to disguise the writing. She meticulously documented every detail–the type of ink, the paper's texture, the slightest variations in pen strokes.

Tobias, meanwhile, focused on the strategic defense of Shole Creek. He knew the terrain better than anyone, having spent years traversing the mountains and the valleys surrounding the town. He proposed a three-pronged approach: reinforce the mine's security, set up watch points around the perimeter of the town, and organize a network of scouts to monitor the surrounding wilderness.

He enlisted the help of the miners, the townsfolk, even Stan Korte, who, despite his initial reluctance, finally understood the gravity of the situation. The unity they had forged earlier was tested but not broken. They worked tirelessly, their collective effort creating a formidable defense against their unknown enemy.

Days turned into weeks, filled with constant vigilance and the ever-present threat of attack. Tobias's determination fueled their efforts. He tirelessly worked alongside the townsfolk, offering medical care to the injured, providing strategic guidance, and instilling hope where fear had once reigned. He was their leader, their protector, their symbol of unwavering courage.

One night, under the pale glow of the moon, a scout reported suspicious activity near the abandoned mine on the outskirts of town. Tobias, leading a small group, cautiously approached the old mine. The silence was eerie, broken only by the rustling of leaves and the occasional creak of the mine's timbers. The air was thick with anticipation.

As they neared the mine's entrance, they found it partially blocked by debris. They cleared the debris, and the sight that greeted them chilled them to the bone. A large group of men, heavily armed and masked, were loading boxes of explosives onto wagons. They were the ones behind the sabotage, their operation meticulously planned and flawlessly executed. They were ready to unleash their final assault.

The battle was swift and brutal. Tobias, his skills honed by years of hunting and trapping, led the counterattack. He fought with the ferocity of a cornered bear, his determination unshakeable. The townsfolk fought alongside him, their unity and resolve stronger than ever.

IN THE END, THEY OVERWHELMED the attackers, capturing most of them. The leader, however, managed to escape. He vanished into the night, leaving behind a trail of unanswered questions.

The captured men revealed their identity–they were hired mercenaries, working for a rival mining company seeking to eliminate Shole Creek's competition. They had been paid handsomely to destroy the mine and destabilize the town.

The aftermath was a mixture of relief and exhaustion. Shole Creek had survived the crisis, but the scars remained. Tobias, exhausted but resolute, knew their fight wasn't over. The escape of the leader indicated a larger conspiracy, a deeper level of malice that needed to be uncovered.

In the quiet moments that followed, with Jen by his side, he recognized that his steadfastness, his unwavering determination, had been the key to their survival. It was more than just physical strength; it was the strength of his spirit, his belief in the people of Shole Creek, and their shared faith in their ability to overcome adversity. He looked at Jen, her face weary but radiant with the triumph of their collective victory. Their love, their strength, their shared faith, had proven stronger than any external threat. The future of Shole Creek was far from certain, but with Tobias's continued determination, and Jen by his side, they were ready to face whatever challenges lay ahead. Their love story, forged in the crucible of adversity, was a testament to the resilience of the human spirit and the enduring power of hope.

The aftermath of the attack left Shole Creek battered but not broken. The air, once thick with the scent of gunpowder and fear, now carried the faint, hopeful aroma of wood smoke from the hastily repaired buildings and the comforting smell of baking bread from Mrs. Gable's kitchen. The victory, however hard-won, was palpable. Men and women alike, their faces etched with exhaustion but their eyes gleaming with a newfound resolve, moved about their tasks with a quiet efficiency that spoke volumes of their resilience.

Yet, beneath the surface of this apparent calm, a deeper current flowed–one of lingering uncertainty and the weight of unspoken anxieties. The escape of the mastermind behind the attack cast a long shadow over the town. The fear wasn't entirely vanquished; it had merely retreated, lurking in the shadows, waiting for an opportune moment to resurface. Tobias, ever vigilant, felt the weight of this responsibility pressing down on him, a burden he bore with quiet determination.

Jen, however, was the unwavering beacon in the storm's aftermath. While Tobias dealt with the logistical fallout—organizing repairs, comforting the injured, and coordinating with the Sheriff—Jen focused on the emotional well-being of the town. She transformed her studio into a makeshift counseling center, offering solace and comfort to those struggling with the trauma they had endured.

Her artistic talent, once a source of personal expression, became a tool for healing. She organized communal painting sessions, encouraging the townsfolk to express their emotions through art. The canvases, once filled with the grim realities of the attack, now began to depict scenes of hope and resilience, vibrant colors replacing the earlier muted tones. The very act of creation became therapy, a shared journey towards healing and a renewed sense of community.

One evening, as the sun dipped below the horizon, casting long shadows across the prairie, Jen found herself sketching by the creek. The familiar sounds of the rushing water, the chirping of crickets, and the distant bleating of sheep seemed to offer a counterpoint to the recent violence. Yet, the image forming on her canvas wasn't idyllic. It depicted Tobias, his face etched with weariness, his eyes burdened by the weight of his responsibility.

She had seen the toll the events of the past weeks had taken on him. The lines around his eyes seemed deeper, his shoulders more stooped. He moved with the same quiet strength, but his usual easy smile was less frequent, replaced by a more serious, contemplative expression. The burden of leadership, of protecting Shole Creek, weighed heavily on him.

She knew he needed her now, not just as a lover, but as a partner, a confidante, a source of unwavering support. Her love for him transcended mere romantic affection; it was a deep, profound bond forged in the crucible of shared adversity, a testament to their shared strength and their unwavering belief in each other.

The following day, Jen approached Tobias, her heart filled with a quiet determination. She found him in his makeshift medical tent, tending to a minor wound on a young miner's arm. He was efficient and focused, his hands moving with practiced ease.

"Tobias," she said softly, her voice barely audible above the sounds of the bustling town.

He looked up, his eyes meeting hers. A faint smile touched his lips. "Jen. How are you holding up?"

"I'm fine," she replied, her voice steady, "But you're not. I know you're carrying the weight of the world on your shoulders."

He sighed, setting down the medical supplies. "It's my duty, Jen. I have to protect this town, protect you."

"I know," she said, stepping closer, "But you can't do it alone. You need to let others share the burden."

He looked at her, his eyes softening. "I appreciate your support, Jen. More than you know."

"Support isn't enough, Tobias," she said, her voice firm but gentle. "You need rest, you need to let go of some of the responsibility. The town will survive. We will survive."

He nodded slowly, a deep sigh escaping his lips. "You're right, Jen. I've been so focused on the external threats that I've neglected my own well-being, and yours as well. I'm sorry."

She reached out, taking his hand. Her touch was a source of comfort, a reminder of the strength they shared, the bond that had weathered so many storms.

"It's okay, Tobias," she murmured, "We'll face this together, as we always have. And we'll find a way to heal, to rebuild, not just the town, but ourselves as well."

In the weeks that followed, Jen actively encouraged Tobias to delegate tasks, to trust in the abilities of others. She helped him create a more structured system of governance, ensuring that the burden of responsibility was shared more equitably. She became a vital part of the town's rebuilding process, her organizational skills and artistic flair proving invaluable in coordinating efforts and raising morale.

She also found ways to express her own grief and anxieties through her art, creating a series of powerful paintings depicting the town's resilience and the strength of its spirit. These paintings became a symbol of hope for the community, a testament to their ability to overcome adversity.

Her actions were more than just acts of support; they were acts of courage, quiet yet powerful. She faced her fears, acknowledging the trauma she had endured while simultaneously working tirelessly to help others heal. She remained the heart of Shole Creek, the embodiment of unwavering resilience and the source of inspiration for its people.

As the town slowly began to heal, a new sense of unity and purpose emerged. The threat of the escaped leader still loomed, but the experience had forged an unbreakable bond between the townsfolk. They had faced death, despair, and destruction together, and they emerged stronger, more resilient, their spirit unbent.

Jen and Tobias, hand in hand, watched as the community rebuilt, their love story woven into the very fabric of Shole Creek's history. Their resilience, their shared faith, and their unwavering commitment to each other became a powerful symbol of hope, a testament to the enduring power of the human spirit in the face of adversity. The future was uncertain, yet they faced it together, their love, a beacon of hope amidst the rugged beauty and challenges of Shole Creek. The scars of the past remained, but they were now interwoven with the threads of a new beginning, a stronger community, and a love that had only grown deeper in the face of danger and uncertainty.

The weeks that followed were a blur of activity, a whirlwind of rebuilding and reconciliation. Shole Creek, though scarred, was slowly healing. The vibrant colors of Jen's artwork, depicting scenes of renewed hope and the resilient spirit of the community, adorned the walls of homes and businesses, a tangible manifestation of the town's gradual recovery. Tobias, though still burdened by responsibility, had begun to delegate tasks more effectively, trusting the capable hands of his fellow townsfolk. He was learning to lean on others, to share the weight of leadership, a lesson Jen had patiently and persistently taught him.

But the shadow of the past remained. The escape of the mastermind behind the attack loomed large, a constant reminder of the fragility of their peace. Stan Korte, Jen's father, remained a complex figure, his gruff exterior masking a deep-seated grief and a lingering sense of guilt. He had been distant, preoccupied with the business of the mine, seemingly indifferent to the suffering of the community. His disapproval of Tobias, fueled by a blend of old-fashioned prejudices and a fear of losing his daughter, had only intensified the tensions in the already fragile situation.

One crisp fall afternoon, Tobias found himself walking along Shole Creek, the familiar tranquility of the scene a stark contrast to the turmoil he had recently witnessed. He was lost in thought, contemplating the future of Shole Creek and the delicate balance of his relationship with Jen, when he noticed an unusual sight. Stan Korte stood at the edge of the creek, a solitary figure against the backdrop of the vibrant fall foliage. He appeared older, his shoulders slumped, his usually stern face etched with weariness.

Hesitantly, Tobias approached him. "Mr. Korte," he said, his voice quiet and respectful. The older man didn't flinch, merely turned to face him, his gaze unwavering.

"Doctor Adams," Korte replied, his voice gravelly. There was a strange vulnerability in his tone, something Tobias had never witnessed before.

An uncomfortable silence hung between them, broken only by the gentle murmur of the creek. Tobias knew he needed to bridge this gap, to address the unspoken tension that had lingered between them for so long.

"I...I wanted to apologize for my earlier behavior," Tobias began, choosing his words carefully. "I understand your concerns, your protectiveness towards Jen. But I hope you can see that my intentions have always been honorable."

Korte remained silent for a long moment, his eyes fixed on the water. Then, he spoke, his voice barely a whisper. "My daughter...she's a remarkable woman. She's stronger than me, stronger than I ever realized." He paused, his throat tightening. "I've been a fool, Doctor Adams. A blind, stubborn fool."

Tobias listened patiently, offering no interruption, allowing Korte to express his remorse. He spoke of his regrets, his harshness, his failure to appreciate the depth of his daughter's character and the sincerity of Tobias's intentions. He confessed that his preoccupation with the mine, his relentless pursuit of wealth, had blinded him to the importance of family, of love, of human connection.

He spoke of the recent attack, admitting that the vulnerability of Shole Creek had finally pierced his hardened exterior. He had witnessed the community's resilience, their collective strength in the face of adversity, and it had shaken him to his core. He had seen Jen's unwavering spirit, her selfless dedication to the healing of the community, and it had humbled him.

He spoke of the fear he had harbored, the fear of losing Jen, not just to another man, but to the dangers inherent in life in Shole Creek. This fear, he admitted, had driven his actions, his resistance to Tobias, his gruff disapproval. He had been afraid of losing his daughter, of losing a part of himself.

"I've been so focused on building my empire," Korte confessed, his voice cracking with emotion. "I've neglected what truly matters. I've neglected Jen. I've been a terrible father."

Tears welled in his eyes, and for a moment, the formidable mine mogul appeared as fragile as a child. Tobias watched him, his heart filled with a mix of compassion and understanding. He had seen this vulnerability before, briefly glimpsed in the moments of shared concern following the attack, but this was different. This was a full and genuine acknowledgment of his faults, a profound expression of regret.

"Mr. Korte," Tobias said softly, placing a hand on the older man's shoulder. "It's not too late. You can change. You can make amends."

Korte looked up, his eyes red-rimmed, but his gaze steadier now, filled with a newfound resolve. "I want to," he whispered, a glimmer of hope shining through his grief. "I want to be a better father, a better man. I want to be part of this community, not just a detached observer."

This was the turning point. It wasn't a sudden transformation, but a profound shift in perspective, a genuine willingness to change. Korte pledged to help rebuild Shole Creek, to use his resources and influence to support the community. He actively participated in the town's recovery efforts, his considerable wealth contributing significantly to the restoration of homes and businesses. He even offered financial assistance to those who had lost their livelihood in the attack.

He began to spend more time with Jen, actively participating in her artistic endeavors, even offering gentle encouragement and praise. He learned to appreciate her talent, her strength, her unwavering spirit. He began to see her not as a possession to be controlled, but as an independent woman with her own ambitions and desires. He apologized to her for his harshness, for his lack of understanding, for the pain he had caused her.

The reconciliation wasn't immediate or easy, but it was genuine. Jen, ever forgiving and resilient, embraced her father's newfound commitment to change. She recognized the sincerity of his remorse and the genuineness of his desire for redemption. Their relationship, once strained and distant, began to heal, strengthened by a shared experience and a newfound understanding.

The news of Stan Korte's transformation spread quickly through Shole Creek. The formerly feared mine owner was now viewed as a symbol of hope, a testament to the power of redemption. His actions brought a new level of unity to the community, demonstrating that grief, loss, and the unwavering love of family could soften even the most hardened hearts.

As the town continued to rebuild, the presence of Stan Korte, actively participating, symbolized a new era of hope and unity. The future still held challenges, but Shole Creek, once a town divided by fear and mistrust, was now united in its resilience, its spirit unbroken, its people stronger than ever. And at the heart of it all was a love story that had transformed not only the lives of Jen and Tobias but also the very soul of Shole Creek. Their love, a beacon of hope amidst the rugged beauty of the American West, had inadvertently sparked a ripple effect of redemption, healing wounds both physical and emotional, and ultimately forging a stronger, more united community. The scars remained, etched into the landscape and the hearts of the townsfolk, but they were now interwoven with the threads of a new beginning, a stronger community, and a love that had only grown deeper in the face of danger, uncertainty, and profound personal change.

The crisp fall air carried the scent of woodsmoke and damp earth, a familiar fragrance that usually brought a sense of peace to Shole Creek. But this time, a palpable tension hung in the air, a silent undercurrent that ran deeper than the meandering creek itself. The recent attack, though resolved, had left an indelible mark on the community, a scar that time would slowly heal, but never entirely erase.

Greg Moore, the town sheriff, a man known for his quiet strength and unwavering loyalty, was bearing the weight of this unspoken anxiety. He had been instrumental in the investigation following the attack, his diligence and sharp intuition leading them to several key breakthroughs. However, the mastermind remained at large, a shadow lurking in the periphery, a constant reminder of the vulnerability of their peaceful existence.

Moore, a man of few words but profound actions, had always been a pillar of the community. He was respected, not just for his badge, but for his inherent decency, his unwavering commitment to justice, and his quiet compassion. He had seen the raw fear in the eyes of the townsfolk, the uncertainty in their hearts, and he felt the responsibility acutely. He understood the weight of his duty to protect them, to ensure their safety, to provide a sense of security in a world that felt increasingly unpredictable.

But this time, the weight felt heavier than ever. The escape of the main perpetrator haunted him, gnawing at his conscience. He blamed himself, not for a lack of effort, but for the inherent limitations of his resources, the inability to fully safeguard the community from the malevolence that existed in the shadows. The sleepless nights were taking their toll, etching lines of fatigue around his usually strong eyes, casting a shadow over his once robust frame. His usual stoicism was slowly cracking under the relentless pressure.

One evening, as the sun dipped below the horizon, painting the sky in hues of fiery orange and deep crimson, Moore found himself alone in his small office at the back of the saloon. The flickering lamplight cast long shadows across the room, creating an eerie atmosphere. He sat at his desk, his head resting in his hands, the weight of his responsibility pressing down on him with crushing force.

He had been reviewing the evidence, poring over details, searching for any overlooked clues that might lead them to the elusive mastermind. But the trail seemed to have gone cold, leaving him with a chilling sense of frustration and failure. He had done everything he could, he told himself, but it wasn't enough. The community was still vulnerable, exposed, still living in the shadow of the recent violence.

Suddenly, a thought struck him, a risky, desperate plan that could potentially resolve the situation, even if it meant making an ultimate sacrifice. It was a plan born out of desperation, a last resort to ensure the safety and security of his beloved Shole Creek, a desperate gamble that might save the town from further harm.

The plan was audacious, fraught with peril, bordering on reckless. It involved confronting the mastermind directly, a dangerous confrontation that could result in his own demise. But he knew he couldn't live with the guilt of inaction, the weight of knowing that he could have done more. His loyalty to the town, his devotion to its people, outweighed his own self-preservation.

He spent the next few hours making meticulous preparations. He carefully organized his papers, his belongings, preparing for the eventuality of not returning. He wrote a letter to Jen, a poignant message expressing his love and admiration, a heartfelt farewell to the woman he secretly admired. He also wrote a letter to the town, outlining his plan, a heartfelt farewell to the community he was sworn to protect.

As the moon cast its pale light over Shole Creek, Moore set off, his silhouette a dark figure against the moonlit landscape. His heart pounded in his chest, a mixture of fear and determination driving him forward. He knew the risks, he accepted the potential consequences, he had made his peace with fate. His sacrifice was not one of cowardice, but of unwavering courage, a selfless act fueled by his deep love for the community.

His confrontation with the mastermind was a tense standoff, a battle of wits and will. Moore, though outnumbered and outmatched, fought with a ferocity born of desperation, a fierce determination to protect his town.

The fight was brutal, a desperate struggle for survival. The outcome was uncertain, a toss of fate, a gamble he was willing to take. His sacrifice ensured the safety and future of Shole Creek.

The news of Moore's sacrifice spread like wildfire through the town. The initial shock gave way to grief, to a profound sense of loss. Moore was more than just a sheriff; he was a friend, a neighbor, a pillar of the community. His selfless act cemented his place in the hearts of the townsfolk, transforming him into a legend, a symbol of unwavering courage, loyalty, and selflessness.

Jen, heartbroken by his loss, found solace in his letter, a testament to his deep affection for her and his devotion to the town. She painted a portrait of him, a powerful depiction of his strength and quiet dignity, a tribute to the man who had sacrificed himself for the safety of the town.

Stan Korte, initially reluctant to acknowledge Moore's sacrifice, eventually came to see the depth of the sheriff's selflessness. He acknowledged his profound impact on the community, and contributed generously to a fund established in Moore's name, supporting the families of those affected by the attacks. He recognized that Moore's sacrifice wasn't just the end of a story, but the beginning of a new chapter, one of healing and unity.

The memorial service for Moore drew the entire community together, united in their grief but also in their gratitude for his sacrifice. It was a testament to the strength of the human spirit, a demonstration of the power of collective sorrow and shared appreciation. Moore's death became a turning point for Shole Creek; his sacrifice created an unbreakable bond within the community. It was a bond forged in grief, but cemented in gratitude. It was a reminder that even in the face of unimaginable loss, the human spirit is capable of profound resilience, and that even the smallest acts of selflessness can have an immeasurable impact. The scars of the attack would remain, but they were now interwoven with the memory of a hero, a reminder that even in the darkest of times, hope and unity can prevail. Moore's sacrifice became a testament to the enduring spirit of Shole Creek, a legacy that would inspire generations to come. His memory lived on, not just in the hearts of those who knew him, but in the very fabric of the community he had protected with his life. The town rebuilt, stronger and more united than ever before, thanks to the ultimate sacrifice of their beloved Sheriff

Greg Moore. His name became synonymous with courage, loyalty, and the unwavering spirit of Shole Creek.

Chapter 9: The Climax

A deeper, more ominous sound–the thud of boots on packed earth, the rasp of breath, the metallic gleam of a shotgun barrel swallowed the rhythmic clang of pickaxes against rock, usually the soundtrack of Shole Creek's lifeblood. Tobias Adams, his usual calm replaced by a simmering fury, stood facing Stan Korte, the mine owner, a man whose steely gaze usually held the power of a winter blizzard. Between them stood Jen, a fragile bridge between the raging storm brewing and the potential for calm.

"This ends now, Korte," Tobias's voice, low and controlled, cut through the tension. The air crackled with unspoken threats, the unspoken accusations hanging heavy like the dust settling over the mine shafts. He hadn't come here for a polite discussion; the events of the past weeks, culminating in the near-fatal attack on Jen, had pushed him beyond the limits of his patience.

Korte's lips curled into a sneer. "Adams, you dare to address me in such a manner? You, a mere...trapper?" His voice dripped with contempt, a venomous antidote to the quiet dignity Tobias usually exuded. He gestured dismissively toward his men, hulking figures who stood silently, their hands resting near the holsters of their revolvers. The unspoken threat hung in the air, heavy and suffocating. This wasn't a fair fight.

Jen stepped forward, her usual artistic grace replaced by a newfound steel. "Father, please. This needs to stop. What you've done is wrong. Tobias has only ever tried to protect me." Her voice trembled slightly, but her eyes held a fierce determination. She'd seen the darkness in her father's eyes, the ruthless ambition that had driven him to such desperate measures.

Korte's eyes narrowed. "Protection? From what? From the dangers of a life outside the security I provide?" He laughed, a harsh, grating sound that echoed across the deserted mining claim. "You're a fool, Jen. He's nothing but a commoner, a mountain man. He doesn't belong in our world."

Tobias moved, his large frame radiating a controlled power that silenced the men around Korte. "Your world? Your world is built on the backs of men who risk their lives in your mines, on the exploitation of this land, and the disregard for the lives of those around you. You threaten the stability of this entire town for your own greed!" He didn't raise his voice; there was no need. His words, clear and measured, carried the weight of his conviction.

The confrontation intensified, becoming a clash of wills. Korte's men shifted uneasily, their loyalty wavering between their employer and the respected trapper who had become a local hero after his bravery in recent events. The unspoken tension between them hung heavier than the dust in the air. Korte, sensing the shift, spat on the ground. "You think you can intimidate me, Adams? I have power here; you have nothing."

"I have Jen," Tobias responded simply, his gaze unwavering. He met Korte's glare, his eyes reflecting a fierce determination that mirrored Jen's own. The unspoken threat hung in the air: he was willing to do whatever it took to protect her.

The standoff escalated. Korte's men began to circle Tobias, their hands moving toward their weapons. The air crackled with the promise of violence. Jen screamed, her voice sharp and shrill, a desperate plea for reason in the face of escalating violence. Suddenly, a gunshot shattered the tense silence.

It wasn't Korte or his men. A figure emerged from the shadows–Sheriff Moore, his face pale, but his eyes filled with a steely resolve. He'd been watching from afar, observing the unfolding confrontation, weighing his options. The single shot had been a calculated risk, designed to interrupt the escalating violence and bring the confrontation to an immediate halt. It was a last-ditch effort to prevent a bloody showdown.

The unexpected intervention startled both sides. The tension momentarily eased as all eyes turned towards the sheriff. Moore, his hand still on his weapon, stepped forward, his voice firm and unwavering. "This ends now," he declared, his tone carrying the authority of his badge, and the weight of the silent understanding within the community. "I've seen enough. This is my town, and this kind of violence is not acceptable."

Korte, taken aback by the sheriff's sudden intervention, hesitated. He recognized the steely resolve in Moore's eyes, the quiet strength that had always held the town together. He knew he was outmatched, not just by Tobias's strength, but by the silent support Moore held within the community. He could feel the change in his men; their loyalty, which he had always taken for granted, now hung precariously in the balance.

The tense standoff continued, punctuated by the silence of the surrounding hills, the looming threat of violence, and the uncertain future. The night was heavy with the weight of unspoken words and pent-up emotions. Korte's anger gradually cooled into a reluctant acceptance, and he signaled to his men to stand down.

The sudden shift was palpable. The atmosphere, once thick with animosity, began to clear. The potential for a bloody confrontation had been averted, but a deep-seated conflict still lingered; a resolution that required more than just a cessation of immediate violence. The confrontation had only scratched the surface of the deeper issues plaguing Shole Creek. The tension remained, a silent undercurrent, hinting at the complexities of resolving the long-brewing conflict.

Tobias stood his ground, his gaze fixed on Korte, a silent warning. The silent threat remained, a grim reminder of the power he wielded, a testament to the intensity of the confrontation that had almost broken out. Jen rushed to Tobias's side, her relief palpable. She threw her arms around him, clinging to him in silent gratitude for his courage, and his unwavering love.

Sheriff Moore watched, a quiet observer. He knew this wasn't the end. The resolution was fragile, a temporary truce in a much larger conflict. The underlying issues that had fueled the conflict remained unresolved. He watched as Tobias and Jen sought solace in each other's arms. He felt a bittersweet sense of relief, a grim understanding of the precarious peace they had just achieved. The quiet tension remained, a lingering reminder that the true resolution of the conflict required more than just a dramatic confrontation. The silent, unresolved issues loomed large, casting a long shadow over the fragile peace that had descended on Shole Creek. The true test of their unity was yet to come.

The following days were filled with a tense quiet. The confrontation had changed the dynamics of Shole Creek. Korte, though outwardly compliant, hadn't truly relinquished his grip on power. He watched Tobias and Jen, a palpable resentment simmering beneath his surface politeness. The uneasy truce was fragile, a thin veneer over the underlying tensions that still plagued the town. The incident had served to highlight the power imbalances inherent in the community, the deep-seated resentment that lay beneath the surface of daily life.

Jen, though relieved by the averted violence, couldn't shake off the unease. She felt a profound sense of responsibility; she found herself caught in the middle of a simmering conflict, a delicate balance between her loyalty to her father and her profound love for Tobias. The incident had profoundly changed her perception of her family and their relationship with the town. She began to see the cracks in the façade of her father's seemingly unshakeable power, the subtle undercurrents of fear and resentment that permeated their perfect world.

Tobias, while outwardly calm, felt the weight of the confrontation. He was keenly aware of the unresolved tension. He understood that the confrontation hadn't solved the deeper problems, that the fragile peace could shatter at any moment. He resolved to continue fighting for Jen, not just against her father, but against the systemic issues that threatened the stability of Shole Creek. His quiet strength and unwavering determination were now focused not only on Jen's safety but also on the well-being of the entire community.

Sheriff Moore, ever vigilant, knew the fragile peace wouldn't last long. He stepped up his patrols, his presence a silent reminder of the need for order and stability in the town. He began to work towards a long-term solution that addressed not just the immediate threat, but the root causes of the conflict. His actions highlighted a growing awareness of the need for true reconciliation, for a deeper understanding between the various factions within the community. He understood that their conflict was not just a personal feud but a reflection of larger societal issues, issues that needed addressing. The confrontation had been a turning point, but the path to lasting peace was long and uncertain. The fight for Shole Creek's future had just begun. The uneasy truce hung heavy in the air, a testament to the deep-seated issues that lay beneath the surface of the town. The shadow of the confrontation still loomed over the community, a haunting reminder of the fragile peace that had been achieved.

The uneasy truce held only as long as the setting sun cast long shadows across Shole Creek. As darkness deepened, a lone rider emerged from the west, a silhouette against the fiery horizon. He was lean, his movements fluid and silent, the very embodiment of the untamed wilderness. This was not a friendly visitor; his hard eyes and the glint of a rifle strapped to his saddle spoke of a different purpose. This was Silas Blackwood, Korte's hired gun, a man known for his ruthlessness and his unwavering loyalty to the mine owner. Blackwood's arrival shattered the fragile peace, his presence a chilling reminder of the volatile nature of Shole Creek.

He rode directly to Korte's mansion, a stark contrast to the humble dwellings that lined the creek. The house, a testament to Korte's wealth, stood as a symbol of the power imbalance that had fractured the community. Blackwood dismounted, his boots crunching on the gravel path, his every movement deliberate and precise. He delivered a message, short and to the point, that sent a fresh wave of icy dread through Korte's heart. The message was simple but deadly: Tobias Adams was leaving Shole Creek, and Korte would not stand in his way. But it was a carefully constructed deception meant to lure Tobias into a trap.

Meanwhile, Tobias and Jen, unaware of Blackwood's arrival, were preparing for a clandestine meeting. Their love, forbidden by Korte, had thrived in secret, their stolen moments a testament to their defiant spirits. They were planning their escape, a desperate bid for freedom, their hearts filled with a mixture of hope and fear. The weight of Korte's oppression was a palpable force; their relationship, a beacon of defiance in a town steeped in fear and resentment. The possibility of a life away from Shole Creek, filled with the promise of a future away from the mine's shadow, fueled their determination.

Their escape route was a treacherous path through the mountains, a winding trail known only to Tobias, a route familiar from his years as a trapper. They planned to leave under cover of darkness, their escape shrouded in the cloak of night, relying on the silence of the wilderness to conceal their departure. The wilderness was their ally, a protector against Korte's reach.

As they made their preparations, a shadow fell across their plans. A piercing scream echoed through the night, followed by the rhythmic thud of hooves, the unmistakable sound of a horse galloping at full speed. It was Jen's younger sister, Lily, her face pale with terror, her breathless words carrying a message of impending doom. Blackwood had discovered their plan and was pursuing them, aided by Korte's henchmen. The pursuit had begun.

Tobias grabbed his rifle, his eyes filled with a cold fury. The escape plan was ruined; the pursuit had become a desperate race against time, a high-stakes gamble with death. He knew Korte would stop at nothing to keep Jen from him. He knew this was not just about their freedom, but about their survival. The peaceful, hopeful departure was replaced with the raw, harsh reality of survival. Their clandestine escape had turned into a desperate fight for their lives.

The chase was relentless, a furious ballet of horse and man against the breathtaking but unforgiving backdrop of the rugged landscape. Tobias, a master of wilderness navigation, led them through dense forests and along treacherous mountain paths, his knowledge of the terrain their only defense against Blackwood's relentless pursuit. Jen, despite her fear, displayed a courage that surprised even Tobias. She rode with a newfound determination, her will matched by her physical stamina. Her art, usually a calming pursuit, became insignificant compared to the urgent need for survival.

The sounds of the chase echoed through the stillness of the night; the thud of hooves, the sharp crack of twigs underfoot, the harsh breathing of the men in pursuit. Every turn brought them closer to danger, every shadow harbored the possibility of an ambush. The pursuit was a blur of adrenaline-fueled action, a test of their physical and mental strength. The darkness, once their ally, now seemed to conspire against them, the shadows lengthening, the silence filled with the ominous sounds of their pursuers.

Blackwood, a skilled tracker, relentlessly followed their trail. The scent of their escape hung heavy in the air, a challenge he could not ignore. His ruthlessness matched his determination, making him a formidable opponent. His pursuit was not merely a professional obligation but a personal vendetta fueled by his unquestioning loyalty to Korte. The mountainous terrain offered them some reprieve, but it also offered advantages to Blackwood, a master of using his environment to his advantage.

The chase reached its peak at the precipice of a deep canyon. Blackwood and his men were closing in. Tobias, with his back against the canyon wall, prepared for a final stand. The air crackled with tension, the silence broken only by the pounding of their hearts and the distant echo of the pursuing riders. The canyon, a natural barrier, offered them some temporary safety. It was also a perfect trap.

In a swift, decisive move, Tobias used the canyon's narrow opening to his advantage, ambushing Blackwood's men, causing confusion and allowing them a precious moment to regroup and escape. It was a battle of wits and skill, a display of survival that tested the limits of their endurance. Tobias's years of wilderness survival skills made the difference, his knowledge of the terrain and his calm under pressure proving to be their salvation.

The escape from the canyon led them towards a hidden network of caves, a labyrinthine passage known only to Tobias. They navigated the treacherous tunnels, the darkness clinging to them like a shroud. The pursuit, though relentless, became a dangerous game of cat and mouse, testing their endurance, their courage, and their love.

Emerging from the caves, exhausted but alive, they found themselves on the outskirts of a neighboring town, the lights of civilization twinkling in the distance, a beacon of hope in the darkness. They had escaped Korte's grasp, but the battle was far from over. Their flight had been a grueling fight against nature and the ruthlessness of a determined enemy. The victory was bittersweet.

Their escape to the neighboring town marked the end of one chapter and the beginning of another. The pursuit, though successful, left a lasting impact; the scars of their escape etched deeply into their memories. The victory, albeit hard-won, was temporary. Korte would not give up that easily; the danger still loomed. The future remained uncertain, but for now, they had found safety, together, in a new beginning. The pursuit had tested the limits of their strength, their endurance, and their love, forging an unbreakable bond, proving that their love could conquer even the most daunting obstacles. The echoes of the relentless pursuit and the tension of their perilous escape would forever resonate within their hearts. The knowledge that Korte would inevitably hunt them down again soon tempered the quiet relief. Their escape was a victory, a testament to their courage and love, but also the beginning of a new and potentially even more dangerous chapter in their lives.

The relative safety of the neighboring town felt fragile, a thin veneer of peace over the simmering resentment and fear that still clung to them like the dust of the trail. They sought refuge in a small, dimly lit inn, the flickering candlelight casting long, dancing shadows on the rough-hewn walls. Exhaustion weighed heavily on them, the adrenaline of the chase replaced by a bone-deep weariness. Tobias cleaned and oiled his rifle, the rhythmic motion a calming ritual, while Jen, her hands trembling slightly, tended to her wounds–a deep gash on her arm, a testament to the ferocity of their escape.

The innkeeper, a wizened old woman with eyes that had seen too much, offered them a meager meal, and a shared room, her silence a comforting presence in the tense atmosphere. As they ate, the sounds of the town–the distant murmur of conversations, the rhythmic creak of a nearby wagon wheel–felt both alien and comforting, a stark contrast to the echoing silence of the mountains.

Sleep offered only fleeting respite. Nightmares of Blackwood's relentless pursuit haunted their dreams, the image of his cold, calculating eyes a recurring motif in the tapestry of their subconscious. They awoke with a shared sense of unease, the knowledge that their respite was temporary, that Korte's shadow stretched far beyond the confines of Shole Creek. The quiet moments were punctuated by the unspoken question: what now?

The following morning, a sense of urgency pushed them into action. They needed to plan their next move, to decide whether to continue their flight or to attempt a more assertive strategy. Their escape had been a desperate act of survival; now they needed a plan, a strategy to ensure their long-term safety. They needed to consider every contingency. The weight of their decision pressed heavily on them.

It was Jen who broke the silence, her voice low and resolute. "We can't just run," she said, her eyes burning with a newfound determination. "We need to fight back. We need to make Korte understand that he can't simply take what he wants." Her words were a bold declaration that shifted the balance of power. Tobias had been prepared to continue fleeing, to fade into the anonymity of the vast American West, but Jen's words ignited a different path, a path of defiance.

Jen's proposal was audacious, a risky gamble with potentially dire consequences. Her plan was to use her father's own network against him, a daring maneuver that involved leveraging her knowledge of the mine's operations and her father's business dealings. She proposed to expose Korte's illegal activities, his corrupt dealings with the sheriff, and his manipulation of the local Native American tribe. She knew the intricacies of her father's empire; she had witnessed his greed and ruthlessness firsthand. This intimate knowledge gave her a unique advantage.

Her conviction swayed Tobias. Her plan was a long shot, fraught with peril, but it offered a chance to not only protect themselves but also to dismantle Korte's empire, to free Shole Creek from his tyrannical grip. It was a fight for their freedom, but also a fight for the town itself. The risk was immense, but the potential reward–justice for the people of Shole Creek, and a future where they could live without fear–made it worthwhile.

Their plan required meticulous preparation. Jen, with her innate understanding of her father's business dealings and her sharp eye for detail, meticulously gathered evidence–letters, receipts, financial records–anything that could expose Korte's illicit activities. She used her artistic skills to her advantage, creating detailed sketches of the mine's layout and the secret pathways she knew existed. Her keen observation skills, honed by years of meticulous artistic practice, proved to be invaluable.

Tobias, meanwhile, leveraged his knowledge of the wilderness, his understanding of human nature, and his reputation as a skilled tracker to establish contact with reliable sources of information. He contacted an old friend, a former lawman who had been forced out of Shole Creek by Korte's influence. The former lawman, sympathetic to their cause, agreed to help, offering crucial insights into the town's power dynamics and the network of Korte's informants.

Their collaboration was seamless, a testament to their shared determination and their growing trust. They worked late into the night, their efforts fueled by a potent cocktail of fear and determination, their actions a bold declaration of defiance against an oppressive force. Their days in the inn were spent gathering evidence, analyzing information, and formulating their strategy. The nights were filled with anxiety and the planning of their next move, a chess game played against a ruthless opponent.

The plan unfolded in stages. First, Jen, using her connections, anonymously leaked selected pieces of evidence to a newspaper in a nearby city, carefully chosen to maximize its impact. The newspaper, known for its investigative journalism, published the leaked information, revealing some of Korte's illicit activities. The initial news created ripples of shock and uncertainty. Korte, realizing he had been betrayed, began to retaliate. This was precisely when Jen's next move would take place.

Jen then stepped forward, contacting the newspaper directly with additional evidence. She revealed her identity and made a public statement, accusing Korte of various crimes. She spoke with the eloquence and courage of someone who had been silenced for too long, her voice a powerful counterpoint to Korte's reign of terror. Her appearance surprised everyone. It was a brave act, a direct challenge to Korte's power.

The revelation sent shockwaves through Shole Creek. Korte's reputation, previously untouchable, crumbled under the weight of the accusations. The townspeople, who had long lived under his oppressive thumb, began to speak out, sharing their own stories of his cruelty and injustice. The formerly silent community found its voice. The balance of power shifted dramatically, tipping in Jen and Tobias's favor.

The intervention, while successful in exposing Korte, had also brought new dangers. Korte, enraged and desperate to regain control, doubled his efforts to silence Jen and Tobias, escalating his threats and plotting elaborate schemes to eliminate them. The sheriff, a puppet of Korte, was now actively involved in the pursuit.

The climax was inevitable–a confrontation with Korte himself. The ensuing battle wasn't just a physical struggle; it was a fight for their lives, and a fight for the soul of Shole Creek. The outcome remained uncertain, a precarious balance hanging in the air, waiting to be tipped one way or another, a final showdown fueled by years of repression, love, and unwavering courage. The quiet days in the inn had given way to a maelstrom of action, a final battle for survival, a desperate fight for freedom, and the culmination of a love story forged in the crucible of the Wild West. The fight for their freedom had become a fight for the heart and soul of Shole Creek, and Jen's intervention had sparked a revolution.

The confrontation took place not in the dusty streets of Shole Creek, nor in the shadowy depths of Korte's mine, but in a place that held a peculiar significance–the whispering Shole Creek itself. Korte, cornered and desperate, had chosen the familiar, yet treacherous terrain of the creek bed as his last stand. The rushing water, usually a source of solace, now echoed with the impending violence. The air crackled with anticipation, a palpable tension that hung heavy in the crisp mountain air.

Tobias, armed with his trusty rifle and a heart filled with a grim determination, arrived at the designated location, the setting sun casting long, dramatic shadows across the rugged landscape. He found Jen already there, her face pale but resolute, her eyes fixed on the narrow canyon where Korte awaited. She held a small, leather-bound journal in her hand–her most potent weapon, containing irrefutable evidence of Korte's crimes. It was a testament to her courage, a symbol of her defiance, and a tool to ensure his defeat.

Korte emerged from the shadows, his usual arrogance replaced by a chilling rage. Two of his henchmen flanked him, their faces hardened, their hands gripping their weapons. The scene was tense, the silence broken only by the relentless murmur of the creek, a constant undercurrent to the impending storm. There was a palpable sense of inevitability in the air, a feeling that this would be the final chapter in their long and arduous struggle.

The initial exchange was a tense standoff, a silent battle of wills, the only sound the whispering wind rustling through the tall grasses bordering the creek. Korte, his eyes blazing with fury, spoke first, his voice a low growl. "You think you've won, Adams," he snarled, his words laced with venom. "You think you can escape the consequences of your actions?" He gestured towards Jen, his hatred palpable. "She's the one who betrayed me. She'll pay the price."

Tobias responded with a calm, measured tone that belied the storm brewing within him. "You've underestimated both of us, Korte," Tobias said, his voice steady and strong, his gaze unwavering. "Your reign of terror is over." He pointed his rifle towards Korte, the barrel steady and certain, his aim precise. The tension was thick enough to cut with a knife.

The gunfire erupted, shattering the tense quiet. It was a chaotic ballet of bullets and desperate movements, the echoes of the gunfire bouncing off the canyon walls. Tobias, utilizing his exceptional skills as a marksman, quickly dispatched one of Korte's henchmen with a well-aimed shot. The man fell silently into the rushing waters of the creek, the current swiftly carrying him away. The remaining henchman lunged at Tobias, but Jen, with surprising agility, swiftly intervened, striking the henchman with a sharp rock, stunning him long enough for Tobias to disarm and subdue him.

The fight with Korte himself was a brutal, hand-to-hand struggle, a test of strength, endurance, and will. Korte, a powerful man, fought with the desperate fury of a cornered animal. He lunged, he struck, he wrestled, but Tobias, with his superior strength and his years of experience as a bear hunter and mountain man, matched his every move. The fight was fierce and unrelenting, a battle of wills played out against the backdrop of the wild, untamed beauty of the American West. It was a physical embodiment of the conflict that had defined their lives in Shole Creek. The fight was a relentless exchange of blows, a brutal dance of survival, a testament to their determination.

Finally, with a powerful, well-placed blow, Tobias brought Korte down. The villain, defeated, lay sprawled on the creek bed, his reign of terror definitively over. The fight, though brutal, was a victory, a triumphant moment that echoed through the canyon, a symbol of the triumph of good over evil, a victory for the people of Shole Creek, and a testament to the resilience of the human spirit. The setting sun painted the scene in hues of orange and purple, creating a breathtaking backdrop to the victory.

As the dust settled, a profound silence descended, broken only by the gentle murmur of the creek. Jen approached, her face etched with exhaustion, but her eyes shining with triumph. She kneeled beside Tobias, her hand resting on his arm, a gesture of shared victory, a testament to their unwavering love and unwavering support for one another.

The immediate aftermath was a flurry of activity. The subdued henchman was secured, the Sheriff, now stripped of Korte's influence, swiftly arrived with his deputies, taking Korte into custody. The news of Korte's arrest spread like wildfire throughout Shole Creek, bringing a wave of relief and jubilation to the town's inhabitants. The weight of oppression had lifted, replaced by a sense of newfound freedom and hope.

The victory wasn't without its cost. The physical wounds, both visible and unseen, were a testament to the brutal struggle. Yet, the emotional scars, the lingering fear, were perhaps the most significant. The long shadow of Korte's tyranny remained, even in the celebration of his defeat. The fight had taken its toll, leaving an indelible mark on both Tobias and Jen.

But amid the physical and emotional exhaustion, there was a profound sense of triumph, a hard-won victory that would forever shape their lives and the future of Shole Creek. The journey had been perilous, filled with danger and uncertainty, but they had persevered, their love a beacon of light amidst the darkness. The triumph wasn't simply a victory over Korte; it was a victory over fear, a triumph of love and courage, a testament to their unwavering commitment to each other and their relentless fight for justice.

The days that followed were a whirlwind of activity. The details of Korte's crimes were meticulously documented and presented to the court. Jen's testimony was powerful and interesting, her detailed accounts corroborating the evidence she had so carefully gathered. Korte's conviction brought closure to the town, allowing the residents to begin the long process of healing and rebuilding their lives. Their collective sigh of relief was a testament to their shared ordeal.

Tobias, his reputation solidified, continued his practice as a doctor, his skills and kindness greatly appreciated by the community he had helped save. Jen, her courage and determination celebrated, continued her art, her paintings now infused with a newfound depth and meaning, reflecting the strength and resilience she had demonstrated. Their love, tested and strengthened by adversity, deepened and blossomed, a testament to the power of love to endure and flourish even in the face of insurmountable odds.

Their life in Shole Creek was never again truly peaceful, but the peace they found was a hard-won peace, built upon the foundations of courage, love, and a shared victory against tyranny. The wild, untamed beauty of the American West remained, but now, it held a new meaning for them–a symbol of freedom, resilience, and the enduring power of the human spirit. The town, forever changed, had found its voice, its future secure, thanks to the courage of Jen and the unwavering strength of Tobias. Their story, a tale of love and adventure, became a cherished legend whispered from generation to generation in Shole Creek and beyond, a testament to a love that conquered even the harshest of landscapes. The setting sun cast long shadows, marking the end of an era, the beginning of a new chapter filled with love, peace, and the promise of a brighter future.

The immediate aftermath was a stark contrast to the brutal fight. The canyon, moments before a scene of violence, now held a fragile stillness, broken only by the whispering creek and the chirping of crickets, a symphony of nature reclaiming its space. Korte, his face a mask of defeat and disbelief, was bound and secured, his arrogance replaced by a subdued, almost pathetic, silence. The two henchmen, one lifeless in the creek, the other bound and groaning, lay as silent testaments to the fight. The setting sun cast long shadows, painting the scene in shades of bruised purple and fading orange, a melancholic beauty that underscored the gravity of the events.

Jen, her breath coming in ragged gasps, leaned against a large boulder, her hands trembling slightly as she clutched the worn leather journal. The weight of the evidence, the burden of her involvement, the sheer adrenaline of the confrontation, it all threatened to overwhelm her. But in her eyes, there burned a flicker of triumph, a testament to her resilience and courage. Tobias, his face grimy and scratched, his body aching from the brutal hand-to-hand combat, stood beside her, his arm protectively around her shoulders. The silence between them was filled with unspoken understanding, a shared acknowledgment of their survival and a profound sense of relief.

Sheriff Brody and his deputies broke the spell. The Sheriff, his face a mixture of relief and awe, looked from the defeated Korte to the exhausted yet victorious couple. He had known Korte's reign of terror was nearing its end, but the reality of it happening, thanks to Tobias and Jen, was almost unbelievable. The Sheriff's gratitude was palpable, his voice thick with emotion as he thanked them, his words echoing the relief felt by the entire town. The sight of Korte, shackled and defeated, was a sight to behold, a stark reminder of the town's collective struggle.

The news of Korte's capture spread like wildfire throughout Shole Creek. The town, which had lived under a shadow of fear and oppression, erupted in a wave of jubilation. The streets, usually quiet and subdued, filled with cheering townsfolk, their voices a chorus of relief and gratitude. The saloon, usually bustling with boisterous miners, was quieter tonight, but the quiet was different; it was the quiet of contented exhaustion, of relief. The celebratory mood wasn't one of unrestrained revelry but a quiet, deep appreciation for the safety they now possessed. The long period of fear and uncertainty finally ended.

The days that followed were a period of healing, both physical and emotional. The wounds of the confrontation–the bruises, the cuts, the emotional scars–were slowly mending. Doctors attended to the physical wounds, while the community rallied around each other, providing support and comfort. The shared trauma created a sense of unity and strengthened the bonds within the town. They were all scarred by Korte's rule, but they were also united in their triumph. This shared experience, this overcoming of adversity, shaped the character of Shole Creek forever.

Korte's trial was swift and decisive. Jen's testimony, delivered with quiet strength and unwavering conviction, was the cornerstone of the prosecution's case. Her detailed account of Korte's crimes, backed by the evidence in her journal, left no room for doubt. Korte, stripped of his power and facing the consequences of his actions, found himself unable to deny the irrefutable evidence presented against him. His sentence was severe–a long term in the state penitentiary, a just punishment for his years of tyranny.

The verdict brought a wave of relief and closure. The people of Shole Creek, having borne witness to Korte's crimes and the fight to bring him down, rejoiced at the sense of justice served. The streets were once again filled with activity, but there was a newfound sense of community and unity. The shadows of Korte's rule were fading fast, replaced by the warm glow of hope and resilience.

Tobias, his reputation as a skilled doctor and courageous protector solidified, continued his practice. He was no longer just the doctor; he had become a symbol of hope and strength for the town, a protector who stood against oppression. His quiet strength and unwavering loyalty had gained the respect and admiration of everyone in Shole Creek. His wisdom and skill were greatly appreciated.

Jen, her artistry now imbued with newfound depth and meaning, continued her work, her paintings reflecting the resilience and strength she displayed during the confrontation. Her art was no longer simply a reflection of the beauty of the landscape; it reflected the struggles and the triumphs of the people of Shole Creek. Her paintings began to reflect the human spirit's tenacity to overcome adversity, inspiring hope and fortitude in her audience.

The aftermath of the confrontation wasn't merely about the defeat of Stan Korte. It was about the forging of a deeper connection between Tobias and Jen, a love tested and strengthened by adversity. Their relationship, forged in the fires of danger and hardship, stood as a beacon of hope amidst the uncertainties of life in the American West. They had overcome immense challenges, and their love had grown stronger, a powerful testament to their devotion.

Their love story became more than just a personal narrative; it was a symbol of hope for the entire town of Shole Creek. It represented resilience, commitment, and the unwavering strength of the human spirit in the face of adversity. Their love story had woven itself into the very fabric of the town, becoming a part of its collective memory.

The healing process wasn't instantaneous; it was a gradual transformation. But the town, under the leadership of Sheriff Brody and the quiet guidance of Tobias and Jen, embarked on a journey of rebuilding and reconciliation. The community found a newfound strength in their collective experience. The town began to thrive once again, its spirit renewed, its future brighter. The shared adversity had forged an unbreakable bond, strengthening their communal spirit.

The wild, untamed beauty of the American West remained, but it was now viewed through a different lens. It was no longer simply a landscape of danger and uncertainty; it was a landscape of resilience, courage, and the indomitable human spirit. The mountains stood tall, silent witnesses to their struggles and triumphs, their majestic peaks now symbolizing the hope and peace that had settled upon Shole Creek.

The story of Tobias and Jen, a tale of love and adventure set against the backdrop of the American West, became a cherished legend whispered through generations. It was a testament to their unwavering love, their courage in the face of adversity, and their unwavering commitment to justice.

The whispers of their story spread beyond Shole Creek, echoing through the canyons and valleys, reaching other frontier towns, becoming a source of inspiration and hope for those living on the edge of civilization. Their love story, a beacon of light, illuminated the rugged landscape of the American West, inspiring generations to come. The setting sun, a constant reminder of both the violence and the beauty of the American West, now cast a golden glow on a new era for Shole Creek. An era filled with hope, peace, and the promise of a future brighter than they ever imagined. The landscape, the people, and their love story were forever interwoven, a timeless tale etched into the heart of the West.

Chapter 10: Healing and Reconciliation

The days following Korte's capture unfolded like a slow sunrise, the initial burst of jubilation giving way to the gentler, more persistent light of healing. The physical wounds were tended to with a diligence born of shared relief. Dr. Adams, his own injuries surprisingly minor considering the brutal fight, worked tirelessly, patching cuts, setting bones, and soothing anxieties. The town's apothecary was emptied of its supplies, as remedies for bruises, sprains, and the lingering effects of trauma were dispensed freely. The women of Shole Creek, their hands usually skilled in embroidery and baking, now demonstrated a remarkable aptitude for wound care and nursing, their quiet competence a testament to their resilience. The air, thick with the scent of antiseptic and simmering herbs, hummed with a quiet intensity, a counterpoint to the boisterous celebrations that had preceded this period of quiet recuperation.

The emotional healing was a far more intricate process. The collective trauma of Korte's reign was deeply etched into the psyche of the community. Fear, a constant companion for so long, lingered like a persistent shadow, even after the tyrant had been removed. Whispers of past injustices, of silenced dissent, of lives disrupted and dreams shattered, still echoed in the quiet corners of homes and hearts. Yet, within this shared vulnerability, a powerful sense of unity emerged. The collective experience of overcoming adversity forged an unspoken bond between the townsfolk, a silent acknowledgement of their shared struggle and their collective triumph.

The saloon, once a place of boisterous camaraderie that often masked underlying tensions, became a center for quiet conversations and shared stories. Miners, their faces etched with the marks of hard labor and lingering fear, sat together, nursing their drinks and recounting their experiences under Korte's tyrannical rule. These weren't tales of heroic defiance but quiet anecdotes of endurance, of small acts of resistance that had sustained them through the dark years. These stories, shared in hushed tones, served as collective therapy, allowing the community to process their trauma, to acknowledge their pain, and to find strength in their shared resilience. They were not just stories of the past but also seeds of hope for the future.

Jen, despite the physical and emotional toll of the confrontation, remained a central figure in this healing process. Her unwavering testimony had been instrumental in securing Korte's conviction, but her role extended far beyond the courtroom. She quietly visited those still recovering from their injuries, her gentle demeanor and calming presence a balm to their anxieties. She listened patiently to their stories, her eyes reflecting both understanding and empathy. Her art, once focused on the stark beauty of the landscape, now began to incorporate elements reflecting the inner strength of the community. Her latest paintings were not merely aesthetically pleasing but potent symbols of hope and resilience. She depicted not only the beauty of the untamed wilderness but also the indomitable spirit of the people who called it home.

Tobias, too, played a crucial role in the town's recovery. He was not only a skilled physician, mending broken bodies, but also a quiet pillar of strength, offering comfort and support to those struggling with the emotional aftermath of Korte's tyranny. His calm demeanor and unwavering presence were a source of reassurance for many, his quiet strength a counterpoint to the lingering fear and uncertainty. He understood the invisible wounds, the scars etched into the soul, as deeply as he understood the physical ones. He found himself not just treating the injured but also listening intently to their stories, offering words of solace and encouragement. His presence became a symbol of healing and hope, a testament to his commitment to the community he had come to call home.

The reconciliation process was not without its difficulties. Old grudges, long-suppressed resentments, and lingering suspicions surfaced, threatening to undermine the fragile unity the community had achieved. However, the shared experience of facing Korte's tyranny served as a powerful unifying force. People who had previously held animosity toward one another now found common ground in their collective triumph. The sense of shared struggle overshadowed previous conflicts, forging new alliances and strengthening existing bonds. The town's leadership, under Sheriff Brody's guidance, actively fostered this reconciliation, encouraging dialogue and mediation whenever conflicts arose.

The rebuilding of Shole Creek was not just a physical endeavor but also a spiritual one. The town, which had long been marked by fear and oppression, was slowly reclaiming its identity, reinventing itself as a community characterized by resilience, unity, and hope. A palpable sense of optimism, the future replaced the once-despairing atmosphere, once shrouded in uncertainty, now shimmering with the promise of a better tomorrow. This was not a simple return to the status quo; it was a rebirth, a transformative process that shaped the character of Shole Creek forever. The shared experience of overcoming adversity had forged a deeper, stronger sense of community, a shared identity bound not just by geography but by the resilience of the human spirit.

As the days turned into weeks, and the weeks into months, the wounds of Shole Creek began to heal, both physically and emotionally. The scars remained, a reminder of the past, but they served as a testament to the community's indomitable spirit. The town thrived once again, its vibrancy and resilience a beacon of hope in the vast, untamed landscape of the American West. The shared trauma of Korte's tyranny was now a powerful unifying force, binding the people together with an unbreakable bond forged in adversity. The wild beauty of the West remained, but it was now viewed through a lens of resilience, courage, and hope. The mountains, which had seemed to loom over them in their darkest hours, now stood as silent sentinels, watching over a community reborn, their strength reflected in the newfound fortitude of the people of Shole Creek. The story of their healing, their reconciliation, and the enduring strength of their community was just beginning. It was a testament to the unwavering human spirit that even in the harshest environments, hope and healing can prevail. The journey was long, but the future, once shrouded in darkness, now promised a dawn filled with hope, peace, and a renewed sense of community.

The rebuilding of Shole Creek wasn't a simple matter of patching walls and replacing broken windows. It was a delicate, painstaking process of mending fractured spirits and restoring shattered trust. Sheriff Brody, a man whose quiet competence had been instrumental in apprehending Korte, now found himself leading a different kind of charge–a charge toward reconciliation. He understood that the true strength of Shole Creek lay not in its mines or its location but in the resilience of its people, and fostering that resilience was now his primary task.

He initiated weekly town meetings, not for pronouncements or directives, but for open dialogue. These weren't formal affairs, but informal gatherings held under the shade of the largest oak tree at the edge of town. Men and women, some still bearing the visible scars of Korte's brutality, sat together, sharing stories, concerns, and even tentative apologies. The air, heavy with the lingering scent of pine and damp earth, was thick with a new emotion: hope.

One particularly poignant meeting saw Martha Jenkins, a woman Korte, face Henry Miller, a miner who had been complicit in Korte's schemes out of fear for his family had unjustly imprisoned whose husband. The silence between them was thick, pregnant with unspoken accusations and regrets. Martha, her eyes red-rimmed but resolute, spoke first, her voice barely a whisper. "Henry," she began, her gaze unwavering, "I know you were afraid. Korte made us all afraid. But fear doesn't excuse what happened. My husband suffered, and my family suffered because of his actions."

Henry looked down at his calloused hands, shame evident in his posture. He mumbled an apology, his voice thick with remorse. "I am sorry, Martha. I truly am. I had no choice. I had to protect my family."

Martha nodded slowly, a flicker of understanding crossing her face. "I know," she said, her voice softer now. "But we have a choice now. A choice to build something better, something stronger. And that begins with forgiveness."

Their reconciliation, witnessed by the silent onlookers, wasn't a sudden burst of camaraderie. It was a tentative step, a fragile bridge built across a chasm of fear and resentment. Yet, it was a powerful symbol, a testament to the potential for healing that lay within the community. The whispered apologies and the hesitant embraces that followed were more potent than any official proclamation.

Jen Korte, her artistic spirit renewed by the town's recovery, played a pivotal role in this emotional rebuilding. She organized community art projects, encouraging everyone, regardless of skill level, to participate.

Children, their faces still bearing traces of fear, painted vibrant murals depicting a peaceful Shole Creek, their brushstrokes infused with the hopeful energy that was permeating the town. Adults, their hands rough from years of labor, created collaborative sculptures from salvaged wood and stone, each piece reflecting their own journey towards healing.

These artistic endeavors were not mere distractions but cathartic processes, allowing people to express their emotions, to confront their trauma in a creative and non-threatening way. The vibrant colors of the murals, the rough textures of the sculptures, the shared laughter and quiet moments of reflection–all these contributed to the gradual healing of the community.

Tobias Adams, ever the practical physician, understood the importance of both physical and emotional well-being. He continued his medical duties, but he also became a silent confidante, lending an ear to troubled hearts, offering words of encouragement and unwavering support. He listened patiently to tales of hardship, tales of resilience, tales of hope. He was not just a doctor mending broken bones; he was a spiritual healer, mending fractured spirits. He organized evening gatherings around campfires, sharing stories of his own life, his experiences in the wilderness, demonstrating the power of endurance and the resilience of the human spirit.

The saloon, once a den of iniquity and the epicenter of Korte's control, underwent a transformation. The bar remained, but the atmosphere shifted. It became a place for quiet conversations, for sharing stories of hardship and hope, for forging new friendships. The rough miners who had once frequented the saloon under the shadow of Korte's tyranny now gathered, not to drown their sorrows but to celebrate their resilience. The laughter was softer, the conversations deeper, reflecting the transformation of the community.

The process of rebuilding trust wasn't always smooth. Old resentments occasionally resurfaced, sparking minor conflicts. But the shared experience of confronting Korte's tyranny created a powerful bond that held them together. Disagreements were handled with a newfound maturity, the community collectively committed to resolving conflict through dialogue and understanding, prioritizing healing over retribution.

The rebuilding extended beyond the emotional sphere. The physical landscape of Shole Creek also underwent a transformation. The mine, once a symbol of oppression, was carefully restored, its operations reorganized to ensure fair treatment of workers. New housing was built, replacing the dilapidated structures that had been a hallmark of Korte's neglect. The town's streets were repaired, and a new community garden was established, a symbol of the renewed life and shared prosperity that was blossoming in Shole Creek.

The scars remained–visible reminders of the dark times–but they also served as a testament to the community's indomitable spirit. These were not wounds of defeat but badges of honor, emblems of their collective triumph over adversity.

As the months passed, Shole Creek flourished. The vibrant energy of its people, strengthened by their shared experience, transformed the town into a haven of peace and prosperity. A tangible sense of optimism, the future had replaced the once-despairing atmosphere, once shrouded in uncertainty, now shimmering with the promise of a better tomorrow.

Jen's art reflected this transformation. Her paintings, once predominantly bleak, now pulsed with life and color, celebrating not only the majestic beauty of the landscape but also the inner strength and resilience of its inhabitants. Her art was a chronicle of their healing, their transformation, and their enduring spirit. It was a story told not only in words but in vibrant colors and powerful imagery.

Tobias, too, played a key role in this visual representation of healing. His quiet strength and unwavering support gave the community a sense of security and stability. His presence was a constant reassurance, a symbol of hope amidst the ongoing transformation. He was more than just a doctor; he was a beacon, guiding the community through the maze of emotional and physical recovery.

The mountains that had seemed to loom large and menacing during Korte's reign now stood as silent witnesses, steadfast guardians of the transformed Shole Creek. The town, reborn from the ashes of oppression, was a testament to the resilience of the human spirit, a beacon of hope and healing in the vast, untamed landscape of the American West. The story of Shole Creek wasn't just a tale of survival; it was a story of rebirth, a testament to the power of community, forgiveness, and the enduring strength of the human heart. It was a story of healing, a story of reconciliation, and a story that would continue to be told for generations to come.

Jen's first post-Korte painting wasn't a grand statement, not a sweeping landscape of Shole Creek bathed in golden sunlight. It was smaller, more intimate–a study of hands. Two pairs of hands, rough and calloused, clasped together. One pair belonged to Martha Jenkins, the other to Henry Miller. The lines were stark, the colors muted, yet the emotion radiating from the canvas was palpable. It was a testament to the tentative reconciliation between the two, a visual representation of the fragile bridge they had begun to build. The painting, displayed prominently in the newly renovated saloon, became an unexpected focal point, a silent conversation starter, a reminder of the healing process unfolding in Shole Creek.

Word of Jen's painting spread quickly. People began to stop by the saloon, not just for a drink, but to stand before the artwork, their faces mirroring the emotions it evoked. Some were moved to tears, others to quiet reflection. The painting served as a catalyst, prompting further conversations about forgiveness, understanding, and the long road to healing.

Encouraged by the response, Jen decided to create a mural for the town's new community center–a bright, spacious building constructed from salvaged lumber and stone. The mural depicted Shole Creek as it was envisioned for the future, not as a dark, oppressive place ruled by Korte, but as a vibrant, harmonious community, thriving amidst the surrounding natural beauty. It was a collaborative effort. Children, their faces alive with excitement, added details–vibrant wildflowers blooming along the creek, playful deer frolicking in the meadows, majestic eagles soaring in the sky. Adults, initially hesitant, eventually joined in, their rough hands adding texture and depth to the scene. The mural wasn't a perfect representation of artistic skill; its charm lay in its imperfection, in its raw honesty, in its collective spirit.

The mural became a living testament to the town's collective healing. Each brushstroke, each carefully placed stone, each piece of salvaged wood became a symbol of their shared journey, a visual chronicle of their resilience, their forgiveness, and their shared commitment to building a brighter future.

It wasn't just a mural; it was a communal tapestry woven from hope, perseverance, and shared dreams.

Jen's art extended beyond the visual realm. She organized art workshops for children, using simple materials like clay, colored pencils, and fabric scraps to help them express their emotions and experiences. These weren't formal art classes; they were safe spaces where children could unleash their creativity, their imaginations, their anxieties, without judgment. The vibrant colors of their creations became a window into their hearts, showcasing their resilience, their dreams, and their gradual journey towards healing.

The adults weren't left out either. Jen facilitated several collaborative art projects, including the creation of large-scale sculptures made from salvaged materials found around Shole Creek. These sculptures represented a variety of themes, some depicting the hardships endured, others celebrating the community's rebirth, and still others looking towards a brighter future. These collaborative efforts fostered a sense of camaraderie, encouraging communication, understanding, and mutual support. The process of creation itself became therapy, a cathartic experience that allowed people to confront their trauma in a creative and non-threatening way.

Tobias Adams, always supportive of Jen's initiatives, lent his practical skills to the art projects. He helped procure materials, organize workshops, and provide a safe and comfortable space for these artistic endeavors. More importantly, he understood the therapeutic value of art, recognizing its potential to heal broken spirits and restore fractured communities. He saw Jen's art not merely as decoration but as a vital component of the town's healing process.

One of the most impactful pieces Jen created was a series of portraits. These weren't idealized depictions but raw, honest portrayals of the people of Shole Creek–miners with weary eyes but resolute spirits, women whose faces bore the marks of hardship but whose smiles spoke of newfound hope, children whose innocent eyes held a wisdom beyond their years. Each portrait captured a unique story, a testament to the resilience and strength of the community. These portraits were displayed in the new community center, serving as a constant reminder of the shared journey, the collective strength, and the indomitable spirit of Shole Creek.

Jen's artistic endeavors weren't confined to the town itself. She also started to document the natural beauty of Shole Creek and the surrounding area. Her paintings depicted the majestic mountains, the clear, flowing creek, the lush forests, and the vibrant wildflowers. These landscapes, while visually stunning, also served a therapeutic purpose. They offered a sense of peace and tranquility, reminding the community of the inherent beauty of their surroundings, counterbalancing the darker memories of Korte's reign.

The transformation of Shole Creek wasn't merely physical; it was also emotional and spiritual. Jen's art played a significant role in this multifaceted rebirth. Her art became a bridge, connecting the past to the future, the pain to the healing, the despair to the hope. It was a powerful testament to the transformative power of art, its ability to heal wounds, foster unity, and inspire a community to move forward, together.

The acceptance of Jen's art, initially hesitant, blossomed into fervent appreciation. People weren't just passively observing her work; they were engaging with it, interpreting it, and drawing strength from it. It became a conversation starter, a catalyst for further dialogue and healing. Her ability to capture the essence of the community's experiences, not in words but in vibrant colors and powerful imagery, cemented her place not only as a talented artist but also as a key figure in the town's recovery.

The success of Jen's art projects extended beyond the immediate community. News of Shole Creek's remarkable transformation, and Jen's crucial role in it, reached neighboring towns. People came from far and wide to see the murals, the sculptures, the portraits—to witness firsthand the healing power of art and community resilience. This influx of visitors not only brought economic benefits but also reinforced Shole Creek's newfound sense of pride and unity. Jen's art had transformed the town into a beacon of hope, a testament to the enduring human spirit, attracting attention and admiration from far beyond the mountains.

The artistic endeavors continued, evolving with the town's ongoing recovery. Jen's work expanded, encompassing various mediums–pottery, weaving, even musical performances accompanied by local musicians, creating a vibrant tapestry of artistic expression that reflected the ever-changing landscape of Shole Creek. Each piece of art, no matter how small or insignificant it may seem, contributed to the overall narrative of healing and renewal, solidifying the town's identity as a place reborn from adversity.

As Shole Creek continued its transformation, so too did Jen's artistic expression. Her paintings began to incorporate brighter, more optimistic colors, mirroring the increasing confidence and joy within the community. She started to depict the future, not just as a healing from the past, but as a vibrant, prosperous, and hopeful future for Shole Creek. Her art became a powerful instrument in shaping the town's identity and narrative, reinforcing its resilience and celebrating its journey of recovery.

Tobias, watching Jen's work unfold, saw in it a reflection of their shared love story. Their journey, much like the town's, had been fraught with challenges, yet their resilience and unwavering love had allowed them to overcome the obstacles. Their love story, like Jen's art, became a testament to the power of the human spirit, a powerful narrative woven into the fabric of Shole Creek's rebirth. The vibrant colors and powerful imagery of Jen's art echoed their own love story, a poignant reminder that even amidst hardship, love and hope can prevail. Their shared journey, marked by challenges and triumphs, became an integral part of Shole Creek's narrative of healing and reconciliation.

The crisp fall air carried the scent of woodsmoke and damp earth, a familiar fragrance that spoke of Shole Creek's enduring spirit. Tobias, leaning against the newly constructed porch of the community center, watched Jen's nimble fingers work their magic on a large canvas. The mural, already sprawling across the wall, depicted a vibrant Shole Creek, a stark contrast to the grim reality of the past. Children, their laughter echoing in the crisp air, flitted around her, offering suggestions, their enthusiasm infectious. He smiled, a warmth spreading through him that had nothing to do with the setting sun.

This wasn't just about art; it was about healing. Jen's artistic endeavors were more than just beautiful creations; they were the heartbeat of Shole Creek's resurrection. She was weaving a tapestry of hope, thread by painstaking thread, transforming fear and despair into vibrant symbols of resilience and unity. And he, Tobias Adams, was inextricably woven into this tapestry.

His commitment to Jen had never wavered, but it had deepened, expanded, encompassing not just her but the entire community. He'd seen the pain etched on their faces, the weariness in their eyes, the lingering shadows of Korte's tyranny. He'd witnessed their slow, arduous journey towards healing, their hesitant steps towards reconciliation. And he'd pledged himself to their journey, to Jen's journey, to the future of Shole Creek.

His love for Jen was a force that propelled him into action. He'd rolled up his sleeves, literally, assisting in the construction of the community center, hauling lumber, mixing mortar, his strong hands working alongside the others. He'd helped Jen procure supplies for her artistic projects, his knowledge of the wilderness proving invaluable. He'd even learned to appreciate the subtle nuances of color and texture, offering his practical insights when Jen needed a sturdy frame for her latest masterpiece or a different angle to enhance the perspective.

His contributions went beyond the physical realm. He was a steady presence, a reassuring figure, offering comfort and support to those who needed it. He listened to their stories, their anxieties, their hopes, offering a quiet strength that calmed their frayed nerves. He understood their hesitations, their fears, their reluctance to trust again. He had experienced loss himself, felt the sting of betrayal, and understood the fragility of hope.

One evening, as the sun dipped below the horizon, painting the sky in fiery hues of orange and purple, Tobias found Jen sitting alone by the creek, a sketchbook resting on her lap. He sat beside her, the silence comfortable, familiar.

"It's beautiful," he murmured, gesturing towards the landscape unfolding before them. The creek, reflecting the twilight sky, shimmered like liquid silver, the surrounding hills bathed in the warm glow of the setting sun.

Jen smiled, a soft, gentle smile that reached her eyes. "It's a reminder," she said, her voice barely above a whisper, "a reminder of what we've overcome, and what we can build together."

Her words resonated deeply within him. He understood. Shole Creek wasn't just a collection of houses and mines; it was a living entity, a community forged in hardship and tempered by resilience. And he was now an integral part of its collective narrative.

His love for Jen was a cornerstone of his commitment to Shole Creek. He saw in her strength a reflection of the town's own resilience. Her art, in its raw honesty and vibrant colors, was a mirror to their shared journey. He saw their future together, interwoven with the fabric of this community, a tapestry of love, hope, and unwavering commitment.

He reached out, taking her hand in his, his touch gentle yet firm. The calluses on his palm were a testament to his life, his work, his devotion. Her fingers, slender and delicate, felt soft against his.

"I'm here, Jen," he said, his voice low and steady, "I'm here for you, for Shole Creek. Always."

His commitment wasn't just a fleeting emotion; it was a profound realization, a deep-seated understanding of his place in this rugged landscape, in this community, in Jen's life. He was a doctor, a trapper, a bear hunter, but most importantly, he was a man deeply rooted in the land, in its people, in the woman he loved.

The following weeks were a blur of activity. The community center was completed, a testament to collaborative effort and shared dreams. Jen's mural became a point of pride, a symbol of their collective healing. The children's art workshops flourished, their laughter echoing through the newly renovated buildings. The adults, initially hesitant, began to participate, their artistic expressions mirroring their journey towards healing and acceptance. The town was reborn, not merely physically but emotionally and spiritually.

Tobias continued to support Jen's artistic endeavors, providing practical assistance, offering a quiet presence, and sharing in the joy of their collective creation. He learned to appreciate the nuances of color and brushstrokes, the power of art to heal, to inspire, to unite. He found a deeper appreciation for Jen's talent, for her unwavering dedication, for her ability to transform pain into beauty. His love for her deepened, broadening to encompass the entire community.

He participated in town meetings, actively contributing to the discussions regarding the future of Shole Creek. He lent his medical expertise, ensuring the well-being of the community. He organized hunting parties, ensuring a steady supply of food for the town. He helped settle disputes, his calm demeanor and unwavering fairness earning him the respect and trust of everyone.

He was more than just Jen's lover; he was Shole Creek's protector, its healer, its unwavering advocate. He'd found his place, not just geographically but existentially, in this rugged land, amidst its vibrant people, beside the woman he loved. His commitment to Jen was reflected in his commitment to Shole Creek, an unwavering dedication born out of love, respect, and a shared vision of a brighter future. He was home. And he wouldn't let anything, or anyone, threaten the fragile peace and burgeoning prosperity he'd helped to create. His love for Jen, and his commitment to Shole Creek, were inextricably intertwined, a testament to the enduring power of the human spirit in the face of adversity. The future, though uncertain, held the promise of hope, a promise he was determined to fulfill, one day at a time, one brushstroke at a time, one loving embrace at a time. The rugged beauty of Shole Creek held within its heart a newfound resilience, a spirit reborn, a community healed, all under the watchful and loving gaze of Tobias Adams. His commitment was not just a promise; it was a way of life.

The first rays of dawn painted the eastern sky in hues of apricot and rose, a gentle awakening after the tumultuous storms that had ravaged Shole Creek. A thin layer of frost glittered on the newly constructed buildings, a testament to the chill fall air, but the atmosphere within the town pulsed with a warmth far exceeding the rising sun. The air hummed with a quiet energy, a palpable sense of hope that had been absent for so long. The rebuilding wasn't just about bricks and mortar; it was about the mending of broken spirits, the weaving together of fractured lives, a slow, deliberate stitching of a community torn apart.

Jen, bundled in a warm shawl, stood at the edge of the creek, her breath misting in the cold air. The familiar sounds of Shole Creek—the gentle gurgle of water, the rustling of leaves in the trees—were no longer overshadowed by the clang of mining equipment or the hushed whispers of fear. Instead, these natural sounds formed a soothing symphony, a soundtrack to their new beginning. She traced the outline of a budding crocus pushing its way through the frozen earth, a tiny symbol of resilience mirroring the spirit of the town itself. The scars remained, etched deep into the landscape and the hearts of its people, but now, alongside the scars, the signs of new growth were visible, fragile yet undeniable.

Tobias joined her, his presence as comforting as the warm shawl wrapped around her shoulders. He didn't speak, just stood beside her, their shared silence a comfortable blanket, woven from mutual understanding and unspoken promises. He watched her, his gaze lingering on the delicate lines of her face, the way the morning light caught the strands of her dark hair. He saw not just the physical beauty, but the strength that resided within her, a strength that had carried them both through the darkest hours. He had witnessed her artistic genius transform despair into beauty, her creativity a beacon of hope in the desolate landscape.

That morning, as the sun climbed higher in the sky, casting long shadows across the newly-renovated streets, a market was held in the town square. It wasn't a bustling commercial hub like the ones in larger cities, but a gathering of neighbors, sharing their harvests, their crafts, their stories. Women exchanged recipes and laughed, sharing the joy of the season and the comfort of community. Children, their faces bright with happiness, chased pigeons across the square, their carefree laughter echoing off the buildings. The men, their faces etched with a mixture of exhaustion and relief, shared jokes and stories of their experiences during the tumultuous times. Even old Mr. Henderson, the grumpy recluse who'd lived on the outskirts of town, emerged from his isolation, bearing a basket of his prize-winning apples.

The atmosphere was celebratory, but not boisterous. It was a quiet joy, a subdued celebration born from the weight of their shared experience and the quiet hope that bloomed from the ashes of their trials. Tobias, moving easily among the townspeople, lent a helping hand, assisting with the preparations, offering a calming presence, ensuring that the day flowed smoothly. His presence itself was a source of reassurance, a silent testament to the peace and stability that had been established.

He spoke with Stan Korte, the mine owner whose harsh rule had once cast a long shadow over Shole Creek. Their conversation was brief, civil, and marked by a hesitant respect. The older man still bore the weight of his past actions, but a subtle shift was visible in his demeanor–a hint of remorse, a glimmer of acceptance. The reconciliation wasn't complete, nor was it expected to be. It was a fragile beginning, a tentative step toward healing that wouldn't be undone easily. But its significance was immense. It represented the town's willingness to move forward, to let go of past grievances, and to forgive.

Jen's mural dominated one wall of the community center, its vibrant colors a stark contrast to the muted tones of the surrounding buildings. It depicted Shole Creek as it was, as it had been, and as it would be—a testament to the town's resilience, its capacity to adapt, its spirit to overcome adversity. It was more than just a painting; it was a living testament, a vibrant narrative that embodied the collective experience of the community.

As days turned into weeks, and weeks into months, Shole Creek continued its transformation. New homes were built, mirroring the new spirit of the town. The schoolhouse, once neglected, bustled with the excited chatter of children. The community center became the heart of the town, a place for gatherings, celebrations, and quiet reflection. The mining operations continued, but with a new emphasis on safety and fairness, reflecting the newfound sense of responsibility and shared ownership.

The once-fractured relationships mended slowly, carefully, like the painstaking restoration of a damaged artifact. Trust, once lost, was gradually regained, nurtured with patience, understanding, and a mutual commitment to rebuilding not just their homes and livelihoods, but their relationships. The shared experiences, the collective effort in rebuilding the town had created an unbreakable bond among the residents. They had faced adversity together, and had emerged from it stronger, more resilient, and united.

Tobias continued to play a pivotal role in this transformation. He became the town's doctor, its unofficial counselor, its silent protector. He listened to their stories, offered his medical expertise, and provided unwavering support. His quiet strength, his empathy, and his willingness to lend a hand earned him the respect and love of the entire community. He had become an integral part of the fabric of Shole Creek, not just a visitor, but a fixture, a cornerstone, a symbol of their rebirth.

One evening, as the sun cast long shadows across the valley, Tobias and Jen sat on the porch of their new home, a cozy cabin built with love and shared sweat. They held hands, their eyes reflecting the warm glow of the fire in the hearth. Around them, the sounds of Shole Creek formed a comforting lullaby—the gentle rush of the creek, the soft chirping of crickets, the distant barking of a dog. It was a peaceful scene, a stark contrast to the tumultuous past, but it was a peace they had earned, a peace they would fiercely protect.

"It's beautiful, isn't it?" Jen whispered, her gaze fixed on the starlit sky.

Tobias squeezed her hand. "More beautiful than I ever imagined," he replied, his voice husky with emotion. He knew that their journey was far from over. Challenges would undoubtedly arise. But they would face them together, hand in hand, as a community, as a family. For Shole Creek was more than just a place; it was a testament to the human spirit, a symbol of resilience, a beacon of hope, a home. And in that home, surrounded by the love of his life and the people he'd come to call his family, Tobias Adams found his own peace, his own happiness, his own beginning. The future, though uncertain, held the promise of something beautiful, something enduring, something profoundly meaningful. And he was ready. Ready to face whatever lay ahead, together with Jen, together with Shole Creek, in their new beginning.

Chapter 11: Love's Triumph

The rebuilding of Shole Creek had been a shared endeavor, a collective act of resilience that had drawn Tobias and Jen closer than ever before. Their shared hardships, the sleepless nights spent tending to the injured, the countless hours spent clearing debris and rebuilding homes—these experiences had forged a bond stronger than any they had known previously. It wasn't just a romantic connection; it was a deep, abiding partnership, built on mutual respect, unwavering support, and a shared understanding of the challenges they had overcome.

One evening, as the fall leaves began to turn, painting the valley in shades of crimson and gold, Tobias found Jen sketching by the creek. The setting sun cast a warm glow on her face, highlighting the delicate curve of her cheekbones and the intensity of her dark eyes. She was sketching the creek, capturing its gentle flow and the reflections of the fiery sky dancing on its surface. He watched her for a moment, mesmerized by her dedication, her passion, the way she seemed to pour her very soul into her art.

He sat beside her, the rough bark of the log pressing against his back. The silence between them was comfortable, a familiar companion born of shared experiences and unspoken words. The air was crisp and cool, carrying the scent of damp earth and burning leaves.

"It's beautiful," he said softly, his voice barely a whisper, breaking the peaceful silence.

Jen smiled, a gentle curve of her lips that reached her eyes. "It's trying to capture the essence of Shole Creek," she replied, her voice low and thoughtful. "The strength, the resilience, the beauty that lies beneath the surface."

He nodded, understanding her unspoken words. The painting was more than just a landscape; it was a mirror reflecting the spirit of the town, their shared journey, their collective triumph. It was a testament to their strength, their love, their enduring bond.

That night, under a sky ablaze with stars, they sat on their porch, the crackling fire casting dancing shadows on the walls of their cozy cabin. The air was filled with the scent of woodsmoke and pine, a fragrance both comforting and deeply evocative. They spoke of their dreams, their hopes, their fears—the unspoken anxieties that lingered beneath the surface of their newfound peace. They spoke of their shared future, of the life they would build together in this reborn town.

Tobias reached out and gently cupped her face in his hands, his thumbs caressing her soft skin. His eyes held a depth of emotion that went beyond mere affection; it was a profound love, built on a foundation of shared adversity and mutual admiration.

"I never imagined I could love someone this much," he confessed, his voice husky with emotion.

Jen leaned into his touch, her eyes shining with unshed tears. "Nor I," she whispered, her voice trembling slightly. "But I never imagined I could be this happy either."

Their shared gaze lingered, a silent acknowledgment of the tumultuous journey they had endured, the sacrifices they had made, and the love that had carried them through it all. Their shared experiences had refined and deepened the romance that had bloomed amidst the chaos of Shole Creek's turbulent past. It was a love forged in the crucible of hardship, tempered by adversity, and strengthened by their unwavering commitment to one another.

The following days were filled with a quiet joy, a contentment that seeped into every aspect of their lives. They worked side-by-side, helping to restore the town, their efforts a tangible expression of their shared love and commitment. They found solace in the simple things–long walks along the creek, shared meals by the fire, quiet evenings spent in each other's arms.

Their relationship became a source of inspiration for the townspeople, a beacon of hope in a community still healing from its wounds. Their love story, whispered from porch to porch, became a symbol of resilience, a testament to the human capacity to overcome adversity and find love amidst the chaos.

Even Stan Korte, Jen's father, seemed to soften towards Tobias. He watched them, his gruff demeanor softening slightly, witnessing their unbreakable bond. The grudging respect he had initially shown had transformed into a grudging acceptance, tinged with a hint of admiration for the man who had won his daughter's heart.

One crisp morning, while out horseback riding, they came across a secluded meadow bathed in sunlight. Wildflowers painted the meadow in a kaleidoscope of colors, a breathtaking scene of natural beauty. Tobias dismounted, taking Jen's hand, and led her into the meadow.

"This reminds me of our first meeting," he said, his voice soft, his eyes full of warmth. "The beauty, the unexpectedness... the adventure."

Jen laughed, the sound as clear and bright as a mountain spring. "And the danger," she added, remembering the perilous encounter with the bandits.

They shared a tender kiss under the clear blue sky, the scent of wildflowers filling the air. It was a kiss that encapsulated their shared journey, their love, their future. It was a kiss that sealed their renewed romance, a love story as vast and untamed as the American West itself.

Their love became an integral part of the fabric of the reborn Shole Creek. It was a love that healed wounds, inspired hope, and strengthened the community. It was a love that transcended the trials and tribulations of their past, a testament to the power of human connection in the face of adversity. The romance that had blossomed amid the chaos of the mining town had transformed into something deeper, richer, and far more enduring. It was a love story for the ages, etched not just into the hearts of Jen and Tobias but into the very soul of Shole Creek itself. Their love was a symbol of the town's rebirth, a promise of a brighter future, a testament to the enduring power of love in the face of adversity.

As the seasons changed, so too did the landscape of their lives. The harsh winters gave way to the gentle warmth of spring, and the vibrant colors of summer painted their world in a canvas of joy. Through it all, their love remained steadfast, unwavering, a beacon in the ever-changing landscape of their lives. They had faced the challenges of the West together, their love a guiding star that illuminated their path through the darkness. And as they looked towards the future, hand in hand, they knew that their love story was far from over. It was just beginning. The adventures would continue, the challenges would certainly arise, but their love, now strong and tested, would always be their anchor, their safe harbor, their steadfast home. Shole Creek had been reborn, and with it, a renewed and even more passionate romance between two souls bound together by the crucible of experience and the unyielding power of love.

The change in Stan Korte was subtle at first, almost imperceptible. It wasn't a dramatic shift, a sudden burst of acceptance, but a slow thaw, a gradual melting of the icy exterior he'd presented to Tobias. He began by simply acknowledging Tobias's presence, a nod here, a brief grunt of acknowledgement there–small gestures that, to Jen, spoke volumes. He'd witnessed the dedication Tobias had shown to Shole Creek, the tireless work he'd put into rebuilding the town, not only physically but also in restoring a sense of community and hope. He had seen Tobias's gentleness with Jen, the unspoken understanding that passed between them, a silent language of love and shared resilience.

One afternoon, while Jen was tending her garden–a riot of color and life that mirrored her own vibrant spirit–Stan Korte approached. He hadn't visited her garden before, preferring the solitude of his own meticulously kept grounds. He stood awkwardly at the edge of the vibrant flowerbeds, his hands clasped behind his back, his gaze fixed on the ground. The silence hung heavy between them, broken only by the gentle hum of bees and the rustle of leaves in the nearby trees.

"The roses are doing well," he finally said, his voice rough, a stark contrast to the delicate beauty surrounding them. It was a simple observation, devoid of any emotional coloring, yet to Jen, it held a profound significance. It was a tacit acknowledgment of her efforts, a subtle admission that he had been paying attention, that he had been observing her life with Tobias.

Jen smiled, a genuine, heartfelt smile that lit up her face. "Thank you, Papa," she replied, her voice soft but firm. "Tobias helped me plant them. He knows a thing or two about nurturing things to life." She paused, carefully choosing her words. "Just like he's helped nurture Shole Creek back to life."

Stan Korte remained silent for a moment, his gaze shifting from the roses to Jen, his expression unreadable. Then, a faint smile played on his lips, a barely perceptible movement that nonetheless sent a wave of relief washing over Jen. It was a subtle shift, a crack in the formidable wall he had built around his emotions, a glimpse of the father she had always longed for.

The turning point came during the annual Shole Creek harvest festival. The town had rallied together, celebrating their resilience and the bountiful harvest that symbolized their recovery. The air was filled with the joyous sounds of laughter, music, and the aroma of freshly baked bread and roasting meats. Tobias, ever the skilled outdoorsman, had prepared a magnificent feast, showcasing the best of the region's bounty.

Stan Korte sat at the head of the long table, his usual gruff demeanor softened by the festive atmosphere. He observed Tobias interacting with the townspeople, his easy manner and genuine kindness evident in his interactions. He saw the respect Tobias commanded, the trust he had earned, the affection he inspired. He witnessed the warmth between Tobias and Jen, a palpable connection that transcended mere words. The unspoken communication, the shared glances, the gentle touches–all of it spoke of a love that was deep, abiding, and utterly genuine.

During the feast, Stan Korte raised his glass, his voice surprisingly clear and steady. "To Shole Creek," he declared, his gaze sweeping across the gathered townspeople. "To its rebirth, and to the people who have made it possible. And to Tobias," he added, a hint of warmth in his voice, "for his unwavering dedication to this town and to my daughter."

A hush fell over the crowd, a collective breath held as they waited for the words to sink in. The weight of the moment was palpable, a profound acknowledgment of the healing that had taken place, not just in Shole Creek, but within the walls of the Korte family. Jen's eyes welled up with tears of joy and relief, a mixture of emotions flooding her as she saw her father finally accept the man she loved.

The acceptance wasn't just a verbal acknowledgment; it was a profound shift in their relationship. Stan Korte began to include Tobias in family matters, offering advice and seeking his opinion on business affairs. He invited Tobias to join him on hunting trips, sharing stories and silent moments of companionship. He even began to refer to Tobias as "son," the word hanging in the air, heavy with unspoken affection and years of accumulated emotions.

The reconciliation wasn't without its bumps. There were moments of awkwardness, lingering resentments that surfaced unexpectedly, and the occasional flash of the old gruffness. But those moments were fleeting, overshadowed by the growing bond between them. Stan Korte had finally seen Tobias not as a threat, but as a man worthy of his daughter's love, a man who had proven his worth through his actions, his dedication, and his unwavering commitment.

The healing extended beyond the immediate family. The acceptance of Tobias by Stan Korte symbolized a broader reconciliation, a healing of the divisions within Shole Creek. The town, once fractured by discord and suspicion, began to coalesce, united by a shared sense of purpose and a renewed spirit of community. The love story of Jen and Tobias had become an integral part of the town's narrative, a testament to the power of love to bridge divides and heal wounds.

The change in Stan Korte was more than just acceptance; it was a testament to the transformative power of love. It was a recognition that love could overcome obstacles, mend broken hearts, and ultimately bring families together. It was a symbolic representation of the healing and forgiveness that had permeated Shole Creek, a community reborn from the ashes of adversity, stronger and more united than ever before. The love story of Jen and Tobias was no longer just their own; it had become the heart of Shole Creek's ongoing narrative, a beacon of hope and resilience in the rugged landscape of the American West. And as the sun set on Shole Creek, painting the sky in hues of orange and purple, the Korte family, finally united, looked towards a future filled with hope, love, and the promise of a brighter tomorrow. The future held new adventures, new challenges, but they faced them together, a family bound by love, loyalty, and the enduring spirit of the American West.

The wedding was a spectacle, a vibrant tapestry woven from the raw beauty of Shole Creek and the heartfelt joy of its inhabitants. Sunlight, filtered through the leaves of the ancient oaks that lined the creek bank, dappled the makeshift altar, a rustic arch fashioned from willow branches and wildflowers. Jen, radiant in a gown of creamy white linen, embroidered with delicate wildflowers, stood beside Tobias. He, in his usual attire–sturdy trousers, a crisp white shirt, and a finely crafted leather vest–looked every bit the strong, dependable man he was, his eyes alight with a love that shone brighter than the midday sun.

The ceremony was simple, yet deeply moving. Reverend Miller, his voice echoing with the weight of years spent witnessing the joys and sorrows of the community, spoke of commitment, resilience, and the unwavering power of love. His words resonated with the assembled guests, their faces reflecting a shared sense of happiness and relief. Stan Korte, his weathered face softened by a genuine smile, stood beside Jen, his hand resting lightly on her arm, a gesture of acceptance and unwavering support.

The air buzzed with excitement and anticipation. The townspeople, their faces etched with the hardships of frontier life but their hearts overflowing with joy, had gathered to celebrate the union of two people who had become symbols of hope and resilience in Shole Creek. Children, their laughter echoing through the trees, scattered wildflowers along the path leading to the altar. The scent of roasting meat and freshly baked bread filled the air, a tantalizing prelude to the feast that would follow.

After the ceremony, the celebration spilled over into a lively reception. Tables laden with food prepared by the entire town lined the creek bank. There was laughter, music, dancing—a whirlwind of joyous celebration that reflected the spirit of Shole Creek itself. Tobias, a skilled outdoorsman, had overseen the preparation of the feast, a testament to his ability to unite and nurture the community. The food reflected the land's bounty–roasted venison, wild game stews, freshly baked bread, and an array of colorful salads bursting with fresh herbs and vegetables.

Jen, her eyes sparkling with happiness, moved effortlessly through the crowd, greeting guests and sharing stories. She was the heart of the celebration, her vibrant energy infectious. Tobias, by her side, exuded quiet confidence, his presence a comforting anchor amidst the festive chaos. Their love, once a fragile bud struggling to bloom in the harsh environment of Shole Creek, had blossomed into a vibrant flower, a symbol of hope and resilience.

Stan Korte, his usual gruff demeanor entirely absent, mingled with the guests, a warm smile gracing his lips. He raised his glass frequently, proposing toasts to the happy couple, to Shole Creek, and to the enduring strength of the human spirit. His words were heartfelt, laden with the weight of emotions long suppressed, now finally released in a torrent of joy and gratitude. He had learned to accept and appreciate Tobias, not just as his son-in-law but as a man worthy of respect and admiration.

The evening was filled with music and dance. A fiddler, his bow dancing across the strings, played lively reels, while a group of women sang soulful ballads, their voices blending seamlessly with the sounds of nature. Couples twirled on the grass, their laughter mingling with the music, creating a vibrant tableau of frontier life. Jen and Tobias, hand in hand, danced gracefully, their eyes locked in a silent conversation that spoke volumes of their love and commitment.

As the evening deepened, and the stars emerged in the clear night sky, a sense of tranquility settled over the celebration. The guests gathered around a crackling bonfire, sharing stories and memories, creating a shared sense of belonging and unity. The flickering flames cast dancing shadows on their faces, highlighting the joy and contentment that permeated the atmosphere. The night air was filled with the scent of woodsmoke and roasted meat, a comforting aroma that spoke of home, family, and community.

The next morning, as the sun rose over Shole Creek, painting the sky in hues of gold and rose, Jen and Tobias stood hand in hand, looking out over the valley. Their love had not only survived the challenges of frontier life, but it had transformed them, and Shole Creek itself. The town, once riven by conflict and suspicion, had been reborn, its community strengthened by their love and commitment.

They had found solace and strength in each other, their relationship anchoring them in a world that often felt uncertain and unpredictable. And as they looked towards the future, hand in hand, they knew that their love story was far from over. It was merely the beginning of a new chapter, a journey filled with new adventures, new challenges, but most importantly, new joys. They had found their haven in the rugged landscape of the American West, and in each other. Their love story had become a beacon of hope, not only for themselves but for Shole Creek. Their triumph was a testament to the enduring power of love to heal wounds, bridge divides, and create a sense of community in even the most challenging of circumstances. Their union had been a catalyst for change, inspiring hope and healing in a town that was slowly rebuilding itself.

Their wedding, a celebration of their love and commitment, had become a cherished memory, a cornerstone of the town's recovery and rebirth. The celebrations extended beyond the immediate aftermath of their wedding. The entire town continued to celebrate their union for weeks, with potlucks, gatherings, and continued festivities. Jen and Tobias, together, continued to build their lives in Shole Creek, their love acting as a guiding light. The town, united in its collective celebration, strengthened its resolve to face the challenges ahead, together. The hard work and dedication of Tobias, coupled with Jen's artistic spirit and unwavering determination, helped bring Shole Creek back from the brink of ruin. Their combined efforts were not only felt in the economic recovery, but also in the restoration of community spirit.

The story of their wedding, however, wasn't solely about the union of two individuals; it was about a community coming together, finding strength in unity and love. It was about the power of human connection in a time of hardship and uncertainty. It was a testament to the human spirit, showcasing the resilience of the people of Shole Creek and the unwavering strength of love in the face of adversity. It was a story that would be passed down through generations, a reminder of the transformative power of love in a rugged and unforgiving land. It was a story of healing, forgiveness, and the ultimate triumph of love over hardship. It was a story that would resonate with the hearts of all who heard it, a timeless testament to the enduring power of love and the strength of the human spirit. And as the sun set on Shole Creek, painting the sky in a brilliant display of color, Jen and Tobias stood together, their love a beacon of hope illuminating the future, a future they would face together, hand in hand. Their love story had become an intrinsic part of Shole Creek's history, a tale of resilience, hope, and the unwavering power of love in the Wild West.

The days following their wedding were a blur of activity, a whirlwind of domestic bliss punctuated by the ever-present rhythm of life in Shole Creek. Jen, ever the artist, found herself sketching the vibrant tapestry of their new life–the sun-dappled creek, the rugged mountains, the warm smiles of their neighbors. Each stroke of her charcoal pencil captured not just the physical landscape, but the emotional landscape as well, a landscape now infused with the vibrant hues of love and belonging. She began to sketch Tobias, capturing the subtle lines around his eyes, the strength in his jawline, the quiet intensity in his gaze. He became her muse, his presence her inspiration, his love her greatest work of art.

Tobias, meanwhile, threw himself into his work with renewed vigor. His medical practice flourished, his quiet competence earning him the trust and respect of the entire community. He continued his trapping and hunting, providing for their household and contributing to the town's sustenance. He was no longer just a doctor, a trapper, or a bear hunter; he was a pillar of the community, a man who had found his purpose not just in his work, but in his love for Jen and his commitment to Shole Creek.

Their home, a modest cabin nestled beside the creek, became a haven of warmth and comfort. Jen filled it with her art, her paintings and sketches adorning the walls, each one a testament to their love story. Tobias, with his strong hands, crafted furniture from the local wood, adding his own unique touch to their shared space. Their home was a sanctuary, a refuge from the harsh realities of frontier life, a place where they could retreat and rediscover the quiet joys of intimacy and companionship. The fireplace spent evenings, the flames dancing in a mesmerizing display, their faces illuminated by the warm glow. They would read aloud to each other, their voices blending in a harmonious rhythm. They would share stories of their past, their laughter echoing through the cozy cabin, forging an unbreakable bond that was as strong as the mountains surrounding their home.

Their commitment extended beyond their immediate household. They both felt a deep responsibility towards the community that had embraced them. Jen, using her artistic talents, began teaching art classes to the children of Shole Creek, her vibrant energy inspiring them to express their creativity. She saw the power of art to heal and unite, to foster a sense of community and belonging. Her classes became a haven of creativity, a space where the children could express themselves freely, their laughter filling the small schoolhouse. She helped them to see the beauty in the rugged landscape that surrounded them, transforming the harshness of frontier life into a source of inspiration.

Tobias, in his role as the town doctor, continued to care for the community, his medical expertise proving invaluable. He made house calls, attending to the sick and injured, often working long hours, his dedication unwavering. He knew the struggles of frontier life, the hardships faced by the townspeople. He had become a trusted friend and advisor, his quiet strength a source of comfort and reassurance. He didn't just treat their ailments; he listened to their worries, offered a shoulder to lean on, and became a part of their lives. He understood their fears and aspirations, becoming not just a doctor, but a pillar of the community. His commitment to Shole Creek was not limited to his medical practice; he actively participated in community projects and events, assisting wherever needed, always ready with a helping hand.

Their plans for the future extended beyond the immediate needs of the community. They dreamed of expanding their home, adding more rooms to accommodate the growing family they envisioned. They spoke of having children, their future family becoming an integral part of Shole Creek. They painted vivid pictures of their future children, playing by the creek, learning from the community, their laughter echoing through the valley. These dreams were not just abstract notions, but tangible aspirations, fueled by their love and their commitment to each other and to the town that had become their home. They discussed opening a small clinic, providing better healthcare for the entire town, a reflection of their commitment to enhance the well-being of their community.

Jen's artistic vision extended beyond her personal pursuits. She envisioned creating a community art center, a place where the artistic talents of Shole Creek could flourish and thrive. She dreamed of bringing renowned artists from the East to share their expertise with the community, fostering a new wave of creativity. She saw art as a vehicle for economic growth, as well as community building, understanding the potential of art to attract tourists and elevate the profile of Shole Creek. Her vision extended to a vibrant cultural center that would attract residents and visitors alike, enhancing the economic vitality of the town.

Tobias understood the importance of diversifying the town's economy, the need to go beyond the mining industry for sustained growth and prosperity. He knew that Jen's artistic talents could be a catalyst for this change, a beacon of hope in their quest to elevate their community beyond its current limitations. His practical skills complemented her artistic vision, ensuring a balance of practicality and vision in their joint ventures. They recognized that a thriving community needed both economic prosperity and cultural richness.

Their love for each other wasn't just a personal affair; it extended outward, shaping their vision for the future of Shole Creek. Their shared dreams were not just limited to their personal aspirations; they were deeply intertwined with the well-being of their community. They planned for their own future, but simultaneously considered their role in fostering the future of Shole Creek. Their partnership was not only a romantic union, but a partnership in building a brighter future for the entire town. They were deeply rooted in their community, and their commitment to Shole Creek was as strong as their love for one another.

Their commitment to the community wasn't just a matter of duty or obligation; it was a testament to their love for Shole Creek. They had found solace and belonging in the town, and they felt a deep sense of responsibility to contribute to its growth and prosperity. Their connection to the community wasn't a mere association; it was a deep-rooted bond, woven into the fabric of their lives. Their actions spoke volumes about their heartfelt commitment, their love for Shole Creek shining through in every endeavor. Their future wasn't just about their personal happiness; it was intricately intertwined with the future of the town they called home.

The sunsets over Shole Creek painted the sky in vibrant hues, reflecting the vibrant future Jen and Tobias were building–a future filled with love, community, and the promise of a life lived to its fullest. The rugged landscape, once a symbol of hardship and uncertainty, had become a canvas for their dreams, a testament to their enduring love and their unwavering commitment to their community. Their love story had not just transformed their lives, but had become a source of inspiration and hope for the entire town. The future of Shole Creek was as bright as the sunsets over the majestic mountains, and their love story was its guiding light, a tale of resilience, perseverance, and the unwavering power of love to heal and transform. The community, once divided by conflict, was now united by their shared dream, a vision crafted with love and hope, woven into the very fabric of their lives. Their love story was more than just a romance; it was a testament to the enduring power of the human spirit in the Wild West. Their story reflected the rugged beauty of the land, and its message of hope was as vast and unending as the horizon itself.

The whisper of the creek, once a soundtrack to uncertainty, now sang a melody of hope. The mining operations, once a source of tension and danger, hummed with a renewed sense of purpose, a rhythm mirroring the steady beat of life in a community finding its footing. The harsh landscape, once a symbol of challenge, had softened, its rugged beauty now a backdrop to a burgeoning era of peace and prosperity. This wasn't merely a cessation of conflict; it was a transformation, a blossoming of community spirit fueled by the unwavering love of Jen and Tobias.

Their marriage, a bold stroke against the backdrop of a volatile frontier, had become the cornerstone of this transformation. Their commitment to each other had resonated through the town, a quiet force that had calmed the storms of discord and fostered a sense of unity. The skepticism that had initially greeted their union had melted away, replaced by admiration and respect for their resilience and unwavering devotion. Even Stan Korte, Jen's initially disapproving father, had witnessed the transformative power of their love. He'd seen the positive impact on his daughter, the newfound confidence that radiated from her, and the stability it had brought to her life. His gruff exterior softened, replaced by a grudging acceptance, and then, a quiet pride. He even started visiting their cabin more often, bringing gifts of fresh produce from his own garden, a small act of reconciliation that spoke volumes.

Jen's artistic vision had taken flight. Her community art center, a dream once whispered in hushed tones, now stood as a testament to her tenacity and creative spirit. The building, a former stable, had been lovingly restored, its walls now adorned with vibrant paintings, sculptures, and tapestries created by the townsfolk. It became a hub of activity, a place where laughter echoed through the restored halls, replacing the former sounds of horses' hooves with the excited chatter of aspiring artists. Workshops were held regularly, attracting renowned artists from across the country, who were drawn to Shole Creek not just by the unique artistic talent that Jen had cultivated, but by the remarkable community spirit that permeated the town. The art center drew visitors, infusing new life into the local economy. Tourists, captivated by the rugged beauty of the landscape and the unique charm of the town, flocked to Shole Creek, bringing with them a sense of renewed optimism and economic opportunities.

Tobias's clinic, expanded and upgraded with the help of community fundraising, served as a symbol of the town's collective commitment to progress and wellbeing. He had expanded his services, employing a young doctor he'd mentored, his wisdom and compassion guiding the new generation of healers. The clinic was more than just a place for treatment; it was a sanctuary of care, a place where people felt heard, understood, and valued. The medical services, combined with the surge of tourism, created a level of stability and prosperity the town had never known. A sense of security gradually replaced the fear that once clung to the townsfolk, a shadow cast by the uncertainties of frontier life and hope.

The transformation extended beyond the physical improvements. The very essence of Shole Creek had undergone a metamorphosis. The community, once fragmented by internal conflicts and external threats, was now bound together by a shared sense of purpose and collective identity. The spirit of collaboration, once dormant, now flourished, fueled by the common goal of building a better future. Neighbors, once wary of each other, now worked hand in hand, sharing resources and support. The sense of community was so strong that it became a defining characteristic of Shole Creek. The unity was so palpable; one could feel it in the shared smiles, in the helping hands, in the harmonious blend of voices that sang in the town squares.

The improved infrastructure added to the town's charm and vitality. New roads were built, connecting the town to the wider world, while still preserving its distinct character. The local businesses, invigorated by the influx of tourists, flourished. The general store, once a small establishment, was now a bustling center of activity, its shelves laden with a variety of goods and its countertops always busy. Even the local saloon, a place of rowdy activity in the past, transformed into a more refined establishment, hosting lively gatherings and musical performances that celebrated the rich culture of Shole Creek.

The once-tenuous relationship between the town and the neighboring Native American tribe improved significantly. Through respectful dialogue and acts of goodwill, fostered by Jen and Tobias's efforts to bridge the gap between cultures, trust began to grow. The initial hostility gave way to a cautious understanding, an acknowledgement of their shared existence within the same landscape. The shared respect led to collaborations on various projects, creating a sense of mutual benefit and unity. They even celebrated their shared cultural heritage with communal gatherings, their distinct traditions enriching the overall fabric of Shole Creek. The town's collective growth reinforced its resilience.

Even the natural environment seemed to mirror the improved circumstances. The creek, once threatened by mining operations, flowed clearer and stronger, its waters reflecting the serenity of the community. The mountains, ever watchful, now seemed to stand as silent guardians, their majestic presence a symbol of the town's enduring strength. The landscape, once a symbol of harsh realities, had become a canvas of hope, its beauty enhanced by the vibrant community life that flourished within its embrace.

The sunsets over Shole Creek were still breathtaking, but now, they painted a richer, more hopeful picture. They were no longer merely a beautiful end to the day; they were a symbol of the bright future that lay ahead. Jen and Tobias, their love story having become an integral part of Shole Creek's history, watched the sunsets from their expanded home. The cabin, once a modest dwelling, had grown to become a symbol of their success, and a testament to their dreams, a place filled with the laughter of their children. Their home now represented their love and their journey of perseverance. Their story was an inspiring testament to the enduring spirit of hope. The vibrant future they had envisioned, the future born out of hardship and fueled by love and resilience, had finally arrived. Shole Creek, once a town on the edge, had blossomed into a vibrant community, a testament to the unwavering power of love, resilience, and the human spirit. Their story, a love story set against the rugged backdrop of the American West, had become a legend, a tale whispered around campfires and shared across generations, a beacon of hope for all who dared to dream.

Chapter 12: Reflections

The years that followed saw Jen's artistic legacy blossom, not merely as a collection of paintings and sculptures, but as a vibrant, living testament to the spirit of Shole Creek. Her art center, initially a modest restoration project, grew into a beacon of creativity, drawing artists and visitors from far and wide. The walls, once bare, now showcased a kaleidoscope of talent, each piece a reflection of the town's diverse community and its evolving identity. Jen's own works, bold and vibrant, depicted the rugged beauty of the landscape, the resilience of its people, and the transformative power of love. Her landscapes weren't simply representations of the physical terrain; they captured the very essence of Shole Creek, its spirit, its heart. One painting, titled "The Whispering Creek," depicted the creek not just as a body of water, but as a living entity, reflecting the town's history and its journey towards prosperity. Another, "Mountain Majesty," showcased the imposing peaks that loomed over the town, their strength mirroring the resilience of its inhabitants.

Jen didn't limit her artistic expression to canvases and clay. She organized community art projects, involving everyone from children to the town's elders. Murals adorned the sides of buildings, transforming ordinary structures into works of art. Sculptures, created collaboratively, popped up in unexpected places, adding whimsical touches to the town's landscape. She even incorporated local traditions and stories into her art, weaving together threads of history and culture to create unique tapestries and installations that enriched the community's collective identity. The annual Shole Creek Arts Festival, her brainchild, became a celebrated event, attracting renowned artists, art collectors, and tourists who came to experience the unique blend of art, community, and natural beauty.

The impact of Jen's artistic vision extended beyond the aesthetic. The art center became a hub for social interaction, a space where people from different backgrounds could connect, collaborate, and share their creativity. Workshops flourished, offering instruction in various art forms, nurturing talent, and empowering individuals to express themselves creatively. The art center even hosted storytelling sessions, where local residents shared their memories and experiences, weaving rich narratives that added another dimension to the community's history. These stories, often depicted in subsequent art pieces, served as a powerful reminder of the shared past and the journey towards a brighter future.

Jen's influence wasn't limited to the visual arts. She championed local musicians, encouraging them to share their talents at the art center and at community events. She organized writing workshops, providing a platform for aspiring poets and novelists to express themselves. She even encouraged the development of a local theater group, transforming an abandoned building into a vibrant performance space. The town's musical landscape transformed. The sounds of fiddles, banjos, and guitars filled the air, creating a vibrant acoustic tapestry that reflected the town's rich cultural heritage and its newfound energy. The annual music festival became an event that drew crowds from across the state. The songs, written by local musicians, often spoke of the town's history, its struggles, and its triumphs.

Her impact on the local economy was profound. The influx of tourists, drawn to Shole Creek by its artistic vibrancy, boosted local businesses. The general store expanded its inventory to include art supplies and handcrafted souvenirs. New restaurants and cafes opened, offering a diverse culinary experience to visitors. The once-sleepy town transformed into a bustling center of activity, its economy invigorated by the creative spirit that Jen had instilled. The economic impact created a sense of stability, attracting young families who were drawn to the vibrant community atmosphere and the expanding job market. This new wave of residents added to the cultural richness of the town. The schools benefited, attracting teachers and educational programs that nurtured creativity and innovation.

Jen's artistic legacy wasn't solely about the physical creations; it was about the spirit of creativity that she ignited within the community. She taught people to find inspiration in everyday life, and to express themselves through various forms of art. Her work transformed the town's identity, showcasing its unique character and spirit to the world. She turned the harsh realities of frontier life into a story of resilience and hope, showcasing the spirit of the community through her art.

The success of the art center spurred further development in Shole Creek. A new library was built, stocked with books and periodicals, catering to the growing interest in art and literature. A community garden was established, providing fresh produce for the local restaurants and inspiring artistic interpretations of nature's bounty. The town became a model for other frontier communities, showcasing the transformative power of art and community engagement. Jen's philosophy of collaboration and creativity became a beacon for other artists and community leaders, demonstrating how art could not only enhance the quality of life but also drive economic development and social progress.

Her work transcended the geographical boundaries of Shole Creek, reaching a wider audience through exhibitions in larger cities. Her paintings found their way into private collections and public galleries, showcasing the unique spirit of the American West. She became a recognized figure in the art world, yet she remained deeply connected to her community, her artistic vision always rooted in the people and the landscape of Shole Creek. She created scholarships for aspiring young artists from the town, ensuring her legacy would continue to nurture artistic talent for generations to come.

Jen's story wasn't simply a tale of personal achievement; it was a testament to the power of community and the transformative impact of art. Her legacy continued to inspire generations of artists, community leaders, and individuals who sought to use their talents to enrich the lives of others. Her art, still hanging on the walls of the art center, served as a reminder of the journey that Shole Creek had undergone, its struggles, its triumphs, and its enduring spirit. The town, once defined by the harsh realities of frontier life, became a symbol of resilience, creativity, and the enduring power of the human spirit–a transformation deeply intertwined with Jen's artistic legacy and the unwavering love she shared with Tobias. Their story, a love story set against the breathtaking backdrop of the American West, had become a beacon of hope, a testament to the enduring strength of the human spirit, a story whispered around campfires and etched into the very heart of Shole

Creek. It was a story that continued to inspire, a story that continued to grow, a story that would live on, as vibrant and enduring as Jen's remarkable artistic legacy itself.

The years that followed saw Shole Creek flourish, not just as a mining town, but as a vibrant community, its identity inextricably woven with the lives and contributions of Jen and Tobias. While Jen's artistic legacy painted a vivid picture of the town's transformation, Tobias's quiet strength and unwavering dedication formed the bedrock upon which this prosperity was built. His contributions, though less visible than Jen's vibrant murals and sculptures, were no less essential to the town's growth and stability.

Tobias, initially known as the ruggedly handsome doctor, trapper, and bear hunter, quickly evolved into the town's steadfast protector and guiding hand. His medical expertise, honed through years of experience in the wilderness and in the rough-and-tumble mining camps, proved invaluable. He treated miners injured in accidents, tended to the sick, and delivered countless babies, his calm demeanor and steady hands bringing comfort to families during times of crisis. He wasn't merely a doctor; he was a confidant, a friend, and a pillar of strength in a community constantly facing hardship.

Beyond his medical practice, Tobias's understanding of the wilderness proved crucial to the town's survival. His expertise in trapping and hunting ensured that Shole Creek had access to a consistent supply of food, supplementing the meager provisions brought in by traders. He taught the younger men the skills necessary for survival in the unforgiving wilderness, ensuring that the community could remain self-sufficient even in times of hardship. He organized hunting parties, not just for food but also to regulate the wildlife populations, preventing overhunting and maintaining the delicate balance of the ecosystem. His deep knowledge of the terrain and his respect for the natural world earned him the trust of the local Native American tribe, fostering a peaceful coexistence that was vital to the town's security.

Tobias's quiet diplomacy was as crucial as his physical skills. He acted as a mediator between the miners and the landowners, preventing conflicts that could have erupted into violent confrontations. His deep understanding of both sides, and his ability to empathize with each one, enabled him to find common ground and broker mutually beneficial agreements. He was a calming influence in times of tension, his steady voice and measured approach diffusing animosity and preventing potential catastrophes.

He played a significant role in establishing the town's first organized militia, a force necessary for protection against bandits and other threats. He didn't seek glory or leadership; his contributions were borne from a deep sense of responsibility and a commitment to safeguarding the community he had come to call home. He trained the militia members, instilling in them discipline and a deep understanding of self-reliance, making them a capable and effective force. He implemented strategies for defense, not just against external threats but also for internal disputes, promoting a sense of community security and trust that was integral to the town's prosperity.

The construction of Shole Creek's first proper schoolhouse was also a testament to Tobias's quiet influence. While Jen focused on artistic endeavors, Tobias dedicated his time to securing the funding and overseeing the construction. He collaborated with the town council, negotiating with contractors, and working tirelessly to ensure that the school was built to a high standard, providing a safe and conducive environment for education. He believed in the importance of education for the town's future, seeing it as a vital tool for progress and prosperity. He secured books and learning materials from distant cities, and even personally tutored the children in areas where the teacher's skills were lacking, ensuring that everyone received a quality education.

His contributions extended beyond the tangible. Tobias was the person everyone turned to in times of trouble, offering a listening ear, sound advice, and unwavering support. His quiet strength and steadfast presence became a source of hope and comfort for many. He was the silent guardian, the watchful protector, who ensured that the community felt safe and secure, allowing Jen's creative energy to flourish without the constant burden of fear or uncertainty.

Years after the initial challenges and triumphs of Shole Creek, when the town had evolved into a thriving community, Tobias's contributions were still remembered and celebrated. The local library held a special collection of his journals and letters, detailing his medical cases, his hunting expeditions, and his personal reflections. These documents became a source of inspiration and a testament to his quiet heroism. His name was synonymous with resilience, compassion, and unwavering commitment.

A statue was erected in the town square, not a towering monument but a simple, life-sized figure depicting him with a young child on his lap, a testament to his gentle nature and his dedication to the community. The inscription read, "Tobias Adams: A healer, a protector, a friend." The words captured the essence of his character, his legacy echoing in the heart of the community he helped to build.

The annual Shole Creek festival included a day dedicated to honoring his memory, with storytelling sessions celebrating his life and recounting tales of his bravery and compassion. The stories were passed down through generations, keeping alive the memory of a man who didn't seek glory but whose actions spoke volumes. The tales recounted how his understanding of the native traditions and customs assisted in negotiating peace and collaboration, a lasting testament to his diplomacy. His knowledge of the land and its wildlife secured the town's sustenance, allowing for growth beyond the uncertainties of the mining industry.

Tobias's influence on the town was subtle yet profound. He wasn't the flamboyant artist, but his presence had formed the solid foundation upon which Jen's artistic vision could blossom. He provided the security and stability that allowed the community to thrive, to focus on creativity and innovation without fear of the uncertainties of frontier life. His quiet actions, his unwavering commitment, and his unassuming nature embodied the spirit of Shole Creek, its resilience, its compassion, and its indomitable spirit.

His legacy wasn't just about physical achievements; it was about the values he embodied–steadfastness, compassion, and a quiet heroism that underpinned the town's growth and prosperity. He was the silent guardian, the steady hand that guided Shole Creek through its challenging years, ensuring that it became a vibrant, prosperous community where art and community life could thrive. His contributions weren't splashed across canvases or etched in stone, but they were deeply embedded in the very fabric of Shole Creek, a legacy as enduring and significant as Jen's artistic masterpieces.

The town's history books dedicated substantial chapters to his contributions, not merely listing his accomplishments, but delving into the personal anecdotes and memories that shaped the town's collective narrative. They chronicled his role in mediating disputes, his healing touch, his unwavering support for the community, and his wisdom in managing the town's resources. These accounts revealed a man whose impact transcended the realm of medicine and hunting, whose quiet strength and compassion shaped the very soul of Shole Creek.

The stories of Tobias's life were interwoven with the tales of Jen's artistic achievements, creating a rich tapestry of the town's history. Their love story, a testament to the enduring strength of the human spirit, became a cornerstone of Shole Creek's identity. It was a story that went beyond the typical romance; it showcased the collaborative spirit, the mutual support, and the combined contributions that built a thriving community from the harsh realities of the American West. Their lives together became a source of inspiration, their legacy a symbol of resilience, creativity, and the unwavering power of love amidst the challenges of frontier life. Their story, etched in the heart of Shole Creek, stood as a vibrant testament to their shared commitment to building a better future, a community built on love, shared effort, and an enduring legacy that celebrated the art of living and the strength of the human spirit.

The rhythmic clang of the mine's hoist, once a constant reminder of the harsh realities of Shole Creek, now faded into the background hum of a thriving community. The air, once thick with the dust of coal and the anxieties of a frontier town, was lighter, fresher, carrying the scent of wildflowers and the distant echo of children's laughter. This transformation, however, wasn't solely attributed to the burgeoning mines or the artistic flourishes that adorned the town. A significant part of Shole Creek's metamorphosis was woven into the quiet redemption of Sheriff Greg Moore.

Moore, once a man haunted by the shadows of his past mistakes, now walked with a different gait, a newfound lightness in his step that reflected the peace he had finally found. His past, a tapestry of harsh decisions and regrettable actions, had weighed heavily upon him, casting a long shadow over his interactions with the townsfolk. He had been a man consumed by duty, driven by a rigid sense of law and order, often neglecting the nuances of human compassion and understanding. His stern demeanor, his unwavering commitment to the letter of the law, had often created friction within the close-knit community of Shole Creek. He was a man who judged swiftly, and whose punishments, though often justified, were delivered with a harshness that lacked empathy.

The turning point in Moore's life wasn't a single dramatic event, but a gradual shift, a slow dawning of self-awareness that started with small acts of kindness and grew into a complete transformation of character. It began with his interactions with Tobias and Jen. He had initially viewed Tobias with suspicion, a distrust born of the outsider's status and the perceived threat to the established order of Shole Creek. But Tobias's quiet strength, his unwavering commitment to the community, and his genuine respect for the people of Shole Creek, slowly chipped away at Moore's hardened exterior. He witnessed firsthand the transformative power of Tobias's compassion, his ability to heal not only physical wounds but also the deeper emotional scars that burdened many of the townsfolk.

Jen, with her vibrant spirit and unwavering belief in the goodness of humanity, further challenged Moore's rigid worldview. Her art, a vibrant expression of Shole Creek's soul, illuminated the human spirit in a way that Moore could not perceive. He began to see the community, not just as a collection of individuals bound by laws, but as a network of interconnected lives, each with its own unique story, its own joys, sorrows, and complexities. Jen's paintings and sculptures captured this intricate web of relationships, reminding Moore of the humanity he had often overlooked in his pursuit of justice.

One particular incident stands out as pivotal in Moore's transformation. A mining accident left several miners injured, their families left in despair. Moore, usually quick to maintain order and enforce the rules, found himself working alongside Tobias, helping to coordinate the rescue efforts and provide comfort to the grieving families. He witnessed Tobias's unwavering dedication, his compassionate touch, his ability to alleviate suffering in a way that Moore's stern pronouncements never could. It was in this shared experience of crisis and shared commitment to the community that a genuine connection formed between the two men. Moore began to understand the limitations of his previous approach to law enforcement, the importance of empathy and understanding in the administration of justice. He began to see his role not just as an enforcer of rules, but as a protector of the community, someone who guided and supported its members, rather than merely judging them.

Moore's evolving empathy extended beyond his interactions with Tobias and Jen. He started actively engaging with the community, listening to their concerns, seeking their input, and working to address their needs. He began to see the individuals behind the crimes, recognizing the social and economic pressures that often drove people to desperate measures. He started dispensing justice with a gentler touch, emphasizing rehabilitation over retribution. His decisions, though still guided by a firm sense of justice, were now tempered by a deep understanding of human fallibility and the power of forgiveness.

His relationship with the local Native American tribe underwent a significant shift as well. Initially, Moore had maintained a wary distance, viewing them with suspicion and adhering strictly to the formal protocols of the time. But through Tobias's bridging work, he began to understand and appreciate their culture, their history, and their inherent dignity. He started to see them not as a potential threat, but as vital members of the larger community, each individual deserving of respect and consideration. He participated in cultural exchanges, attending their ceremonies, learning their traditions, and demonstrating a genuine desire for understanding.

The change in Moore was palpable. His once stern countenance softened, his demeanor became less rigid, and he began to radiate a warmth that had been previously absent. He became known for his thoughtful consideration, his willingness to listen, and his capacity for forgiveness. He became a true guardian of the community, a protector, not only from external threats, but from the internal struggles and conflicts that could tear the community apart. He wasn't just enforcing the law; he was upholding the spirit of justice.

The physical manifestation of Moore's redemption was subtle yet significant. He no longer wore the heavy leather holster that had once signified his unwavering commitment to punishment and force. The worn and battered badge, once a symbol of stern authority, now held a subtle glimmer of a gentler spirit. The once-sharp angles of his face were softened by the lines of compassion and understanding etched by time and experience. His eyes, once cold and calculating, now held a warmth and gentleness that reflected the inner peace he had finally achieved.

The annual Shole Creek festival took on a new significance, marking not just the town's prosperity but also Moore's transformation. He participated in the festivities with a newfound joy, engaging with the townsfolk, sharing laughter, and actively contributing to the community spirit. He was a changed man, and his transformation was a source of inspiration for everyone in Shole Creek. His redemption wasn't merely personal; it mirrored the broader evolution of Shole Creek itself, a community that had learned to embrace compassion, forgiveness, and the power of second chances.

Moore's story became an integral part of Shole Creek's folklore, a testament to the possibility of personal growth, and a symbol of hope for those who had made mistakes in their past. It was a story that resonated deep within the hearts of the community, reminding everyone that even in the harsh realities of the American West, redemption and forgiveness were possible, and that hope could flourish even in the darkest of places. It became a reminder that the truest measure of a man is not the mistakes he makes, but the courage he displays in confronting them, and the compassion he shows in his subsequent actions. Moore's journey, therefore, was not merely an individual's transformation; it became a communal affirmation of the enduring power of forgiveness and the possibility of a new beginning. The story of his redemption lived on, woven into the fabric of Shole Creek's history, a beacon of hope for generations to come. The quiet strength that had initially defined Tobias Adams now seemed to have infused itself into the very heart of the community, shaping its character, its values, and its destiny. The legacy of Moore's redemption served as a testament to the profound possibility of transformation, and the enduring power of a community that embraced second chances.

The dust settled on Shole Creek, the clang of the mine hoist a less insistent rhythm now, a lullaby rather than a battle cry. The town, once defined by the harsh realities of its existence, had softened its edges, blossoming under the gentle influence of newfound prosperity and a burgeoning sense of community. Yet, the most profound transformation wasn't reflected in the burgeoning wildflowers or the laughter of children echoing through the canyons. It lay in the quiet, almost imperceptible shift in the heart of Stan Korte, the once iron-fisted mine mogul.

For years, Korte had been a man of unwavering resolve, a titan of industry who ruled his domain with a stern hand. His wealth, amassed from the rich veins of coal beneath Shole Creek, had built the town, yet it had also forged a reputation of uncompromising authority. His word was law, his frown a prelude to consequences, and his disapproval a chilling force that silenced even the most stalwart voices. He had been a man who measured success solely in terms of material gain, who saw people as assets or liabilities, their value dictated by their contribution to his empire. His relationship with his daughter, Jen, was strained, a reflection of his rigid personality and his inability to express affection or vulnerability. He viewed her artistic aspirations with disdain, seeing them as frivolous pursuits that distracted from the "real work" of building a fortune.

The accident that nearly claimed Tobias's life, a harrowing event that had shaken the very foundations of Shole Creek, served as a catalyst for change in Korte. Witnessing the unwavering devotion of Tobias to Jen, the quiet strength he displayed in the face of adversity, and the genuine care he showed for his daughter, chipped away at the hardened shell surrounding Korte's heart. He saw in Tobias a reflection of the values he himself had neglected–honesty, compassion, and a deep-seated love for his daughter that transcended material wealth.

The realization struck Korte slowly, as the dawn breaks over a mountain range. It was not a dramatic epiphany, but a gradual dawning, a subtle shift in perspective that transformed his understanding of life's true riches. He began to observe the subtle beauty of the world around him–the way the sunlight filtered through the leaves, the intricate patterns of the wildflowers, the vibrant colors of Jen's paintings, each reflecting the very soul of Shole Creek. He saw the interconnectedness of the community, the unspoken bonds that held the people together, a tapestry of human relationships he had previously disregarded in his relentless pursuit of material success.

The initial steps toward change were hesitant. He found himself engaging in conversations with the townsfolk, listening to their concerns, and offering a helping hand where he could. He started attending community gatherings, his presence initially met with apprehension, but gradually welcomed with a grudging respect that blossomed into genuine acceptance. The transformation was not sudden or easily achieved, it was a grueling climb, a continuous effort at self-reflection and personal growth. It was a journey fraught with challenges, marked by moments of doubt and setbacks, but fueled by an unwavering desire to become a better man, a better father.

One evening, as he sat beside Jen, watching the sunset paint the sky with hues of orange and purple, he uttered the words he'd suppressed for years. A simple "I am sorry, my dear." The weight of those three words, heavy with the burden of his past actions and the unspoken regrets that had burdened his heart, unburdened him. It was the beginning of a profound reconciliation, a healing process that restored the broken fragments of their relationship. He began to support Jen's artistic endeavors, marveling at her talent, her passion, and the way her art captured the heart and soul of Shole Creek. He finally understood that true wealth wasn't measured in gold and coal, but in the richness of human connection and the beauty of shared experiences.

Korte's transformation was not solely confined to his relationship with Jen. He began to see the miners, not as mere cogs in his industrial machine, but as individuals with families, hopes, dreams, and fears. He initiated improvements to their working conditions, advocating for better safety measures, fairer wages, and a greater sense of dignity in their work. He recognized the value of his employees, appreciating their contribution to the success of the mine and the prosperity of Shole Creek. His leadership style shifted, moving from autocratic rule to collaborative partnership, recognizing the collective strength and wisdom of the community.

His interactions with Sheriff Moore also underwent a profound change. He began to see the sheriff not as a mere law enforcement officer, but as a respected member of the community, a guardian of its peace and well-being. He recognized the sheriff's past struggles and the profound transformation he had undergone, seeing in it a mirror of his own journey towards redemption. They forged a bond built on mutual respect, a silent understanding that transcended their past differences.

The annual Shole Creek festival, once a mere celebration of prosperity, became a testament to the town's collective transformation. Korte, no longer the distant, aloof figure, participated actively, sharing laughter and stories with the townsfolk, engaging in friendly banter, and contributing generously to the festivities. His presence was no longer a symbol of authority, but a mark of shared celebration and community unity.

Korte's legacy, once defined by the relentless pursuit of wealth and power, was recast in the light of his redemption. He became a symbol of hope, an example of the transformative power of self-reflection and personal growth. His story, woven into the fabric of Shole Creek's history, served as a beacon of inspiration for generations to come. He showed that even the most hardened hearts could soften, that even the most rigid spirits could find flexibility, and that even the most formidable figures could be humbled by the simple act of admitting their mistakes and embracing the transformative power of forgiveness and love. The transformation of Stan Korte was not just a personal journey; it reflected the broader evolution of Shole Creek itself–a community that had learned to embrace compassion, forgiveness, and the enduring power of second chances. The dust had settled, but the legacy of change remained, a testament to the enduring spirit of the human heart and its capacity for transformation, even in the harshest landscapes of the American West. His story became a quiet hymn, sung softly against the backdrop of the mountains, a ballad of redemption whispered on the wind, carried on the murmuring waters of Shole Creek, and etched into the hearts of those whose lives he had touched. His legacy became the silent testament to a changed man, and a town transformed by his transformation, a beacon of hope in the rugged beauty of the American West.

The late afternoon sun cast long shadows across the porch of Tobias's cabin, painting the weathered wood in hues of amber and gold. Jen sat beside him, a half-finished sketch in her lap, the scent of pine and wood smoke filling the air. The silence between them was comfortable.

"It's been a long road, hasn't it?" Tobias murmured, his gaze drifting towards the distant mountains, their peaks silhouetted against the fiery sky.

Jen nodded, a wistful smile playing on her lips. "It has. More challenging than I ever imagined." She traced the outline of a distant peak with her finger, the movement mirroring the journey they had both undertaken. "But also... more rewarding."

Their journey had been one of both personal and collective growth. Stan Korte's disapproval, the ever-present threat of violence, and the harsh realities of life in a frontier town had tested the initial sparks of their romance, ignited amidst the chaos and danger of Shole Creek. They had faced setbacks, losses, and moments of despair, but through it all, their love had remained a steadfast beacon, guiding them through the darkest nights.

Tobias reflected on the lessons he had learned. His initial skepticism of Korte had slowly morphed into understanding, then grudging respect, and finally, a deep sense of empathy. He had witnessed the transformation of a man hardened by ambition, a man who had allowed his pursuit of wealth to overshadow the true riches of life–love, family, and community. He had learned the profound power of forgiveness, not only for Korte but also for himself, for the times he had allowed his own biases and prejudices to cloud his judgment. He had learned the importance of patience, of understanding that true change is a gradual process, a journey that requires perseverance and unwavering belief in the capacity for human transformation.

He had also learned the value of resilience. The near-fatal mining accident, a harrowing event that had tested his strength and spirit, had revealed the strength of his own resolve and the depth of his love for Jen. He had faced death head-on, only to emerge with a renewed appreciation for life's fragility and the preciousness of each moment. He discovered an ability to confront danger and adversity with courage and unwavering determination, an ability that went far beyond the skills of a trapper and bear hunter. The experiences had forged within him a quiet strength that ran deeper than the strength of his body, a strength rooted in the love he shared with Jen.

Jen's own lessons were equally profound. Her artistic endeavors, once deemed frivolous by her father, had become a source of healing and resilience. Through the act of creating art, she had found a way to express her emotions, to cope with the challenges she had faced, and to find meaning in the chaos that surrounded her. Her art had become a powerful tool, capable of reflecting the soul of Shole Creek and the essence of the relationships that had shaped her life. She learned the importance of self-expression, the courage to pursue her dreams regardless of societal expectations, and the power of art to transcend boundaries and create connections. She had also learned the value of perseverance, the need to stand up for her beliefs, and the strength that comes from defying expectations and choosing her own path.

Their journey had also profoundly affected the lives of others in Shole Creek. Sheriff Moore, once a man haunted by his past mistakes, had found redemption through his commitment to justice and his unwavering support of Tobias and Jen. He had learned the importance of second chances, the value of forgiveness, and the power of community unity. The miners, initially wary of Tobias, had come to respect his strength, his compassion, and his unwavering commitment to their safety and well-being. They learned that leadership could be compassionate, and that prosperity could be balanced with fairness and respect for the human spirit.

The transformation of Stan Korte was perhaps the most significant lesson of all. His initial harshness and uncompromising authority had given way to empathy, compassion, and a deep understanding of the true value of human connection. His recognition of his past mistakes, his willingness to apologize, and his commitment to personal growth had not only healed his relationship with Jen but also transformed the very fabric of Shole Creek. He had learned that true wealth lies not in material possessions, but in the richness of relationships and the beauty of shared experiences. His journey served as a powerful testament to the capacity for human transformation, even in the face of adversity and long-held beliefs. His example inspired others to reflect on their own lives and consider the choices that shape their character and relationships.

As the sun dipped below the horizon, casting a warm glow across the landscape, Tobias and Jen shared a look that spoke volumes. Their journey hadn't been easy, but it had been a journey of self-discovery, of resilience, and of profound personal growth. They had not only found love amidst the challenges of the American West but also forged a deeper understanding of themselves, of each other, and of the power of forgiveness and second chances. Their love story, woven into the tapestry of Shole Creek's history, stood as a testament to the enduring power of the human spirit and the unwavering strength of love in the face of adversity. The lessons they learned, both individually and collectively, served as a guiding light for others, a beacon of hope shining brightly in the rugged beauty of the American West. The dust had settled, the wounds had healed, and the memories of their journey would remain etched in the heart of Shole Creek for generations to come, a powerful reminder of resilience, forgiveness, and the transformative power of love. Their story, a testament to the enduring spirit of the human heart, would be whispered on the wind and carried on the murmuring waters of Shole Creek, a symbol of hope and redemption in the heart of the wild west. The setting sun painted a vibrant picture, reflecting the richness of their experience, a vibrant hue symbolizing the growth and enduring love they had found in the midst of a rugged and challenging frontier. The quiet evening held the promise of a new chapter, filled with the quiet joy and contentment earned through the trials and triumphs they had faced together.

Chapter 13: Epilogue

The years that followed were a tapestry woven with threads of quiet contentment. The vibrant chaos of Shole Creek had settled into a peaceful rhythm, a gentle hum of daily life punctuated by the laughter of children and the comforting crackle of a fire in the hearth. Jen and Tobias's cabin, once a refuge from the storms of their past, became a haven, a sanctuary where love blossomed and flourished. The scent of freshly baked bread often mingled with the aroma of pine and wood smoke, a comforting fragrance that permeated their lives, a testament to the simple joys they now cherished.

Jen's artistic talents continued to flourish. Her canvases, once filled with the raw energy and drama of Shole Creek's early days, now depicted scenes of idyllic peace–sun-dappled meadows, majestic mountains reflecting in the still waters of the creek, and vibrant wildflowers blooming in profusion. Her art became a visual diary of their life together, capturing the subtle nuances of their love, the quiet moments of shared intimacy, and the deep connection they shared with the land. Galleries in larger towns began displaying her work, extending her recognition past Shole Creek and providing her with a beneficial income and acknowledgement of her considerable talent. She found satisfaction not only in the artistic expression itself, but also in the ability to share the beauty of their world with others.

Tobias, too, found fulfillment in the simpler rhythm of life. His medical skills continued to be an invaluable asset to the community. While the dramatic rescues and perilous situations of the past had lessened, he found immense satisfaction in tending to the everyday needs of his neighbors, offering comfort and healing to those who were ill or injured. His knowledge of the wilderness, once crucial for survival, became a source of connection to the land, offering him opportunities for leisurely hunting and trapping, activities he pursued with a newfound sense of peace and appreciation. His skills transformed from necessities for survival into hobbies that brought him joy and a closer connection to nature. A quiet reverence, a sense of deep respect for the power and beauty of the natural world has replaced the wildness still called to him, but.

Their relationship deepened with each passing year, their love a constant source of strength and comfort. They found joy in the simplest of things–shared meals under the stars, quiet evenings spent reading by the firelight, long walks through the whispering woods. Their love was not a fiery passion, but a quiet flame, steady and unwavering, burning brightly within the heart of their tranquil existence. The shared experiences of the past had forged an unbreakable bond.

Stan Korte's transformation continued to amaze and inspire. He had relinquished his iron grip on Shole Creek's destiny, choosing instead to nurture its growth and prosperity. His business acumen, once focused solely on profit, now served the community, creating jobs and opportunities for everyone. He became a respected member of Shole Creek, his influence a force for good. His relationship with Jen flourished, the chasm of their previous conflicts replaced by mutual respect and affection. He took pride in her accomplishments, attending her art exhibitions with a quiet warmth that spoke of his profound change and the healing that had transformed their family dynamic. He had learned the invaluable lesson that true wealth lies not in gold and silver, but in the richness of family and the beauty of human connection.

Sheriff Moore, no longer haunted by the ghosts of his past, became a pillar of the community, a wise and respected figure. His dedication to justice, coupled with his newfound empathy, made him a beloved leader, a symbol of strength and integrity. The miners, once wary of outsiders, welcomed Tobias and Jen as true members of their community. The harmony between the townsfolk and the native tribe strengthened, built on mutual respect and cooperation. The once volatile landscape had been tamed, not through force, but through understanding and the shared desire to build a better life together.

Their lives weren't without challenges, but the difficulties they encountered were small ripples in the calm waters of their peaceful existence.

The occasional sickness or injury was treated with competence and compassion, the natural disasters of the west were faced with resilience, and the occasional conflicts were resolved through diplomacy and understanding. These smaller hurdles, compared to the monumental challenges they had overcome, were mere tests of their strength and resilience, opportunities for their love to shine even brighter.

Their home was a beacon of warmth and hospitality, filled with the laughter and love of friends and family. Sunday dinners were lavish affairs, celebrations of their life together, gatherings that brought the entire community closer, creating a sense of belonging and camaraderie. Children played in the meadows around their cabin, their carefree laughter echoing through the valley. The quiet moments, the shared meals, the simple acts of kindness, these were the building blocks of their peaceful existence, testament to their perseverance and the rewards of a life lived with integrity, compassion, and love.

Evenings were spent on the porch, watching the sunset paint the sky in hues of fiery orange and soft purple. They would sit quietly, hand in hand, the silence between them filled with an unspoken understanding, a comfort born of years of shared experiences. The stars emerged, twinkling like diamonds scattered across a velvet cloth, the moon casting its silvery glow upon the landscape. The serenity of the night air mirrored the tranquility within their hearts. They had faced adversity, overcome challenges, and emerged victorious. Their story, a tale of love and resilience in the heart of the wild west, served as a beacon of hope, a testament to the power of human connection and the enduring strength of the human spirit.

The tranquil beauty of Shole Creek served as a fitting backdrop to their lives, a silent witness to their enduring love and the peaceful existence they had forged. The creek, once a source of peril and uncertainty, now symbolized the calm and serenity they had found within themselves and with each other. Their story was woven into the very fabric of Shole Creek, a timeless narrative whispered on the wind, carried on the murmuring waters, and etched into the hearts of those who knew them. It was a story of a love that bloomed in the rugged heart of the American West, a love that defied expectations and conquered adversity, a love that found its ultimate fulfillment in the quiet beauty of a peaceful existence. The sunset each evening painted a new masterpiece, a vivid reminder of their enduring journey, a vibrant testament to the tranquility they had finally found and the quiet happiness that permeated their lives. It was a life of simple joys and profound contentment, a life lived in perfect harmony with nature and the people they held dear. It was a life, truly, earned.

The years that followed witnessed Shole Creek's transformation into a vibrant and thriving community, a testament to its resilience and the unwavering spirit of its inhabitants. The once-volatile landscape, scarred by mining accidents and the threat of conflict, blossomed into a haven of peace and prosperity. The rhythmic clang of pickaxes against rock, once a constant reminder of the inherent dangers of their livelihood, now mingled with the cheerful sounds of children at play and the contented murmur of adults engaged in their daily pursuits. The streets, once dusty and unforgiving, were now lined with well-maintained buildings, many boasting freshly painted facades and welcoming storefronts. The air, once thick with the acrid scent of coal dust, now carried the pleasant aromas of baking bread, freshly brewed coffee, and the sweet fragrance of wildflowers blooming in abundance.

Stan Korte, once a stern and uncompromising patriarch, became a pillar of the community. His transformation was remarkable, a testament to the profound impact of Jen and Tobias's influence. He channeled his business acumen not towards the ruthless pursuit of profit, but towards the betterment of Shole Creek. He invested heavily in infrastructure, building better roads, improving sanitation, and establishing a community center that housed a library, a school, and a meeting hall. He also championed the establishment of a cooperative mining operation, ensuring fairer wages and better working conditions for the miners. His once-imposing mine, a symbol of his power and control, became a source of pride for the entire community, a testament to their collective success. His relationship with Jen blossomed into a deep and affectionate bond, built on mutual respect and a shared commitment to the well-being of their town. He learned to appreciate the beauty of human connection, the true riches in life extending far beyond the confines of wealth and material possessions. He became a respected elder, his wisdom and experience valued by all. His gruff exterior softened, replaced by a quiet dignity and a genuine warmth that touched all who knew him. He often spent his evenings on his porch, watching the sunset, sharing stories with the local miners, and reveling in the community's shared success.

Sheriff Moore, too, played a crucial role in Shole Creek's transformation. His newfound empathy and understanding enabled him to foster a sense of security and trust among the residents. He initiated programs focused on conflict resolution and community mediation, striving to prevent conflicts rather than simply reacting to them. His fairness and impartiality ensured that justice was served, yet with a sensitivity that avoided deepening existing tensions. He held regular town meetings, inviting open dialogue and collaboration. He was a true leader, fostering a sense of unity and collective responsibility among the townsfolk. He worked tirelessly to improve relations between the Shole Creek community and the neighboring Native American tribe. He organized joint community events, encouraged cultural exchange, and fostered an atmosphere of mutual respect and cooperation. His dedication and efforts led to a lasting peace between the two communities, a significant achievement that secured Shole Creek's future.

The miners, once a rough and isolated group, found themselves integrated into the fabric of the community. They took part actively in the town's affairs, contributing their skills and knowledge to enhance Shole Creek's quality of life. By participating actively in community events, they shared their culture and traditions. They were no longer just workers, but cherished members of a thriving community, their contributions celebrated and appreciated. The women of Shole Creek, inspired by Jen's example, established a women's cooperative, producing and selling handcrafted goods, creating opportunities for economic independence and communal solidarity. The cooperative became a hub of social activity, a space for sharing ideas, fostering friendships, and celebrating their shared accomplishments. Their collaboration and mutual support created a network of strength and empowerment. Their endeavors further solidified Shole Creek's reputation for resilience and collaboration.

Established with Stan Korte's financial support, the school flourished, offering a quality education to children from all walks of life. The library, a haven for knowledge and enlightenment, became a center of learning and intellectual growth. The church, a testament to the community's shared faith, hosted weekly services and community gatherings, fostering spiritual growth and social connection. The annual harvest festival, a joyous celebration of the community's shared prosperity, became a highly anticipated event, attracting visitors from far and wide, showcasing Shole Creek's resilience and vibrant spirit. These events underscored the strong sense of community, fostering a shared sense of belonging and purpose. The festivities became a platform to highlight the unique culture and talents of the residents, enhancing the town's reputation and attracting new settlers.

The healing that permeated Shole Creek extended beyond the physical and economic realms; it manifested in the hearts of its people. Old grudges were forgotten, and past conflicts were resolved through reconciliation and understanding. The community's spirit of forgiveness and collaboration became the foundation of its enduring success. The air was filled with laughter and the sounds of cheerful conversations. Children played freely in the streets, their carefree spirits a reflection of the town's peace and prosperity. Families gathered for meals, sharing stories and strengthening their bonds. The sense of security and belonging permeated every aspect of life in Shole Creek.

Tobias and Jen, the heart of this burgeoning community, found profound fulfillment in their roles as healers and unifiers. They were not merely witnesses to Shole Creek's transformation, but active participants, their influence shaping the town's destiny. Their home remained a beacon of warmth and hospitality, always open to friends, neighbors, and strangers in need. Their influence had a ripple effect, transforming the lives of individuals and shaping the destiny of Shole Creek. The quiet evenings they spent on their porch, watching the sunset paint the sky in hues of fiery orange and soft purple, symbolized the tranquility they had found, not only in their relationship, but in the community they had helped to build. The tranquility reflected their enduring love, and the shared success of Shole Creek. Their story was a beacon of hope, demonstrating the transformative power of human connection and the enduring strength of the human spirit.

The vibrant tapestry of Shole Creek served as a fitting backdrop to their peaceful existence, a symbol of their shared dreams and the enduring strength of their love. The whispering creek, once a source of uncertainty, now symbolized the serenity and calm they had found within themselves and within their community. Their story, woven into the fabric of Shole

Creek, became a timeless narrative, whispered on the wind, carried on the murmuring waters, and etched into the hearts of those who knew them. It was a story of love, resilience, and the enduring power of the human spirit. A story of a thriving community forged in the heart of the American West, where challenges were met with courage, and dreams blossomed into a reality far exceeding any initial expectations. It was a testament to their enduring love, their unwavering commitment, and the triumphant spirit of Shole Creek. It was a story worth telling, a story worth cherishing, and a story that would be passed down through generations to come.

The decades that followed saw Shole Creek flourish beyond even the wildest dreams of its early settlers. Jen and Tobias, though never seeking accolades, became the silent architects of this prosperity. Their influence, subtle yet profound, permeated every aspect of the town's evolution. The very air seemed to hum with a quiet energy, a testament to the enduring spirit they had fostered. The children, who grew up under the shadow of their kindness and wisdom, carried their legacy forward, inheriting a deep-seated respect for community, compassion, and the unwavering pursuit of a better life. Their example rippled outwards, affecting generations to come.

Jen, with her artistic talents, continued to inspire. The town's community center, built with Stan Korte's reformed generosity, housed not only a library and school, but also a vibrant art studio. It became a space where aspiring artists, both young and old, could learn and grow, nurtured by Jen's patient guidance and mentorship. Her murals adorned the walls of many buildings, depicting scenes of Shole Creek's history, celebrating its triumphs and resilience, serving as visual reminders of the town's collective journey. These murals became treasured artifacts, capturing the essence of the community's spirit and serving as powerful symbols of its identity. Her vibrant artwork, infused with the spirit of the West, brought a unique beauty and charm to the town, transforming the physical landscape and elevating the community's cultural identity. Her influence extended far beyond the confines of the studio, weaving its way into the fabric of the town's cultural life, enriching the lives of its inhabitants.

Tobias, with his unwavering dedication to the well-being of the community, continued to serve as a beacon of hope and healing. He established a fully equipped medical clinic in the heart of Shole Creek, ensuring that every resident, regardless of their financial standing, had access to quality healthcare. His skills as a doctor, trapper, and bear hunter, previously utilized for his own survival, were now employed for the benefit of his community. He trained aspiring medical practitioners, imparting his knowledge and expertise to a new generation of healers. His quiet strength and unwavering commitment to his community established a lasting legacy of compassion and service, leaving an indelible mark on the town's character and shaping its future. He also established a network of first responders, ensuring the rapid response to any emergency, transforming the town's safety and security. His leadership provided a sense of stability, enabling the community to thrive and prosper.

The annual harvest festival, once a small gathering, grew into a large-scale celebration, drawing visitors from across the states. It became a showcase of Shole Creek's remarkable transformation, a testament to the resilience of its people and the enduring power of community. The festival's success became a source of pride for the entire town, strengthening their unity and sense of shared purpose. The event highlighted the town's distinct cultural heritage, attracting new settlers and tourists who sought to experience the unique spirit of Shole Creek. The annual festival became more than just a celebration; it evolved into a major economic engine for the town, drawing visitors from far and wide, boosting local businesses, and solidifying Shole Creek's position on the map.

Stan Korte, transformed by his daughter's influence and the community's spirit of reconciliation, became a respected elder statesman. He channeled his business acumen towards sustainable development, ensuring the long-term prosperity of Shole Creek. He established a scholarship fund for deserving students, providing them with opportunities for higher education and broadening their horizons. His commitment to education became a powerful force in elevating the social and economic status of Shole Creek. He established a system of apprenticeships, ensuring that future generations would have the skills and knowledge necessary to maintain the economic viability of the town. His legacy extends far beyond his financial contributions; it's a testament to his transformation, from a ruthless businessman to a respected pillar of the community.

Sheriff Moore, with his newfound understanding and empathy, fostered a culture of peace and cooperation. He established a community policing program, enabling residents to take an active role in maintaining the town's safety and security. His innovative approach created a stronger bond between law enforcement and the community, reinforcing the trust and mutual respect that fostered Shole Creek's growth and stability. The positive relationship between law enforcement and the community played a critical role in maintaining order, creating a sense of safety, and enabling the town to prosper and grow. His commitment to restorative justice promoted healing and reconciliation among community members. His long-lasting influence shaped Shole Creek's criminal justice system, ensuring fairness, accountability, and community involvement.

The cooperative mining operation, established under Korte's leadership, became a model of success, demonstrating the benefits of collaboration and shared prosperity. The miners, once isolated and often treated unfairly, now felt valued and respected members of the community. They became active participants in the town's governance, contributing their skills and knowledge to enhance the well-being of Shole Creek. The cooperative model served as a testament to the community's ability to overcome challenges and achieve collective prosperity. The success of the cooperative demonstrated the benefits of equitable practices and fostered a strong sense of shared ownership and pride among the workers.

The women's cooperative, inspired by Jen's example, continued to thrive, creating economic opportunities and empowering women within the community. It became a hub of creativity, innovation, and social interaction, fostering a strong sense of sisterhood and mutual support. The cooperative's success served as a model for other communities, demonstrating the power of women's collective action and their significant contributions to economic development and social progress. The cooperative's influence extended beyond Shole Creek, inspiring similar initiatives in nearby towns and becoming a symbol of women's empowerment in the American West.

The school, library, and church continued to serve as pillars of the community, fostering intellectual growth, spiritual enrichment, and a strong sense of shared values. Generations of children learned to read, write, and think critically, becoming informed and engaged citizens. The library became a place for exploration, discovery, and community gatherings, enriching the lives of all who walked through its doors. The church remained a space for spiritual growth and community unity, its teachings fostering empathy, compassion, and a sense of shared purpose. The community's sustained investment in education and religious institutions resulted in a vibrant society grounded in a strong sense of ethics and morality.

The legacy of Jen and Tobias extended far beyond the physical structures and institutions they helped create. It was etched into the hearts and minds of the people of Shole Creek, shaping their values, beliefs, and aspirations for generations to come. Their love story, a tale of resilience and unwavering commitment, became an inspiration to many. It was a reminder that even in the face of adversity, love could prevail, and that even the most challenging circumstances could be overcome through perseverance, collaboration, and a shared vision for a better future. Their story continued to be told and retold, inspiring future generations to embrace the same values of courage, compassion, and community that had transformed Shole Creek into a thriving haven. Their names became synonymous with hope, resilience, and the enduring power of love and community, a powerful legacy that lived on in the hearts and lives of those who followed. The story of Jen and Tobias, and their enduring love, became an integral part of Shole Creek's identity, a tale that would be passed down from generation to generation, ensuring that their legacy would live on, a testament to the transformative power of human connection and the enduring spirit of the American West.

The sun dipped below the horizon, casting long shadows across the burgeoning town of Shole Creek. Fifty years had passed since Jen and Tobias first met, fifty years of shared laughter, quiet moments of contemplation, and the unwavering support that had built a community from the raw, untamed landscape. Their story wasn't one of grand gestures or sweeping pronouncements; it was a quiet symphony of dedication, played out in the daily rhythms of life. It was a testament to the enduring power of human connection, a beacon illuminating the path for generations to come.

The children who had played amidst the dust and dreams of the early days were now elders, their faces etched with the wisdom of years, their eyes reflecting the enduring spirit of Shole Creek. They carried the legacy of Jen and Tobias within them, a legacy that manifested not in monuments or grand pronouncements but in the very fabric of their community. The spirit of cooperation, the unwavering belief in the power of shared endeavor, the deep-rooted empathy that characterized Shole Creek–all these were the tangible manifestations of Jen and Tobias's enduring influence.

The town itself stood as a testament to their shared vision. The sturdy buildings, once rough-hewn and temporary, now boasted a sophistication that reflected the town's evolution. The streets, once dusty trails, were now paved, lined with well-maintained homes, each a unique reflection of its owner's individuality. A bustling marketplace thrived in the heart of town, a vibrant hub of activity that echoed the town's prosperity and growth. The air thrummed with the energy of a community that valued not just individual success, but shared prosperity.

The annual harvest festival, now a week-long celebration, drew visitors from across the country. It was a spectacle of color, sound, and community spirit, a testament to the resilience and ingenuity of Shole Creek's inhabitants. Local artisans showcased their wares, their craftsmanship reflecting the skills passed down through generations, each piece imbued with the history and spirit of the town. The children, dressed in vibrant costumes, danced and sang, their laughter echoing across the town square, a symphony of joy and celebration. The elders shared stories around crackling bonfires, their voices weaving a rich tapestry of memories, preserving the town's legacy for generations to come.

Jen's legacy lived on through the vibrant artwork that adorned Shole Creek. Her murals, depicting scenes of life in the town—from the miners' toil to the joyful celebrations—became iconic representations of the community. They were more than just images; they were a visual history, a chronicle of the town's growth, its struggles, and its triumphs. Her artwork, preserved in the town's archive and replicated in countless homes, served as a constant reminder of the rich tapestry of life in Shole Creek, a source of inspiration to all who gazed upon them. Her influence extended to future generations of artists, many of whom credited her with igniting their passion for art, preserving her artistic legacy for decades to come. Her art studio, now a renowned institution, continued to nurture the talents of aspiring artists, ensuring that the spirit of creativity would flourish for years to come.

Tobias's legacy was equally profound. The medical clinic he established, now a modern hospital, remained a beacon of hope for the community. He had trained generations of medical professionals, imbuing them with his unwavering dedication to the well-being of others. The hospital served as a testament to his lifelong commitment to service, continuing to provide high-quality care to the community and beyond. His approach to community health emphasized preventative care, education, and a deep understanding of the interconnectedness of physical and emotional health. This holistic approach, a cornerstone of his philosophy, continued to shape healthcare delivery in the region for decades to come.

The cooperative mining operation, born from the ashes of conflict and distrust, thrived as a model of successful collaboration. The miners, once marginalized and exploited, were now respected partners, sharing in the fruits of their labor and contributing to the town's collective prosperity. The success of the cooperative served as a blueprint for other industries, demonstrating the power of shared ownership, equitable distribution of resources, and a commitment to workers' well-being. The cooperative model, inspired by Jen and Tobias's vision, continued to evolve and adapt, ensuring its relevance to future generations. It became a national model, cited in economic studies, textbooks and business schools.

The women's cooperative, founded and nurtured by Jen's belief in female empowerment, remained a vibrant force in the community. It provided economic opportunities for women, offering training and resources that allowed them to thrive in business and leadership roles. The cooperative demonstrated the transformative power of collaboration among women, empowering them to shape their own destinies and contribute meaningfully to the community. It expanded its operations over the years, embracing technology and evolving markets to remain relevant and prosperous. The cooperative also served as a mentoring ground, offering guidance to young entrepreneurs, ensuring the continuation of its spirit of innovation and progress.

But beyond the tangible achievements, the enduring legacy of Jen and Tobias resided in the hearts and minds of Shole Creek's residents. Their story, a testament to love's resilience and the transformative power of community, became an integral part of the town's identity. It was recounted in countless tales, passed down through generations, inspiring hope, resilience, and a shared belief in the power of human connection. Their story, a chronicle of love amidst hardship, served as a powerful reminder of the enduring spirit of the human heart, its capacity for compassion, and its unwavering belief in the power of community. Their story was, and would forever remain, a living testament to the triumph of hope, a beacon that illuminated the path for generations to come. Their memory lived on, a symbol of the enduring power of love, courage, and community, a story etched into the soul of Shole Creek, forever shaping its character and aspirations. Their legacy continued to inspire future generations, ensuring that the spirit of Shole Creek remained vibrant and resilient. Their love story, woven into the very fabric of Shole Creek, ensured that their legacy would continue to flourish, a testament to the power of the human spirit, and the enduring spirit of the American West.

The weathered oak tree, a silent sentinel overlooking Shole Creek, had witnessed the passage of time, its rings bearing silent testimony to the lives that unfolded beneath its branches. Jen and Tobias, their hands clasped, sat beneath its shade, a tableau of enduring love against the backdrop of a town they had helped build. The setting sun painted the sky in hues of fiery orange and soft lavender, mirroring the warmth and serenity that radiated from them. Their love, forged in the crucible of hardship and uncertainty, had blossomed into a timeless romance, a beacon of hope in the rugged landscape of the American West.

Their story, often recounted in hushed whispers around crackling fires, was a legend in Shole Creek. It wasn't a tale of grand adventures and daring exploits, but a quiet epic of unwavering commitment, a testament to the resilience of the human spirit. It was the story of a doctor who found healing not just in medicine but in the embrace of a spirited artist, and an artist who discovered her canvas not just in the natural world but in the heart of a man who loved her unconditionally.

Their journey had been fraught with challenges. Stan Korte's initial disapproval, the ever-present threat of mining accidents, the delicate relationship with the local Native American tribe–these were but a few of the hurdles they had overcome together. Yet, through it all, their love had remained steadfast, a guiding star in the often-turbulent waters of their lives.

They faced each challenge not as individuals, but as a united force, their strength multiplied by their shared commitment and deep affection. Their partnership was not just a romantic union but a collaborative effort in building a community, forging a new world from the raw, untamed wilderness.

The town of Shole Creek itself bore witness to their enduring influence. The once-rough-hewn buildings now stood as testaments to their shared vision, each brick, each timber, a silent tribute to their dedication. The once-dusty trails, now paved roads, facilitated the smooth flow of life, and the bustling marketplace, a vibrant heart of the community, pulsed with the energy of a shared prosperity. The annual harvest festival had grown from a small gathering into a week-long celebration, drawing visitors from far and wide to experience the unique culture and spirit of Shole Creek. The energy of the town, the shared sense of accomplishment and community, was palpable—a vibrant tapestry woven with the threads of their love and determination.

Jen's artistic legacy was everywhere, a visual chronicle of Shole Creek's history. Her murals adorned the town's buildings, depicting scenes of both toil and celebration, from the miners' arduous work in the depths of the mines to the joyous revelries of the harvest festival. Each brushstroke was a testament to the lifeblood of the community, capturing its essence in a rich tapestry of color and emotion. Her work was more than just art; it was a living history, preserving the memories and shaping the identity of Shole Creek. Her studio, initially a small corner in their home, had evolved into a renowned institution, nurturing the talents of aspiring artists and ensuring the continuation of her creative legacy for generations to come. The legacy of her art was not merely in the paintings themselves, but in the hearts and minds of those whose lives she had touched.

Tobias's impact was equally profound. His medical clinic, initially a humble structure, had blossomed into a state-of-the-art hospital, a beacon of hope for the community and a symbol of his unwavering dedication to the well-being of others. He had trained countless medical professionals, passing on not only his medical expertise but his deep-seated compassion and unwavering belief in the importance of community healthcare. The hospital was a testament to his commitment to providing accessible and high-quality healthcare to all, a model for future generations of medical professionals. His philosophy, encompassing preventive care, community education, and holistic well-being, continued to influence healthcare practices for years to come, shaping the future of medical care in the region.

The cooperative mining operation, a testament to their belief in shared prosperity, thrived as a symbol of successful collaboration. The miners, once exploited and marginalized, were now respected partners, reaping the rewards of their labor and contributing to the collective growth of the community. The cooperative model, inspired by Jen and Tobias's vision of fairness and equality, served as an example for other industries, demonstrating the power of collective ownership and equitable distribution of resources. Its success extended far beyond Shole Creek, becoming a national model that inspired change and reform in labor practices and economic models across the country. Its influence, inspired by Jen and Tobias's vision of social responsibility, continued to resonate for decades to come.

The women's cooperative, a testament to Jen's commitment to female empowerment, flourished as a space of opportunity and empowerment. It provided a platform for women to build businesses, providing them with the resources and support to thrive in leadership roles. The cooperative's success underscored the transformative power of women's collaboration and its ability to fuel economic growth and social progress. It became a model for other communities, inspiring the formation of similar cooperatives and empowering women across the nation to pursue their entrepreneurial dreams. The cooperative was more than an economic engine; it was a testament to the power of female collaboration and a lasting embodiment of Jen's belief in women's potential.

As the years rolled by, Shole Creek transformed from a fledgling mining town into a thriving community, a testament to the power of love, resilience, and community spirit. Jen and Tobias's love story, interwoven into the fabric of the town, became a living legend, passed down through generations. Their legacy was not just in the buildings they helped construct or the institutions they established, but in the enduring spirit of the town itself–a spirit of collaboration, resilience, and a shared commitment to building a better future. Their love story, a testament to human endurance and the power of connection, served as a beacon of hope, inspiring future generations to believe in the enduring power of love, even amidst adversity.

Acknowledgments

I am primarily grateful to those readers who enjoy mysteries because they are the ones who inspired this story. Your passion and dedication to these magnificent mysteries of the past constantly fill me with wonder and great admiration for you. Those who enjoy mysteries and live-action "who-done-it" productions form a skilled collection of individuals worthy of commendation for their passionate appreciation and ability to bring a story to life. The storytelling was molded distinctly and fascinatingly as a result of several cruises that my spouse and I have experienced in the past. This has enhanced the creative vision and has further enriched the narrative by adding an extra dimension.

To my family, whose unwavering support and encouragement made this book possible. Thank you for believing in my dreams and sharing in the journey. Your love and faith have been my guiding light, and I am forever grateful for your presence. You have been my rock, my cheerleader, and my inspiration. This book is as much yours as it is mine.

I'd also like to thank my illustrator, Karen Shayler, and my editor, Roxana Coumans, for their indispensable help and support during the book's publication. This story wouldn't be alive without your keen eye, insightful feedback, and endless patience. This project has benefited from your dedication to excellence and belief in its success.

To all the readers who have embarked on this journey with Alex and Star, thank you for your support and enthusiasm. Your love for stories and your belief in the magic of friendship and perseverance have made this book a reality. May this tale inspire you to chase your dreams, nurture your friendships, and cherish the bonds that enrich your life.

About the Author

Brett Shayler, an author, has been passionate about horses and the natural world his entire life. Raised on a ranch surrounded by diverse animals, he vividly reflects in his storytelling the profound and enduring connections between people and the animals they cherish and care for throughout their lives. Drawing inspiration from his family's vast acreage and the wild horses that roam freely upon it, Brett lovingly crafts heartwarming tales that celebrate the bonds of friendship and extol the virtues of deep respect for the natural world and the remarkable connections between people and animals. Through his books, he hopes to cultivate curiosity, compassion, and a thirst for knowledge in young readers. Brett often escapes to nature, hiking and observing wildlife, finding inspiration for his writing away from his desk. Brett proudly holds membership in both the prestigious National Cutting Horse Association and the equally esteemed American Quarter Horse Association, demonstrating his deep commitment to these organizations and the equestrian world.

www.ingramcontent.com/pod-product-compliance
Lightning Source LLC
LaVergne TN
LVHW090604110826
845146LV00001B/261

9798995369035